THE PERUVIAN CONTRACTS

THE
PERUVIAN
CONTRACTS

a novel by

FRANK FOWLKES

G. P. PUTNAM'S SONS
NEW YORK

COPYRIGHT © 1976 BY FRANK FOWLKES

SBN: 399–11710–5

Library of Congress Cataloging in Publication Data

Fowlkes, Frank V   1941—
   The Peruvian contracts.

   I. Title.
PZ4.F789Pe   [PS3556.0873]   813'.5'4   75–34217

For Connie

Prologue

THE arrival of the helicopter caused no great excitement. Though it had been closing on them in full view for more than five minutes, the men on the afterdeck had paid it almost no attention. They seemed to ignore it until it was within twenty-five yards and they could feel, as well as hear, the whudda-whudda of its engine over the ship's own sounds. They were just sailors. No one had told them what was going on. They really didn't care.

An officer appeared on deck now and began to shout instructions. Noise swallowed the words, but the sailors seemed to understand. A heavy cargo net was produced, spread out, then lifted and lashed taut between the rear gun station and the destroyer's stern rail. The helicopter, which had descended to about forty feet, circled and now approached from the rear, its downdraft pressing the foam flat in the wake of the slowly moving ship. In a matter of moments it was over the net, directly in front of where Cardona stood on the bridge. Through the helicopter's open door, he could see blue-jacketed crewmen moving about. At intervals, when the helicopter dipped its nose to keep pace with the ship, he could see the pilot, his face half hidden behind dark yellow-tinted glasses.

Things were moving quickly now. Sailors had positioned themselves at either side of the net. In the helicopter, two crewmen had maneuvered a five-foot steel ammunition caisson to the threshold of the door and were attaching it to a quarter-inch cable that had been threaded through a pulley that protruded from the fuselage above the door. They were finished now. A push and the caisson was out. For an instant it looked as if it would crash to the deck. Four feet above the net, the slack went out of the cable. The caisson bounced wildly. A moment later it was in the net. The caisson had taken the net to within inches of the deck. From the struggles of the sailors to free it, Cardona estimated it might weigh four hundred pounds. He watched the helicopter rise, then bank and fall away. There had been no communication between its crew and the men on deck: no smiles, no waves. The drop had taken less than three minutes.

The deck was now clear of all but a handful of officers. One was kneeling at the caisson's end undoing the snap latches. The man lifted the right end of the top, slipped its roller bearings into the upper track and slid it partway toward the other end.

From where he stood, Cardona could make out in the half-open caisson what appeared to be a gray fiber mailing case bound lengthways and across with steel strapping. It sat high in the open end of the caisson as though resting on some other object beneath it. The officer slipped his fingers under the steel straps, braced one foot on the partially open top and yanked. Instead of extricating the case, however, his efforts were spent in the other direction, sending the caisson top shooting to the end of its track and leaving him straddled across its open top like a hurdler.

Thirty feet above, a ten-knot wind whipping his hair past his ears, Cardona could hear the man gasp. What the officer saw at a distance of no more than a foot, Cardona could see also in the open space beside the gray case. Horribly mottled and blackened with its own dried juices, it was swollen beyond superficial recognition. But there was no mistaking what it was. It was a man's head.

That rendezvous, which took place July 26, 1972, in the Bay of Panama, might not have been front-page news even had the fact of its occurrence not been carefully hidden. That day, the minds of Americans two thousand miles to the north were occupied with events closer at hand.

The newspapers that morning told stories of the Democratic Vice Presidential candidate's having been hospitalized on three occasions for nervous exhaustion. That afternoon, his running mate would declare continued support for his troubled colleague in words that would haunt him for the remainder of the campaign. That same afternoon, the incumbent President, a Republican, would ask the governor of New York, also a Republican, to put his name in nomination for a second term later that summer in Miami Beach. And the wire services would carry a report from Moscow saying that revised estimates of the Russian wheat crop showed it falling twenty million tons short of projections.

No one watching the strange meeting at sea on that afternoon in 1972 would have seen in it any connection to these events. The physical evidence was too slight, too well concealed. But anyone who had watched the event from beginning to end would have some faint clues.

From its markings, he would know that the ship was the Peruvian destroyer *Palacios*. Had curiosity prompted him to inquire further, he might have learned that the *Palacios* was one of Peru's two British-built, Bostwick class destroyers, might have learned also that in an earlier incarnation she had seen service in Her Majesty's Navy as the H.M.S. *Diana.*

If he had thought to confirm the sighting with the Peruvian Naval Registry, he would have found that the *Palacios* spent July 26 on maneuvers off Valparaiso, Chile.

Had he looked closely, he might also have noticed the helicopter's six-digit identification number obscured under a thin overlay of fresh paint. Had he been able to make it out, the number would have identified the helicopter as a Huey Cobra based at Southcom Headquarters, Quarry Heights in the Canal Zone.

That observation would also conflict with official records. The helicopter's log would show it to have spent July 26 on a training exercise with the special forces at Fort Davis forty miles away. This he could have checked out and confirmed.

There would be no records to prove that what he had seen had ever taken place. Nothing to show that the *Palacios,* after twenty-two years of unremarkable service under two flags, had paid for herself twelve times over in a single day. Nothing to document that a U.S. Army helicopter, flying without markings, had spent an afternoon on a most unmilitary mission.

A witness would know two more things. He would know that somewhere at the bottom of the Bay of Panama the sand was swallowing slowly a partially filled ammunition caisson, and he would know that the caisson contained a human body—male, Caucasian, unsuitable for viewing. To know more—certainly to know the whole story—he would have to have been in Lima more than seven months earlier.

THE PERUVIAN CONTRACTS

Chapter

I

"HELLO. Yes. Yes. We know. Thank you very much." Cardona slammed the receiver down. He was annoyed. The phone had been ringing with the same message since eight o'clock that morning. Everyone seemed to feel duty-bound to notify the ministry.

The Instituto del Mar had called first. That was their job. They had scientific equipment. They followed the fish. Their word would have been enough. But there had been at least thirty calls since. From Chimbote, from Pisco, from Huacho, Callao, Mollendo and Ilo; from all the ports. It was not the fishermen calling. They had no phones. They would not think first of their government. Cardona knew where the fishermen would be. They would be calling their prayers up church chimneys in the coastal towns.

"Brinnng." There was another one. The phone's jangle was cut short as Cardona ripped the jack from the baseboard wall box. He had talked to enough processors for one day. They were the ones who bought the fish: bought it, boiled it, dried it, ground it, put it in sacks and shipped it around the world. Bought it cheap because there was no refrigeration, no transportation. They were the ones who got rich.

"Bastards," Cardona muttered to himself.

The phone could not stay unplugged long. He would

have to call the deputy. The deputy would have to brief the minister. Explain the obvious economic consequences. Explain the not so obvious political consequences. An official response would be expected by morning. That was the way it was when El Niño came.

Cardona turned to the window. From the fifth floor of the old building he could look down on the northern wedge of the city gleaming in the January sun. January and February normally were the good months. They were the only months when Lima was fit to live in, or so the diplomatic people had always said. He supposed them right, though he could not fully understand their attitude. His people had always lived in Lima. He did not notice the choking dust, the cheerless aluminum sky. Even the chilling mist, the *garua* had not bothered him until he heard others complain.

But January and February would not be normal this year. There would be meetings early and meetings late. The daily catch would have to be monitored with special care. Provision would have to be made for the displaced. Action would have to be quick and decisive. That, after all, was the justification for military dictatorship.

By morning, El Niño's arrival would be common knowledge. *El Commercio* would see to that. Its report would be straightforward, factual. That would be enough. The people would understand. By afternoon, *Ultima Hora* and the other evening tabloids would be on the street translating the hard economic facts into lurid images of personal hardship.

He pondered what it would mean for him professionally. A big public-relations effort would be required just to hold things together. Worse, the palace would watch the minister closely. He would not like that.

Cardona, Luis Aroyo, twenty-six years old, secretary

to the Minister of the Ministerio de Pesquería, watcher over the fishing industry of Peru, plugged the telephone jack back into the wall and punched out the four-digit extension. The curt hello at the other end of the line confirmed what he had feared. His phone had not been the only one overworked that morning. Despite his assurances, the processors were boring into the ministry without regard for channels.

The deputy's voice was edged with irritation. The President had called a meeting for ten o'clock the following morning, January 6. It would be in the Cabinet room of the palace. The heads of the Finance Ministry and the Military Advisory Council also had been asked to be present. Cardona felt a pang of discomfiture at the last piece of information. The Deputy's last words reinforced the feeling: "Looks like we could get jumped over on this one."

Cardona put down the receiver and went over in his mind what would have to be done. There were fewer than twenty-two hours—eighteen if you subtracted the ones he would sleep. It was not much time. At least there would be no need to work up a background presentation. El Niño would need no explanation.

"El Niño" is short for "El Niño de Navidad." It is the name given by Peruvians to a maverick ocean current which appears periodically and without warning. Ten years, sometimes more, can pass without a sign. Then one morning, always one January morning, El Niño is back, boring south along the coast, pushing the cold water of the northbound Humboldt Current away from the land, displacing it with warmer, more saline equatorial water. The current can linger and linger. And it affects only Peru.

Nobody knows for how many centuries El Niño has

paid its visits. Until the early 1950s, nobody cared. No one was much affected. Bathers noticed the water a little warmer. The people of Lima and the other seaside towns remarked that the mist was heavier and the rains more frequent; the slow Incan rhythms of life were not otherwise changed.

It had taken scientists to expose the dark side of El Niño. Agriculturalists and agronomists. Men who preached the wonders of the fish meal, taught that it would make plants bend under their fruit, taught that it would make cattle fatten faster on the hoof, and most important, taught that it could be made from the *anchoveta*. The fishermen of Peru had used that knowledge well. For twenty years they had pursued the anchovy. The chase had not been difficult. The anchovy abounded in the offshore waters, and each year the catch had grown. Individually the fishermen had not got rich. Their boats, the *bolicheras*, were too small. But in their numbers, the fishermen had given Peru something it had never before had: a substantial foreign income. In 1971, they had mined ten million tons from their watery lode, ten million tons which had brought $250 million from farmers in China, Poland, Russia and Western Europe. Ten million tons which also in that year had made Peru the greatest fishing nation in the world. Fishing was not the biggest industry in Peru. The copper mines were larger. But fishing was the biggest Peruvian industry owned by Peruvians, and that was important. It meant that the $250 million the fish brought in was money that would not leave the country except in exchange for goods.

Cardona knew El Niño would end that. He did not know how El Niño killed. He was not even certain that it did kill. He had heard respected oceanographers argue that the current's warm waters only killed the tiny organisms on which the anchovy fed.

[16

The government had spent millions of dollars to find out what happened to the fish and why, but its efforts had only lengthened the list of questions. When it was over, and the scientists had made their reports, the government knew only what any fisherman could have told it; when El Niño came, the nets went slack.

Cardona remembered only vaguely the last time El Niño had come. He remembered that the grown-ups had talked at night of the hard times. But times had always been hard in Lima. The percentages and statistics, the aggregates by which economic disasters are reckoned, they had meant nothing to him. That there was depression he had understood. But there was also food. Depression was numbers written on papers. One could not see depression in the streets.

He was wiser now, and the numbers, like goblins, talked to him with frightening eloquence. The fish would not be there. The catch would drop eight million tons, perhaps nine million. At $100 a ton, an absurdly conservative price, it would mean a loss of $160 million to $180 million. Peru could not afford it.

The presidential palace in Lima occupies an entire city block. Built at the turn of the last century, its five stories of stone façade spiral and twist to the borrowed music of another culture.

Each week, on Tuesday, in a long narrow and windowless room, the President of Peru meets with his Cabinet. The room has no other use. The meeting of January 6, a Thursday, was, therefore, unusual. Of those in attendance, three besides the President were regular frequenters of the room: Alfredo Checa, Minister of the Ministerio de Pesquería; César Sallas, Minister of the Ministerio de Economía y Finanza; and Ernesto Ferricio, chief officer of the Comité de Oficiales Asesores al Presidencia (COAP), the advisory council of military officers. Each was a member of the club of generals that had run Peru for, at that time, over four years. One other, the head of the Servicio de Inteligencia Nacional (SIN) was not a regular.

Two more men were present: Luis Cardona seated away from the table, holding a folder stuffed with charts and graphs, and the President of Peru.

It was the President who spoke first. His remarks were predictable and short and, to Cardona—preoccupied with what was to follow—no more than a hum. The President was through. The meeting was Checa's. That the Fisheries Minister should speak first was a decision of the organization chart alone. None in the room seemed more conscious of it than the flushed and chinless man who now nervously gripped the folder Cardona had handed him.

The newly created ministry had seemed a safe and custodial culmination to his career when proffered two years earlier. Indeed, it had been precisely that in the past twenty-two months. His role had been that of a regulator: important but, in this case, simple. He had never considered that the ministry could become the focus of a national crisis.

"Mr. President." Cardona wondered if the others detected the same pathos in the voice. For five agonizing minutes he listened as Checa spoke the obvious. The minister's speech was a litany of the already known. Regional offices were reporting smaller catches. Temperature readings seemed to indicate a warm water current. The first reports had come from the northern ports, but by that morning, there had been indications that the current was already south of Lima.

Graphs and charts were spread on the table and referred to. They could have been calendars for the interest they aroused from the others.

It could not be long before boredom would give way to irritation. There was nothing Cardona could do. The presentation was already a disaster.

Checa had finished now. There had been traces of original thought in his conclusion. He had proposed consolidation of the industry, proposed abandoning the inefficient *bolicheras* and using bigger boats which could go outside the current, boats which could chase the fish as the Japanese and the Russians did. Sensible ideas, but hardly redemptive.

For a moment no one spoke. In the presentence pause, Cardona scanned the table, wondering which of the other ministers would know how to use the void, know how to make the moment his.

It was Sallas who finally broke the silence.

"Is the minister aware of the purpose of this meeting?" His tone was predatory. "You may correct me if I am wrong, but it was not my understanding that we had been called into this emergency meeting to discuss futuristic plans for our fishing industry."

There were nods around the table, and Sallas seemed to draw assurance from them. It was clear he was on a safe tack and he spoke more loudly now.

"Our problem is in the present. Soon we will lose much of our foreign income; there will be people with no work, people with no money and with nothing to eat. All this will happen within weeks. It is a pressing matter, my friend. Our house is on fire; do not talk to us of the future."

The observation was, of course, right, but Cardona felt only loathing for the squat, bull-necked Sallas. His scolding tone had no place in a meeting room. With the subject a bare five feet distant, it was indecent. But that was Sallas. He had made a career of stepping on people. By doing so, he had marched rapidly up the ranks of the army. Until 1968 it had seemed that lack of voter appeal would keep him from higher office. But in October of that year, for the second time in a decade, a military junta had seized power from the elected government, and Sallas marched into the Finance Ministry without breaking stride.

Sallas' personality was an extension of uncommon physical ugliness. He had the stubby legs and barrel chest of a hill Indian and, between them, a huge belly, the upper half of which rested now on the lip of the table. His hair had left his head early in life, apparently to take root on his pudgy wrists where it all but obscured a heavy silver watchband.

"Señores." The President was asking for attention.

"Señores, we have heard General Checa's suggestions. I find some merit in them. I am bound to say though that I agree with General Sallas that we must have something offering more immediate results. Are there other suggestions?"

Again it was Sallas who spoke.

"Mr. President, I know little of fishing. But I do know that the answer to El Niño will not be found in the sea. Our problem is caused by the sea, but our problem, for the moment, is not the sea; it is money."

Sallas paused. The others regarded him with expectation. The immoderation of his tone suggested he was about to say something of which he was proud.

"Mr. President."

Cardona's throat tightened with irritation at Sallas' repeated use of that obsequious address.

"Mr. President, by my calculation our first year foreign exchange loss as a a result of El Niño will be at least two hundred million dollars. I say 'at least' because that estimate is based on last year's tonnage and last year's prices. Our loss in terms of what we had looked forward

[20

to will be even greater. Moreover, there will be other costs. We will have scarce credit, reduced spending and unemployment. I am a monetary man. I am not qualified to assess the magnitude of these other costs. But you must agree with me that they will amount to at least another two hundred million. My plan, therefore, assumes four hundred million dollars as the measure of Peru's loss. It is a conservative estimate, I assure you."

Sallas was becoming increasingly didactic and overbearing. Cardona nurtured a hope that it was all leading up to something silly.

It was not. In four minutes, Sallas succinctly laid out his proposal. When he finished speaking, the room was awash in admiration.

The proposal he outlined bore no relation to fishing or to El Niño except as points of departure. It was ingenious. More galling, it was stunningly simple: Sallas proposed to make the problem pay for itself through a massive speculation in the international commodities market.

El Niño would cost $400 million; that could not be avoided. But a shrewd operator, buying the right commodities and buying them at the right time, could turn early knowledge of the anchovy failure into profits of at least as much and perhaps much more. With impressive and persuasive detail, Sallas had just explained how this could be accomplished.

Cardona stared at his notes half hoping to find a flaw in what had been outlined.

The plan had the remorseless logic of a geometric theorem. The failure of the anchovy catch would create abnormal demand for substitute commodities. That could not be doubted.

According to Sallas, printouts from the computerized world protein model at the Ministerio de Economía y Finanza indicated that the commodities most affected would be soybeans and hard wheat, winter wheat, the sort of wheat used for animal feed. Grains were a subject about which Cardona knew little, but Sallas' assertion seemed plausible.

Nor did Cardona know how to assess Sallas' assurance that wheat was already going to be in short supply by summer and its price likely to rise even without El Niño. One thing he did know. The odds Sallas had just described would have kindled gambling instincts in a churchman. Forward contracts on wheat and soybeans could be had in the U.S. market for five cents on the dollar. One did not have to be a mathematician to understand what that meant. If the price of soybeans and wheat were to double, as Sallas had said they would, Peru would have to invest only a little more than $20 million to make back all it stood to lose from the effects of El Niño.

"Excuse me." It was a new voice. The man from SIN was speaking.

"I am impressed with what General Sallas proposes," the man began, "but it occurs to me that it may contain an oversight. The general's plan assumes that our information regarding El Niño is somehow unique, that others will not have the same opportunity as we do to evaluate and capitalize on the consequences. I do not see how this can be so. The newspapers today already have printed much of the story. Within a week, the world markets will have discounted the news entirely. Twenty million dollars is perhaps a small sum compared to the potential profit, but it is more than we can mobilize and invest before this occurs."

Cardona reckoned it a telling point. But Sallas was ready for it.

"The gentleman is correct in observing that the plan

is flawed. But he is only partly correct, for the plan has not one but two flaws." Sallas' contempt, it was obvious, was not reserved for Checa alone. He continued. "The first flaw, the one you mention, is easily corrected. How do you think other people will know the size of the catch? They will not count the fish; they will read the data. And who produces the data? We do. More specifically, General Checa does. The answer then is simple: we falsify the data. What is wrong with that? What do we keep the data for if not to serve the interests of the country? Should we keep data which do not serve the interests of the country? To be sure, if we falsify the data, there will be confusion, there will be conflicting reports. The fishermen will say the fish are not there. But who are the fishermen to say? Each knows only what he catches. And the brokers, the brokers thousands of miles away? What can they know? They are sophisticated men. But they use our data. They do not read Peruvian newspapers.

"The second flaw, the one you have not mentioned, is more difficult.

"There is only one commodities market large enough to absorb twenty million dollars invested over a short period of time without prices rising greatly. That market is in the United States. As you know, our relations with that country have not been good since our seizure of the International Petroleum Company. Moreover, the Congress in that country does not as a rule look kindly on military governments, and I do not have to tell you that it is the Congress of the United States which must approve our foreign aid each year. This year our U.S. aid will total forty million, two hundred and sixty-six million dollars, twice what we must have to make our initial investments. Were it to become known that Peru was using a part of those dollars to speculate in the U.S.

commodities market, the Congress would be considerably less generous. In fact, I have no doubt but that our aid would be cut off."

Sallas paused. He had talked for three straight minutes and was savoring it.

"What are you saying then?"

"I am saying, Mr. President, that we must have a buying agent."

"An individual?"

"Yes, an individual, one who can move quickly and with discretion."

"A Peruvian?"

"No, Mr. President, he cannot be Peruvian; he cannot be traceable in any way to Peru."

"A foreigner, then?"

"Yes, Mr. President, a foreigner."

For what seemed to Cardona like ten seconds, the two men's eyes joined in silent communication. It had become a two-man meeting.

"Bonham-Carter."

Sallas and the President had spoken the name simultaneously.

Chapter

II

FELIX BONHAM-CARTER put down his bag and paused in front of the revolving door. It was almost noon Washington time. Outside, the temperature would be racing the humidity into the nineties. It was Saturday, July 1, 1972.

[24

Lima had been cool when he had boarded the Braniff DC-8 at 12:45 the night before. Since then, through a stopover and cursory customs inspection in Miami, the mobil lounge ride into the Dulles Terminal and twenty minutes of watching the suitcases go round and round, it had been air conditioning all the way.

It had been over four months since the Peruvian authorities located him in San Feliu in his tiny room at the Casa Toni halfway up the hill. He had been impressed. Finding the Casa Toni was by itself an accomplishment. The detective work that must have gone into tracking him across more than nine years and through a half-dozen aliases would have done credit to Interpol. Sallas' men had done it in six weeks.

Spain had seemed the place to be in February with no money and no reason to be anywhere else. Before leaving London, he had toyed with the idea of taking a room in Marbella or Fuengirola. It was warmer on the Costa del Sol, and ten years earlier it would have been the logical choice. But the Costa del Sol had grown expensive thanks to the hoards of Germans and Scandinavians who had chosen the area around Torremolinos to escape from the winter darkness. San Feliu had seen its day as a tourist draw. It was pleasant enough.

The vibration of the airport bus relaxed him and Bonham-Carter dozed. In his lingering consciousness he went over what would be expected of him in the following four or five weeks. The details had taken Sallas less than an hour to explain. They had all been spelled out in the thin orange folder to which had been affixed a gummed label bearing the words *Projecto Belén,* the Bethlehem Project. Bonham-Carter had been slow to grasp the mordant humor in the name Sallas had given the undertaking. His mind had been on the money. The job had struck him as ridiculously simple and risk-free considering it would net him a total of $100,000.

His instructions were to buy futures contracts for selected commodities. The contracts were, in effect, options to buy predetermined amounts of the commodities at a specified price on some future date. If on that future date the market price was higher than the price specified in the contract, the difference would be profit to Peru. The future date he was to specify was August or September. He was to carry no cash other than what he needed for personal use. He was to make the down payment required on the contracts by drawing on a numbered account which Sallas had opened at the Swiss Credit Bank in Zurich. This arrangement meant a short delay while the money was cabled from the Swiss bank to the broker's U.S. bank. It also meant that Peru would be required to pay Switzerland's eight percent surcharge on foreign money inflows imposed earlier that year to slow the influx of capital fleeing currencies weaker than the franc. But it would prevent the transaction from being traced.

One further precaution had been taken. For several years, the U.S. Treasury had been negotiating with the Swiss for access to the names and records of certain numbered account holders. Against the possibility that this hitherto inviolable veil of anonymity would fall under diplomatic pressure, Sallas had established a dummy corporation under Liechtenstein charter. Should U.S. Internal Revenue Service agents penetrate the numbers, they would learn only that the holder of the contracts was the Bethlehem Corporation headquartered in Vaduz.

Until otherwise instructed, Bonham-Carter was to buy only contracts for soybeans and hard red winter wheat and to spread the purchases widely enough so as not to attract attention. Where and from whom he bought the contracts was left entirely to him.

There had been one more instruction. Twice each week, once on Wednesday evening and again on Friday evening, he was to inform Lima of what he had bought. This he was to do by cable and in the form of a crypto-gram. The cables were to be sent to Sallas at his home address.

Bonham-Carter was wakened by metallic scraping noises beneath him. Outside his window, the driver was dragging suitcases from the baggage compartment. He could see passengers for the Washington Hilton filing out the door at the front of the bus. A check of his watch showed he had been dozing for forty minutes. The next stop would be the Mayflower then the Madison.

"Bonham-Carter, Felix; Hays Mews, London, NW 1," he added his signature with a flourish and pushed the registration card across the counter. The fashionable Mayfair address would mean nothing to the clerk; the pretense was for his own benefit.

The clerk was deferential enough. Bonham-Carter put that down to his hyphenated name. It was a familiar reaction. His name was one of his few permanent assets. He had his mother to thank for that.

His mother had not done herself many kindnesses in her lifetime. Booze and loneliness had rotted her out while he was still in his teens. Until then, home for them had been a series of cheap flats in first one and then another dreary London suburb. There had been lovers at times, most of them men he had known only by their first names; but there had been little love, and her death in 1940 had been a rescue for them both.

Of his father's identity, he had no proof, only his

mothers account. According to her, she had been sixteen when he had been conceived out of a union too brief and uncomplicated to be called an affair. At the time, she was living with an aunt in Winchester and working in one of the many small shops that line the High Street below the point at which it intersects the Southampton Road. Although Winchester had once been the capital of England, it was, by 1925, a quiet, somnolent town which, but for its cathedral and a half-dozen lesser tourist attractions, possessed little to distinguish it from many other similar-sized towns in the south of England.

Among the less magnetic attractions of the town was the River Itchen, its claim to fame being that three centuries earlier it had costarred along with another otherwise forgettable stream in Izaak Walton's *Compleat Angler*. While the old men of the town still spent summer afternoons testing Walton's proposition that there were fish in the Itchen, for the young people of Winchester, the Itchen was a resource of more obvious fecundity. In its peregrinations through the hilly countryside, the river had carved out dozens of natural trysting places cloistered by tall stands of poplar and locust which flourished in the rich alluvial soil. It was in one such spot, near the bottom of a place known as Hills Valley, that Bonham-Carter's mother had placed his conception. Though she had recalled the occasion for him with unusual candor, she had been able to summon few details about his father excepting his name, which had pleased her for its aristocratic sound. There had been no common social ground between them. He had been an accidental acquaintance, no older than she, a student at Winchester College, the old public school located at the south side of the city. She had seen him just once afterward, a chance encounter on the street. Though alone,

[28

he had seemed embarrassed and had avoided her. She had been four months pregnant and wondered if he could have noticed.

She never pressed her claim. When the baby came, there had been no help other than that which her aunt could provide. A paternity suit never entered her mind. Of his father, all she had been able to offer her son was the name that had pleased her and that she hoped would one day please the child. Taking the name had meant filling out many forms at the Hall of Records, but it had been free.

Five minutes later, having purchased the bellhop's exit for a dollar and having dispatched his clothes to the laundry somewhere in the bowels of the hotel, Bonham-Carter was climbing into the tub. The shower head, set high on the wall, had plenty of pressure behind it, and he held his face to the stream, letting the hot water wash the nearly twelve hours of road dirt down his body.

After brushing his teeth and shaving, he took a tumbler from the holder beside the sink, filled it with cold water and turned to the door-length mirror now gray with droplets from the shower vapor. The motion of his arm was quick and practiced. The cold water hit the mirror head high and washed to the floor, leaving the mirror momentarily crystal clear. In that moment, he stared at the familiar body. Anyone would have to concede that at forty-seven he was well preserved. Past his prime perhaps, by the conventional wisdom; but prime was an average, and averages could be beaten. There was a little more skin than he needed. That he would allow, but the muscle tone underneath had not given way. With clothes on, it was the body of a thirty-five-year-old man.

Thus assured, Bonham-Carter finished unpacking,

hung his suits and stuffed the empty suitcase into the end of the closet. After asking the switchboard to call him at 9:00 P.M., he crawled into bed. It was 2:30 in the afternoon.

The phone rang promptly at nine. The switchboard girl's voice triggered familiar confusion. Hundreds of wakings in hundreds of hotels had taught him not to panic at strange accents. For a period he lay still, eyes shut, adding up the little bits of information. In twenty seconds, having assembled a convincing concept of where he was, he arose and dressed. He was out of the room by 9:25.

There were perhaps a dozen people in the lobby below. The Madison was a new hotel and like most new hotels its lobby, reflecting the value of the real estate on which it sat, was little more than two wide intersecting corridors.

The newsstand was out of morning papers and it was still too early for the first Sunday editions to have arrived. Bonham-Carter settled for the evening *Star* and, folding it under his arm, made for the bar. The bar was dark, but, after allowing his eyes time enough to adjust, he could make out enough to see that the *Star's* financial page was going to be of no use. He would have to wait and pick up a *New York Times* in the morning.

Sallas had spread *The New York Times* before him the previous week and instructed him in the mysteries of the numbers, showed him where to find the prices of wheat and of soybeans, explained why there was August wheat and September wheat and October wheat and why their prices were different, though when the time came to deliver them they would all look the same. *The Times* was to be his shopping list and his box score unless he bought on the West Coast. There he would have to rely on *The Wall Street Journal.*

Bonham-Carter was not unfamiliar with money. Eleven years earlier the Patrice Lumumba assassination in the Congo had introduced him to the care and spending of large sums. He had received $40,000 for that job and would have netted seven or eight times that sum had he not naïvely agreed to take payment in Congolese francs. He had discovered too late that the black market, which was the only place his wad of beautifully engraved green currency could be converted, applied an eighty-five percent discount to the francs' official exchange value.

No matter, it had been a profitable undertaking. And he had been greatly amused ten months later to read the cautious speculations of the United Nations Commission that had investigated the former premier's death. No fewer than four theories had been advanced. There was the mysterious Belgian mercenary, Captain Ruys, alleged to have administered the coup de grace after Minister of the Interior Munongo had driven a bayonet into Lumumba's chest. Then there was Colonel Huyghe, another Belgian mercenary, who several witnesses swore had admitted—even boasted—that he had shot Lumumba as the former premier pled for mercy on the floor of a villa outside of Elisabethville. And the boozy British mercenary Chalmers who had also claimed responsibility for the deed, saying that he had been hired by an unnamed party to assassinate a man whom he believed to be Lumumba while the man was getting off a plane at the Elisabethville airport.

Finally there was the official account of the Katangan provincial government, for which the UN Commission had professed emphatic disbelief. Bonham-Carter could understand the UN Commission's doubts. It did seem improbable that Lumumba, having been weakened already by four months of captivity, having just been flown from Thysville to Moanda and from there to Elisabethville with Congolese troopers beating him most of the way, and having been locked in the heavy-walled Zumbach villa outside the city, could have, in his depleted condition, summoned the strength and will to dig a hole in the wall, overcome and bind up the two guards outside, locate and start an automobile, cross the guarded bridge leading out of the compound and then, after all this, make the mistake of taking a dead-end road at the end of which he would meet with hostile villagers and spontaneous death.

Indeed, the official account did seem incredible—but only because of what it omitted. The Katangan authorities could hardly have mentioned the European doctor who that afternoon in February 1961 had been admitted to treat the badly battered prisoner, or the bag which the doctor, feigning forgetfulness, had left behind, the bag which contained the razor-sharp, mortar-cracking cold chisel and the other tools which four hours later would have been used to cut the 45-by-35-centimeter hole in the Zumbach villa's wall. They could not mention that the guards found bound with bed sheets remembered no attack, or that, had anyone thought to run blood tests on them, they would, even twelve hours after, have still shown traces of sodium pentothal in their systems. Finally, they could not admit that the Ford in which Lumumba had rocketed out of the compound had belonged to that same European doctor whom they had brought in earlier, or that it had been the doctor whose voice Lumumba had heard calling softly from the bushes by the roadside when, as instructed, he reached the end of the dirt road by the village, or that it had been the doctor who had fired the bullet that stopped the answer in Lumumba's throat, splitting the supra sternal notch in the center of his collarbone and severing in order the former premier's trachea, esophagus, spine and spinal cord before spending itself against the trees of the darkened forest.

It had been a good start, the Lumumba business, part of a run of beginner's luck. He had followed up the next year with $70,000 which the Peruvian army chiefs paid him for providing plausible substantiation for their fraud claims in that year's June elections. There had been other jobs and other paydays since, though, he had to admit, the intervals between them had lately been getting longer.

Still, despite occasional bursts of income, Bonham-Carter knew nothing of investments. His was a feast-and-famine business. When it was feast time, he held cash. Cash could be confiscated, but it had to be found and identified first. Investments in paper and real property were hard to hide. For a man in his line of work, it was an important consideration.

The Montpelier Room was the Madison's major success. It had been treated well by Washington's restaurant critics and in two years of operation had built up a substantial expense account clientele. Like most downtown restaurants its money-maker was lunch, but Friday and Saturday nights were busy, and by the time Bonham-Carter was ready to eat, it was three-quarters full.

Twenty years earlier, his white linen suit would have assured him one of the better tables in any hotel restaurant. But in the Washington of 1972, style and stature were on divergent courses, and the city's maître d's had learned to associate white suits with homosexuals and fops. Accordingly, Bonham-Carter was shown to a table uncomfortably close to where a group of five men were eating and talking in low tones. Apparently, his dinner neighbors were celebrating, for there was a bottle of Montrachet on the table and two more cooling in buckets. From the prices on the wine list, Bonham-Carter reckoned it to be more than $100 worth of wine. He eyed the men with a mixture of respect and envy. For a moment he was tempted to imitate their extravagance but resisted, reminding himself of how broke he had been a short time earlier and of how he had cursed himself then for not being more prudent.

Two of the five men at the table would not have stood out in any crowd of successful businessmen. The other three, however, were dressed in dark winter suits that looked as though they had been picked up in the 1940s—most likely, from the looks of them, in a grab and run robbery at a store catering to outsized men.

Bonham-Carter perused the menu, listening as he did so for bits of conversation from the next table. It was an involuntary reflex. Over several decades of dining alone in public places, eavesdropping had become a habit with him. As a diversion, it had advantages over reading. One could eavesdrop in any restaurant. It required no equipment, nothing to carry around, and it did not interfere with his eating. Moreover, it was infinitely entertaining. Many had been the occasion when he had fabricated whole life histories from fragments of other people's conversations.

But there would be no such entertainment tonight. The five men at the next table were conversing with extreme circumspection. Occasionally a word was audible, but as often as not it was also incomprehensible. He could not be certain, but he thought he detected foreign accents when the men with the baggy suits spoke. By the time the waiter brought the dinner, he had written off the effort as futile and turned his thoughts to other matters.

Bonham-Carter returned to the bar after dinner for cognac and remained there nearly forty-five minutes. It was after 11:00 P.M. when he left. Upstairs, the corridor was empty as he emerged from the elevator. Midway along the corridor, he located his room, fumbled in his pocket for the key and unlocked the door.

The light inside was off. He stepped back, checked the room number, then the number on the key in his hand. They matched. He felt certain he had left the light on. Possibly the maid had turned it off when she had come in to turn down the bed. He reached for the switch, stepping back into the hall as he did so. The precaution was instinctive—but unnecessary. The room was empty, completely empty. Clothes, toilet articles, suitcase—all were gone. The bed had been remade. There was no sign he had ever been there.

A phone call to the desk cleared up the mystery. Apologetically, the desk explained that his belongings had been moved to the room next door, that the room from which he was calling was already taken and had been reserved for a week. They were very sorry. A man would be right up. Five minutes later, for the second time that day, Bonham-Carter was receiving instructions in how to turn on lights, open closets, find the bathroom and operate the airconditioner. The second room was identical to the first in every respect. It struck him as curious that the hotel should have troubled to move him. Probably whoever had reserved the room next door was a frequent customer with a sentimental or superstitious attachment to the room he had just been forced to vacate. Bonham-Carter could appreciate attachments of that sort. Like most men whose lifestyles kept them lonely, he had his own list of out-of-the-way bars, hotels and restaurants which, like old songs, he associated with happy experience. He knew that with each return he diluted their associative value; that enough revisits, and the nostalgic kick would disappear altogether. Still, he went back. One could not bank the small change of the heart in a mattress.

He dispatched the bellhop with another dollar and was just closing the door when he noticed the five men from the table in the restaurant walk past in the corridor. The door blocked his vision, but from the sound of their footsteps, he felt certain that they were stopping in front of the room just beyond the one he had vacated. He pushed the door quietly to and stood for a moment reflecting. Had it been his imagination, or had he heard one of the men mutter a quiet "thanks" to the departing bellhop? Could one of the five men in the restaurant have asked for him to be moved? Why?

Now, hotels make mistakes. They lose reservations, deliver fruit baskets to the wrong room, mix up laundry; they are, in short, susceptible to all the forms of screw-ups that occur in large institutions dependent on underpaid, semicompetent, unmotivated staff. An ordinary hotel customer, a businessman, a tourist would, therefore, have given the matter no further thought. Most customers would have had the sense to understand that if they had a room and the bed had clean sheets on it and the toilet wasn't clogged they were ahead of the game and well advised not to fret over seemingly irrational quirks of hotel behavior. There is no return in it, just as there is no return in worrying about why trains run late and some telephone lines are always busy.

But most people would have had other things to occupy their thoughts. Bonham-Carter, that evening of July 1, did not. The business he had come to transact was as simple as rote, and it would be thirty-six hours before he could get started on it. Besides, if experience had taught him one thing, it was that, when working, it was dangerous to assume anything to be coincidence.

Accordingly, Bonham-Carter did not tarry long in his new room. Twenty minutes after closing the door behind the bellhop, he was in the phone booth in the coffee shop on the first floor. He placed two calls separately but to the same number. Five minutes later, when he left the booth, he had two interesting pieces of information. From the first call, he had learned that there were no vacancies in the Madison Hotel that night. From the second he learned that the room three doors down from his own, the room on the far side of the one the five men from the dining room had entered was empty—or at least that the phone in the room did not answer.

The first of these facts was fortuitous, for without it the second would have been meaningless. Had there been numerous vacancies in the hotel, there would have been nothing to remark in the fact that, at nearly 11:45 P.M., neither of the rooms that flanked the one occupied by the five men had anyone in it. But, with the hotel fully booked, that fact raised an intriguing possibility—the possibility that for some reason the men two doors down had reserved and paid for two extra rooms to serve as buffers between them and their neighbors. It was possible, of course, that the men would later disperse and occupy all three rooms. That seemed unlikely. In that case, one of the men would have had his belongings moved into the room next door at the same time Bonham-Carter was being moved out. One thing was certain. People didn't go to the expense of paying for extra rooms unless privacy was important to them. And privacy—or the violation of it—was something to which Bonham-Carter was professionally addicted.

Turning these thoughts in his mind, Bonham-Carter regretted now having surrendered his first room key to the bellhop. He wondered if he had not volunteered it, whether the bellhop would have asked for it. It was a pointless speculation. There was another way to find out what was going on—though it would take a little time.

Rising from the dressing table where he had been seated, Bonham-Carter went to the door, opened it and studied the lock. It was a cylinder lock, and a good one. There was every probability that the hotel builder, hurrying to complete the job, had installed the locks serially as they were packaged by the manufacturer rather than scrambling them. If so, the lock next door would differ only slightly from his own. Still, he knew its workings would consist of five sliding pins. Even if his key would lift all but one of the pins by precisely the right amount, he would have to determine which pin was preventing the plug from rotating and whether it was because it was lifting too much or too little. That was a simple trial-and-error exercise. But it would require at least ten keys like his own, ten keys he didn't have. He would have to do it the hard way.

Moments later, Bonham-Carter was in front of the room between his own and that which the five men had entered. From his pocket he produced a tight ball of filament-thin nylon thread, gripped the loose end and gave the ball a toss down the hall, watching it quickly unwind until it was gone and all that remained was the nearly invisible thread marking its path. This he doubled over before returning to the door. For a second he studied the slit where the lock would be. The sloping side of the bolt would be facing him. The pull of the thread would have to be toward the inside of the room. That could be a little tricky.

The next step, feeding the folded end of the double-strand over the top of the door, would be the most difficult. He worked patiently, keeping his ear cocked for footsteps at either end of the hall. At the end of three minutes he had passed approximately eight feet over the middle of the door. He had been careful to keep the thread in the middle of the door since it was essential that it fall on the side of the doorknob away from the lock. The rest of the job would be quick.

With a coat hanger, Bonham-Carter fished under the door and pulled the thread loop out into the hall. Then he passed the two loose ends through the loop and drew them tight so that the thread encircled the door from top to bottom like a drawstring. Next, keeping light tension on the end in his left hand, he began to slip the thread across the door from the middle toward the locked side. In a few seconds, the thread cleared the corner of the door and slid down to the level of the lock. He repeated the same procedure with opposite results at the bottom of the door. When he was through, he held all but about eight inches of the thread in his hand. But those eight inches now formed a tiny drawstring encircling the latch bolt and the doorknob on the inside of the door. The doorknob would not move. The only way for the drawstring to constrict when he pulled its loose end was for the pressure of the thread on the sloped face of the latch bolt to force the bolt against its spring back into the door.

He would have to be careful. Driving the latch bolt back into the door was no problem. But this would occur instantaneously. Unless there was something obstructing it, the bolt would immediately pop back into its socket and all he would have to show for the previous five minutes was a drawstring around the inside doorknob. The trick was to make certain that, as the bolt slid away, the thread remained across the socket opening. To be sure of this, he would have to pull the thread directly away from the lock rather than up the face of the door. That meant sacrificing some leverage but he had no alternative. There was one more preliminary. Taking a plastic tube from his pocket, he unscrewed the tiny cap at its end and pressed it to the slit between the door and the doorjamb at the point where the thread emerged and squeezed. Powdered graphite. Dry oil. It would make both bolt and thread as slippery as wet ice.

The last thought entering his head before pulling the thread was what he would do if he found the room occupied after all, found that one, or perhaps several, of the five men from the restaurant had entered the room during the time he had been downstairs phoning from the coffee shop and that, for his curiosity, all he would earn was extraordinary embarrassment—even arrest.

But the room was dark, just as it had been an hour earlier. As he closed the door quietly behind him, he could see light from the window at the far end of the room shining off the smooth surface of the counterpane on the bed ten feet ahead. There were no clothes, no suitcase, no sign that anyone was in the room or had been.

The room was laid out so that one entered along a short hall separating the bathroom on the right from a bank of sliding-door closets set into the wall on the left. Bonham-Carter slipped into the bathroom, closed the door behind him and turned on the light. The maid had done a good job. The floor, which had been covered with water that afternoon, was dry. Next to the sink, the glass which he had used to wash the mirror down had been replaced with a clean one in a new paper wrapper. He took the glass from its holder and slipped it into his jacket pocket. He would need that later.

Next he took a Swiss army knife from his pants pocket and, opening the medicine cabinet above the sink, slipped the knife's largest blade into the razor-blade disposal slot. The slot accepted three-quarters of the knife blade before he felt resistance. For a moment he scratched at the unseen surface behind the metal pan that formed the back and sides of the cabinet. No need for caution. Behind that wall was his own room. He could make as much noise as he wanted.

In a few seconds he had learned all he needed to know. It was cheap construction: dry wall, probably on metal studs. In the bedroom proper, the walls would doubtless contain fiber-glass sound insulation. Not in the bathroom though, not with the next room's clothes closet on the other side. It was the same the world over. One man's cheating was another man's economy. The architects' plans would have called for insulation throughout. But what contractor could stay in business and do everything the blueprints called for? And what architect would know?

Before turning out the light, Bonham-Carter used the thread to measure the distance from the bathroom floor to the middle of the medicine cabinet, also the distance from the middle of the cabinet to the wall separating the bathroom from the outside corridor. Then, after turning out the lights, he left the bathroom, repeated the same measurements on the wall behind the sliding doors of the clothes closet across the hall and marked the corresponding spot with a twist of the knife blade.

It took less than a minute rotating the knife back and forth to grind a three-quarter-inch hole through the dry wall and another five minutes using the saw blade of the knife to turn this small hole into a larger one approximately two and one-half inches in diameter. With the glass inserted in the hole open end first and pressed flush against the metal pan of the next room's medicine cabinet, the result was a double resonating

41]

earhorn. For a makeshift arrangement, it was a device in which an aficionado of eavesdropping technology could take pride.

Bonham-Carter remained in the closet with his ear pressed to the bottom of the glass until nearly 1:30. But, for all his efforts, the results were disappointing. The bathroom proved a less-than-ideal listening post. Most of what he could hear was muffled by the fact that the conversation was taking place in the bedroom. Only on those occasions when someone actually entered the bathroom did he achieve something close to acoustical perfection. In addition, the accents of several of the speakers made even the occasional loud statement difficult to understand.

By the time he tired of crouching in the closet, cleaned up the plaster dust with wet toilet paper and covered the hole in the wall with the five-by-eight-inch card describing the hotel's regulations and check-out time, he had ascertained only one hard fact: a great deal of money had changed or was about to change hands. The figure he had heard repeated several times was $200 million. But despite an obviously unguarded discussion of the details, he had been unable to deduce the nature of the transaction.

Several words had been repeated frequently in the course of the conversation. One of the words was "Durham." The other—actually two words, but always spoken together—was "turkey red." From their tone of voice, he thought it sounded as though the men who spoke with accents looked with favor on the latter and with disapprobation on the former. Bonham-Carter knew "Durham" as a city in England. He believed there was also a city called "Durham" in the United States. But by no contortion of context had he been able to make sense of the antipathy with which the men with baggy suits had seemed to regard "Durham." "Turkey red" was even more of a mystery. To it he was able to attach no meaning whatever. Several possibilities had occurred to him. A tobacco? An exotic dancer? Neither fit. The only thing which seemed clear was that the men with accents had liked turkey red.

It was almost two o'clock when he turned out the light by his bed. As a vicarious experience, he had to admit that his night of eavesdropping had been less than satisfactory. Still, for several hours it had spared him the company of a familiar occupational enemy—boredom. He wondered if he would be as lucky in the weeks ahead.

Chapter

III

DURING that first week in July, the East Coast of the United States was locked in a heat wave which would persist for most of the month. Before it broke, there would be brownouts, blackouts and shutdowns of public facilities in major urban areas. Up and down the Appalachian river valleys, National Guardsmen were still at work twelve hours a day cleaning up the wreckage left by Hurricane Agnes several weeks earlier. If Bonham-Carter had walked fourteen blocks west to Georgetown, he could have seen the ravages of the hurricane firsthand in the dried-up sump of the Chesapeake and Ohio Canal whose embankments, intact since George Washington's day, had been smeared flat by the force of the Potomac's floodwaters.

While baseball fans that morning amused themselves

at breakfast by critiquing the President's all-time, all-star team prominently featured on *The New York Times* sports page, a force of 150 FBI agents was beginning a nationwide search for a man named E. Howard Hunt who was wanted for questioning by a grand jury in connection with a break-in at the Democratic National Committee two weeks earlier. That afternoon, on the West Coast, a young man named Bob Seagren, who looked more like a store mannequin than an athlete, would jam his fiber-glass pole into the box at the end of the runway and ride it higher than any pole-vaulter in history.

If those developments were of consequence to the rest of Washington, they were of little interest to Bonham-Carter whose only concern was how to kill a day until the market opened.

The Mall, normally an open swath of green from the Capitol to the reflecting pool at the foot of the Lincoln Memorial, was that Sunday a gold-rush town of tents, pens and rough pavilions spread harum-scarum across the rain-softened ground which, despite tons of straw and wood chips, had been churned by the feet of thousands of tourists into a steamy, fly-infested quagmire. The Smithsonian Institution, holding company for the battery of museums that line Constitution Avenue, was producing its ballyhooed roundup of rural America, the Sixth Annual Folklife Festival.

Bonham-Carter, his roots an ocean away, could summon little of the nostalgia which seemed to sustain the interest of the rest of the throng.

He paused at the Maryland Pavilion and watched as an eighty-three-year-old rustic with a penknife fashioned a broom from a green hickory sapling, then stopped to observe Zuñi Indians dancing.

The star of the show, which consisted of a half-dozen

semiclothed Indians jumping up and down, was a small child. Bonham-Carter guessed he could be no older than six. Hopping around in anklets, short skirt and headdress all of brightly colored fluffy feathers, the tiny dancer looked more like a fishing lure than the Indians Bonham-Carter knew from the movies. After a few minutes, he moved on and listened for a while to a dark, greasy-haired union spokesman advocating a lettuce boycott.

After half an hour, having had enough, he strolled on up Thirteenth Street into the deadness of downtown Sunday Washington. The strip joints and porno shops, rear guard of the inner city's evacuating economy, would not open until evening, and the street was empty of all but its residual complement of derelicts too weary or addled to move on. Just above H Street, he paused at the Silver Slipper which that week was hawking the attractions of Angelique, whom the poster described as an "international favorite," and one Fanne Fox, described only as "wow." Though he knew neither would do justice to her picture, he felt sure that, for entertainment value, either of them would top the eighty-three-year-old whittler.

He did not return to test this instinct. Instead, after walking for another hour, Bonham-Carter returned to the Madison, ate an early supper in the coffee shop and watched *Modesty Blaise* on the Channel 7 movie.

On the morning of the next day, Monday, July 3, Felix Bonham-Carter went to work.

As Sallas had advised, he picked Merrill Lynch, the biggest of the retail brokerage houses. It would offer the advantage of enabling him to buy in a number of cities on the strength of one credit examination. It was possible that Merrill Lynch would impose a trading limit on

45]

his account and that the limit would be below the total amount he had to invest. If that happened, he would have to open a second account later on with another broker. But initially, at least, his plan was to stick with Merrill Lynch.

The Merrill Lynch offices in Washington are located on Connecticut Avenue, three blocks from the Madison and diagonally across the street from the Mayflower. Bonham-Carter was there by the ten o'clock opening.

The receptionist had all of the requisite qualifications: she was beautiful, she could smile and she could point. She pointed to the far right-hand side of the room where five commodity specialists sat in a row of desks ranged perpendicular to the screen of green numbers traveling endlessly from left to right.

Bonham-Carter picked one of the older men in the row and approached him. Several verbal greetings went unheeded. Bonham-Carter was about to reach out and tap him on the shoulder when the man looked up from his newspaper, started, and introduced himself as Clinton Royer, manager of the commodities division. Apologizing for his inattention, Royer explained that he had been absorbed in a very funny article. It concerned an airline hijacker who had parachuted with a half million dollars in ransom from an American Airlines jet. What had tickled Royer though was that the money, the hijacker, his pants and his gun had landed in four different places. The FBI had picked him up the day before in Peru, Indiana.

"What can I do for you?" he asked affably. "Pig tums, plywood, propane, silver; the price is right, step right up." Put off by this burst of good-fellowship, and suddenly uncertain of the subtleties of the vocabulary with which such matters were conducted, Bonham-Carter told Royer simply that he would like to buy some hard winter wheat.

[46

"Okeydoke, that shouldn't be too tough. Do you have an account with us already?"

Bonham-Carter explained that he did not, nor did he have an account elsewhere.

Undeterred by this piece of intelligence, Royer produced from his drawer a one-page questionnaire to which were affixed carbon duplicates in blue, pink and yellow. "We're gonna have to fill us out a little new account information form. What's your name?"

Item by item they went down the page. New client: yes. Marital status: single. Over twenty-one years of age: yes. Power of attorney: none. Of what country is client a citizen: Bonham-Carter hesitated, then reasoning that he might be asked to produce his passport, answered Great Britain. Home address: again he hesitated, but this time decided to gamble. Would it be acceptable, he asked, to use his business address, since he was rarely reachable at his home address? Royer offered no objection and the line was completed with the entry of Bethlehem Corporation's Swiss office at 41 Sonnenberg-strasse, Zurich. The address would check out except in the unlikely event Merrill Lynch decided to send a man around there in person. Even then the danger was not great. The address was that of Sallas' brother-in-law who had been fully briefed on how to handle inquiries.

The next series of questions had to do with Bonham-Carter's credit worthiness. Before asking them, Royer invited him to a private room explaining that there confidentiality would be assured.

"What is your annual income?" Up to this point, Royer could not know whether he was dealing with an odd-lot trader or on to somebody big—somebody with the resources to pick up his otherwise very slow business. His tone was anticipatory.

The question took Bonham-Carter by surprise. He had expected to be asked his net worth. The $20 million tucked away in Zurich would answer that question. But that money was earning precisely zero interest, and there was no other disclosable income to which he could point. He could hardly tell Royer he had just been given $50,000 from the Peruvian government and would receive another $50,000 in a month or two.

"I don't have, any income." He was gambling again. His mind racing only a step ahead of his tongue, he explained that because he had no family and no fixed residence other than his Zurich business address, he paid himself no salary. As director of the Bethlehem company, his living expenses were drawn on an as-needed basis from company funds and offset in full against the company's revenues. In short, since he had no private life, he had no private income. He assured Royer that the Eidgenoessische Steuerverwaltung, the Swiss federal tax authority, had examined and approved the arrangement and that similar tax treatment was not uncommon in that country in cases where corporations were essentially one-man operations.

Bonham-Carter was pleased with the explanation. Royer seemed to accept it, for he went on to the next question.

"Net worth?"

"Twenty million." For a man who several months before had been washing his own shirts in the sink, they were sweet words.

It was obvious that the words pleased Royer too, for, from the look of him, he couldn't have licked a stamp. The remainder of the interview was brief and perfunctory. Royer seemed hardly to listen to the answers as he filled in the remaining spaces on the form. When he was through, he explained that routine confirmation of balance would have to be obtained from the bank in Zurich before the account could be opened and a trading limit set. That would take several hours by cable. Bonham-Carter agreed to return at 12:30 and left.

Royer was all smiles when he returned. From the respectful looks given him by the other brokers, Bonham-Carter suspected that the membrane of confidentiality may have been ruptured in his absence, but he was more pleased than annoyed.

His credit confirmation had come through in good order. Royer explained that, after discussing it with the office manager, he had assigned Bonham-Carter a $15 million trading limit. The figure, he conceded, was somewhat arbitrary, but, since, in thirty-three years in the business, he had never had a customer buy in anything near that volume, he suspected it would be adequate. If not, the limit could be reviewed and adjusted.

Trading limits are intended to protect the customer because of the extraordinary risks which he assumes in buying on margin. But, since the customer has at risk only what he has put up in cash, the limit applies to the aggregate of those payments, not to the total value of the commodities against which his cash payments give him claim.

In 1972, Merrill Lynch normally required customers to put up eight percent of the face value of a futures contract as margin payment. But, as Sallas had predicted, because of Bonham-Carter's extraordinary cash reserves, Royer and the office manager had agreed to allow him to buy on five percent margin, the minimum permitted by the Chicago Board of Trade.

Wheat is traded in three cities: Chicago, Kansas City and Minneapolis. But unless the customer specified otherwise, Merrill Lynch bought it in Chicago. That day, July 3, the September wheat which Bonham-Carter had been instructed to buy was selling in Chicago at between $1.49 and $1.50 a bushel. That was the price which would appear in the newspapers the next day, it was the price that news commentators would cite and the price by which brokers would measure the direction of the market. But $1.49 to $1.50 was not the price of all September wheat; it was only an average, known in the trade as the contract price. In reality, the Chicago market traded some twenty-two grades of wheat, some of which sold for slightly more than the contract price, others for slightly less. On that day, No. 1 hard winter wheat was selling at a one-cent premium.

There was one more formality. Royer handed him a green three-by-five card which Bonham-Carter signed without reading. It was a commodity account agreement. Had he bothered to read the tiny seven-point type, he would have learned that he had agreed to let Merrill Lynch hold his contracts and to sell them at any time and without notification. The language was only brokerage boiler plate. In fact, as a matter of practice, Merrill Lynch would only liquidate his contracts in the event their market value fell by more than twenty-five percent of the money he had put up, and he refused to put up more.

By the time the paperwork was completed, it was 1:30 Washington time. In Chicago, it would be 12:30, forty-five minutes before the close of the market.

Ordinarily, Royer explained, he would advise making a buy order at a specified price, but if Bonham-Carter wanted the purchase made that day, the only way to assure it was to put the order in at the prevailing market price. It might cost him an extra quarter cent per bushel.

Bonham-Carter agreed, and Royer wrote out a buy order for three hundred contracts of September No. 1 hard winter wheat at the market price. The contract unit varies from commodity to commodity, but for all grains traded on the Chicago Exchange a contract represents five thousand bushels. Royer rolled the scrap of paper, stuffed it into a red cylinder which would alert the teletype room that it was an order to be expedited, and dropped it into the pneumatic tube to the left of his desk. Forty feet away, the cylinder was picked up, and in thirty seconds it was on the wire to Chicago. Moments later, the order chattered out of a machine in the Chicago Board of Trade, was ripped off by a runner and rushed to the wheat pit on the floor. Though, to the untrained eye, the pit more closely resembled a theater fire than a marketplace, the runner knew exactly where to find his man. The coding on the order indicated that it was from Merrill Lynch and for hard wheat; the proper floor broker could be in only one place on only one step of the pit. While Royer and Bonham-Carter were still enjoying their first cigarette, the man in Chicago made the buy. Four minutes from the time it had left, the red capsule was back at Royer's desk with confirmation.

The order had been filled at $1.51 per bushel. For a total of $113,250, Bonham-Carter had just bought control of $2,265,000 worth of wheat—one and one-half million bushels—which would not even exist until September. For every penny by which the price of a bushel now rose, Peru would make $15,000 when he sold. If by September, the price had risen to $3.00, as Sallas had said it would, Peru's profit from that day's transaction alone would be $2,235,000.

Bonham-Carter felt a twinge of uneasiness when Royer informed him that, because he had bought more than two hundred thousand bushels, the law required Merrill Lynch to report the trade to the Commodity Exchange Authority. But it was only a twinge. After all, it was requirements like that which were the reason Peru had needed an intermediary, the reason they were paying him $100,000.

There was one final matter, the confirmation slip.

The next day was a holiday and it would not be ready until the fifth. Royer had to know where to have it sent. Bonham-Carter planned to leave that evening for New York, but had made no hotel reservations. At Royer's suggestion, it was agreed that the slip should be sent to the New York Hilton. The hotel was big, and there was little chance that he would be unable to get a room there.

It was 1:50 when Bonham-Carter got up to leave. Though the transaction had taken less than four minutes to execute, the entire procedure had taken almost four hours. Thereafter, there would be no forms, no questions. He considered it an auspicious beginning. He had only one nagging apprehension. Sallas had been emphatic in instructing him to buy hard winter wheat. There had been nothing on the piece of paper that had popped back up in the red capsule which indicated to him what sort of wheat he had bought. He had asked before, but he would ask again. Was Royer certain that the contracts had been for hard winter wheat?

Royer laughed. "My man, take my word for it," he said. "You got yourself three hundred of number one hard."

"You're certain?"

"Absolutely. Turkey Red. Nothing but the best."

Chapter

IV

SO Turkey Red was a grade of wheat. In the taxi to the airport, Bonham-Carter tried to recall the bits of conversation he had overheard two nights earlier and wondered how they fit with this new piece of information.

One thing was obvious. He had not been the only foreigner in town interested in wheat, possibly not the only
one buying it. If the conversation had meant what it
now seemed to mean, he was a piker alongside the men
in the baggy suits. Unless, of course, the baggy suits
were doing the selling and the other two men the buying. That was a possibility.

But why would anyone be buying in such volume?
Could they, too, know about El Niño? The Ministerio de
Pesquería was still issuing optimistic reports of the anchovy catch. Perhaps that deception had failed. It was a
troubling thought. Another buyer, bigger than himself,
might not take adequate precautions to conceal his activity. A bigger buyer might drive up the price faster
than Bonham-Carter could invest the Peruvian funds.
If that happened, the prices of wheat and soybeans
might reach the levels Sallas had projected and still
leave Peru with far less than its anticipated profit.

By itself, that prospect did not concern Bonham-
Carter. Peru could roll over on its side and sink into the
sea and it would not worry him, so long as it did not sink
before he got the balance of his fee. What did concern
him was the possibility that the balance of his fee might
be cast in jeopardy by something less dramatic—by an
inadequate return on Peru's investment, for example.
The $50,000 that Sallas still owed him had been prom-
ised without condition. But he knew Sallas well enough
to know that the money might be hard to come by if the
minister had to suffer the indignity of seeing his plan go
awry. He understood, too, that if Sallas refused to pay,
there was no potential legal recourse.

Over the long holiday weekend, out-of-town busi-
nessmen were staying away from the city, and Bonham-
Carter had no difficulty getting a room at the Hilton.
Taking his key directly from the desk, he ignored the

overtures of the bellhop and found his way to the thirty-ninth floor.

Half an hour later he was back in the lobby having changed into slacks and a sport jacket.

The only thing that the Hilton had in common with the Madison was newness. The hotel resembled a slender glass slab set on an east-west axis upon a slightly wider, rectangular first floor. Whoever had designed it had taken a good stab at making the first floor pay for itself. The central hall was given over to a long registration desk and several banks of elevators. But the halls parallel to it on either side were lined with bars and restaurants reflecting a business judgment that the hotel's Rotarian clientele would rise to the lure of foreign menus.

Bonham-Carter opted for a room at the lobby's west end which a blue awning announced as the Kismet Lounge. Inside, it turned out to be elaborately done up in a rose motif. He ordered a Scotch and, as he waited for it, tried to guess where the collection of nets and beads and vaguely Eastern bric-a-brac scattered about the place was intended to make him imagine he was. He glanced around him at the rest of the customers. Double-knit checks, string ties, white socks, mustard shirts, black tassel loafers—not the stuff on which illusions of the East were long sustained.

Suddenly the whole scene seemed ludicrous. He had come a zigzag course of some seven thousand miles to get to the United States. Now he was at its center, in a typical hotel, downtown in the middle of the city that was supposed to be the ultimate expression of American character, and what had he found? The whole place was in cultural drag. How long would it be, he wondered, before some American evangelist entrepreneur would build a replica of Westminster Abbey in which to address his flock? He decided to eat in his room.

Preoccupied, Bonham-Carter failed to notice that the elevator door was being held by a slender gray-haired man of about sixty whose British tailoring and continental appearance would have seemed more in place at the Pierre or the Carlyle than the Hilton. The man's warning was too late. Turning into the elevator, Bonham-Carter bumped squarely into over two hundred pounds of muscle headed in the other direction.

The impact was momentarily befuddling. With a smile and a hurried pardon, the man was out of the elevator and gone. But there was no mistaking the face and the accent. They belonged to one of the baggy suits from the Montpelier Room.

By the time Bonham-Carter collected his wits, the elevator had begun its ascent. It would not stop again until the thirty-fifth floor. It was nearly three minutes before he reached the lobby again. Neither man was in view. He would have to wait.

Nearly two hours later, his patience was rewarded. The baggy suit was back, this time without the slender gray-haired man but with one of his colleagues from the Madison.

Bonham-Carter watched the clerk hand them the room key, gave them a ten-second head start, then moved quickly to the desk.

"Excuse me, but could you have room service send up a fifth of Johnnie Walker Red."

The clerk looked confused.

"I'm with those gentlemen," Bonham-Carter said, nodding in the direction which the baggy suits had taken.

For a moment it looked as though the clerk might refuse.

"Look, I've got to run an errand or I'd call from the room. Do me a favor."

The clerk nodded.

When Bonham-Carter reached the bank of elevators into which the two men had disappeared, there were no lights above any of the doors. He backed off and checked the signs at the end of the wall that indicated which elevators served what floors. The bank of elevators on the left were for floors 25 through 34, those on the right for floors 35 through 44. When he looked back, a light had come on over one of the elevators on the right. He watched it move rapidly across the top of the door and then stop, indicating that the elevator was at the forty-second floor. The elevator stopped a second time at the forty-fourth floor before starting back down. The second stop told him he would have to wait for the same elevator, wait to make sure that the second stop, the one at the forty-fourth floor, had been to pick up another party and not to let out one of the two men he was following. Sure enough as he entered the elevator, he brushed past a couple in their mid-thirties on their way out. The woman seemed flushed and held the man's arm closely with both her hands just below his shoulder. As he waited for the door to slide closed, he could hear the man offering to get her a taxi. The Scotch would have to be going to the forty-second floor.

At the forty-second floor, Bonham-Carter emerged from the elevator. Signs on the wall directly opposite him indicated that the floor contained the "tower suites." As he stepped out into the hall, he could see that the doors were set at wider intervals than had been the case three floors below. He made his way quickly toward one end of the hall and ducked into an alcove that contained an ice machine. The design of the building was ideal for his purpose. By leaning out slightly from the alcove, he could see the whole length of the hall. It was possible that there was a service elevator, but whoever used it would also have to use the hall.

In ten minutes, he heard a door open. Halfway down the corridor, a waiter emerged from a fire door at the far end of the hall. As the waiter turned toward him, Bonham-Carter ducked back into the alcove and busied himself with the ice machine, listening carefully to the waiter's footsteps. Ten yards short of the alcove, the waiter stopped, checked his order slip, then knocked on the door. As he did so, he had to step forward to let pass a tall man carrying a wax cardboard ice bucket. By the time the door opened, the man with the ice bucket had disappeared into the elevator and was scribbling the room number on a scrap of paper.

It was pushing 11:30 when Bonham-Carter arrived back in the lobby. With the stores closed the next day, he could waste no time. There were five cabs waiting on the crescent driveway under the hotel marquee. The traffic was light at that hour and in a few minutes the cab had negotiated the several blocks to the top of Times Square. There, Bonham-Carter got out and headed south into the seamy neon world of pimps, pushers and purveyors of stolen merchandise.

Ten minutes later he was in one of the square's dozen or so fluorescent-lit stores that specialize in records, tapes, souvenirs and cheap sound equipment. At a counter in the rear, he found what he was looking for. He paid the man $116 and left with two parcels.

A block farther down the street, he turned into an all-night drugstore, emerging five minutes later with a brown paper bag containing adhesive tape and a pair of inexpensive pliers.

By 12:20 he was back in his room on the thirty-ninth floor of the Hilton.

The tape and the pliers he dropped into the drawer of the bedside table. One of the parcels he tossed into the chair, the other he unwrapped on the bed and spread out its contents: a Fanon FIC3 home intercom consisting of a master station, a remote unit and some forty feet of connecting wire.

After ripping the cable off its terminals, he coiled it and dropped it into his jacket pocket. The master station and remote unit he tossed into the trash basket. Then, after asking the switchboard to wake him in two hours, Bonham-Carter turned out the lights and lay down on the bed.

The call from the switchboard came a little before 3:00 A.M.

The elevator would take him no lower than the lobby level, but an escalator in the northeast corner of the building led one level lower to an underground shopping mall and a coffee shop. Everything was dark and closed. The hotel's maintenance complement would probably be off until about six. Bonham-Carter glanced around him. Directly across the small sunken patio, at the bottom of the escalator, in the facing wall, was a door marked "stairs to main lobby." Behind the door he found a small concrete chamber with two more doors in the wall facing him and a third door in the wall on his right. The latter also was marked "stairs to main lobby." He opened it. He could see stairs leading both up and down. He headed down. The stairs ended in a hall about five feet by seven feet. Again two doors. He tried the one on the right first. It was a closet. Then he tried the one on the left. It was blue and steel and behind it he found what he was looking for.

Two floors below the lobby level, lights burned around the clock. Bonham-Carter paused for a moment and tried to calculate the direction that would put him underneath the hotel telephone switchboard. If the Hilton was anything like other hotels, there would be an enormous wall cabinet, perhaps an entire room of circuitry through which the hundreds and hundreds of rooms in the hotel would be linked to the switchboard jacks and beyond them to the outside world.

In five minutes he had found it: a gray steel cabinet, ten feet high and nearly forty feet long. Access to the cabinet was through twenty-six top-to-bottom doors which gave it the appearance of a bank of several dozen huge metal athletic lockers.

Each door concealed two vertical rows of over one hundred terminals from which sprouted wires in blue, red, green, gray and black. The terminals were numbered but not by room. To match terminal and room, Bonham-Carter had to consult the chart pasted to the inside of each door.

In several minutes, he had located his room and the room he had seen the room service waiter knock on four hours earlier. They were three metal doors apart. He unscrewed the nut that secured a blue wire to his own terminal and pushed the wire aside. His phone and the switchboard were now no longer connected. Then he took the intercom wire from his pocket and, after peeling back the plastic coating, wrapped it around the terminal and secured it with the nut. He then threaded the other end of the intercom wire behind the face of the cabinet from door to door until he reached the terminal belonging to the room on the forty-second floor. After cutting off the excess wire with the pliers and stripping its end of its plastic coating, he undid the second terminal and screwed the intercom wire down on top of the wire already there. His phone was now an extension of that belonging to the baggy suits. Bonham-Carter shut the doors, collected the excess wire and was back in the elevator by 3:45.

Before going to bed, he had one last piece of business to attend to. Without taking his phone off the hook, he unscrewed the mouthpiece and removed the round disc inside. Though the phone would still receive, without the disc it would not transmit. There would be no chance of his eavesdropping being overheard.

Next, he unwrapped the second package he had bought in Times Square. Its contents were identical to those of the first, a Fanon FIC3 intercom set. Buying two sets had been an expensive way to get the extra wire, but at that hour there had been no alternative. He could not have known how much wire he would need for the basement, and it was essential that he have one set intact if he was to know when the line was in use. Though his phone would pick up any call made to or from the room on the forty-second floor, it would not ring. He could hardly spend the day holding the phone to his ear.

He placed the remote unit on the bedside table and, with the adhesive tape from the drawer, bound the earpiece of the telephone receiver to the face of the unit.

The master station he placed on the bureau and plugged the electrical cord into the wall socket. With the volume on high, he would be able to hear what was said on the line from any point in the room except the shower.

After hanging a do not disturb sign on the door, Bonham-Carter turned in. It was 4:30, the morning of the Fourth of July.

It was after ten when he awoke. He had not slept well. For what had seemed like hours he had imagined himself on a train somewhere in Poland. Though racked with fatigue, he had, in his dream, been unable to sleep because of the incessant talking of two men with whom he shared the compartment. Their conversation had been doubly irritating for the fact that he had understood not one word of it. Even in his dawning consciousness the men seemed to talk on. It was almost a minute before he grasped the significance of what he was hearing and sat up.

The voices were coming from the intercom on the bureau. How long had they been talking? Surely not hours. Probably closer to ten minutes. It hardly mattered. His. dream had been faithful to reality in one respect; he could not understand what was being said. Quite possibly it was Polish. It might just as well have been Tagalog. Bonham-Carter had no gift for languages.

Five minutes later the conversation ended abruptly with a click. Bonham-Carter's thoughts turned to food. Breakfast presented a problem. If he ate in the dining room, he ran the risk of missing a call he might understand. But how to get in touch with room service? He had rendered his phone useless.

He slipped into his clothes and opened the door. Down the corridor, he could see the maid's cart. She had passed his room because of the sign he had hung out the night before, but between where he stood and the cart, there were a half-dozen open rooms. They would be stripped but their telephones would work.

He was back in his room in three minutes. By the time he was out of the shower and dressed, the waiter was at the door with breakfast plus a club sandwich, a chef salad, a six-pack of beer and a carafe of white wine. All but the breakfast Bonham-Carter put into the refrigerator. It would be an all-day vigil. There was no telling when he could get to a phone again.

New Yorkers sweltered in the holiday heat that July 4. Wall Street's sizzling canyons were empty of all but a few hundred tourists and strollers who stared with be-mused curiosity at a troup of bluegrass minstrels taking advantage of the trafficless day to test the Brobdingnagian acoustics.

At Shea Stadium that afternoon, New York Mets' pitcher, Tom Seaver, would lose a no-hitter in the ninth inning when a San Diego Padre with the alliterative name of Leron Lee lined a broken-bat single to center field. Bonham-Carter would watch this on television and not understand its significance.

Twice, at noon and again at 3:30, the remote unit crackled with calls from the room on the forty-second floor. Both conversations were in the unintelligible tongue of the men on the Polish train. It was 6:45 when Bonham-Carter got what he had been waiting for, a call in English.

The call was apparently incoming, for the first word over the intercom was heavily accented. Bonham-Carter took it for the name of the answering party. It sounded like "Sockem." The caller seemed to be well known to Sockem since he identified himself only as Michael before getting down to business.

It was clear from the tone of his voice that the information Michael was relating was good news. "We've just got assurances from the Agriculture Department that the subsidy will be allowed to move as necessary to hold the export price. In light of that, we are prepared to sign tomorrow," he said.

"One minute." From the muffled noises amplified by the intercom, Bonham-Carter could tell that Sockem was conferring with someone else in the room.

"Michael." Sockem was back on the line. "I am sorry. I was speaking to Belousov. He agrees that we can complete the arrangements tomorrow morning. He also asks if the contract can be changed from three and one half to four million tons on the same terms. If not, we are prepared to accept the offer as it is now written. I know I do not have to repeat that there is, with respect to the entire transaction, a need for the greatest secrecy."

Michael assured him that the extra half million tons would create no problem, and that secrecy was a mutual concern. After agreeing to meet at ten the following morning at a downtown address, the two men rang off.

Bonham-Carter, who had been scribbling furiously throughout the conversation, was now leafing through a booklet Royer had given him the morning before. In a moment he had what he was looking for, a commodities equivalency table. A ton of wheat was equal to almost thirty-seven bushels. "Sockem" had just committed himself to buy 148 million bushels of wheat. That worked out to 2960 contracts, almost ten times the amount Royer had bought for him the previous day.

Bonham-Carter had no idea what the total size of the market might be, but one thing seemed obvious: if Sockem and his friend were buying wheat, they were buying a great deal of it.

Sallas had warned him that his own purchases would push the price up too rapidly unless spread over a period of time. Once again the possibility occurred to him that the price might be pushed up regardless of what he did. Who were these men with the strange names? Had they bought all they would buy, or were they, as he was, buying in installments? Would Sallas have given him different instructions had he known there would be another major buyer in the market? Could he gamble that the secrecy of which the men had spoken would be maintained? Or should he invest the balance of his funds as quickly as possible and take advantage of the price rise that was sure to occur when Sockem's purchases came to light at some future date? What future date? Perhaps it would be after September, after he was out of the market, too late.

Bonham-Carter was awakened at seven the next morning by the switchboard's call to the room on the forty-second floor.

After showering and dressing, he turned off the intercom. In the lobby, he stopped briefly at the Hertz car rental desk, then went to the coffee shop for breakfast.

At 9:20 the two baggy suits emerged from the elevator and made straight for the hotel's east door. Outside, under the massive marquee, they climbed into a waiting limousine. Neither man seemed to notice the red Plymouth Barracuda parked with motor running at the south end of the crescent driveway.

Two blocks north of the hotel, the limousine turned west off the Avenue of the Americas and headed toward the river. Five seconds later, the Barracuda made the same turn.

The limousine took the long crosstown blocks with authority, and Bonham-Carter was forced to press to avoid losing contact. The two cars hit the southbound ramp of the West Side Highway fifty yards apart.

In the speeding traffic of the highway, Bonham-Carter allowed the limousine a longer lead. He could still see the heads of its two passengers through the rear window.

Five minutes later, both cars left the highway and headed back across lower Manhattan.

At the bottom of Broadway, the limousine stopped and let the two men out in front of a large office building. Bonham-Carter double-parked half a block farther on and hurried back on foot. By the time he reached the lobby, neither man was in sight, and none of the six elevators was open. From the monitor on the wall, he could see that the only ascending elevator was at that moment on the fourth floor. He watched it stop again at the eighth floor then run uninterruptedly to the top of the building and start back down.

By that time, there were several open elevators. Bonham-Carter ignored them and moved instead to the building directory on the lobby's north wall. The directory was alphabetical. In a minute he satisfied himself that there was nothing in the collection of ad agencies and legal offices on the fourth floor that could have interested the baggy suits. He started back through the alphabet, this time looking at eighth-floor entries. Halfway through the list he found the entry he was looking for: Midcontinental Grain. Indented beneath was a list of company officers. At the top of the list was the name Michael Freeport, Chairman.

Several blocks farther up Broadway, Bonham-Carter parked again, went into the Merrill Lynch offices at One Liberty Plaza and bought three hundred more wheat contracts. With his credit check behind him, the transactions took only twenty minutes. The price of September wheat had not changed since two days earlier, so the costs of the two purchases were identical. But this time he also bought two hundred contracts of August soybeans at $3.58 per bushel. For his option on those more than $3.5 million worth of soybeans, he had to put up a margin payment of $179,000. As he left the Merrill Lynch office, he reflected that he would have to pick up the pace of his buying. He had bought twice already and he was only a little over $400,000 into his Swiss account.

Shortly after eleven he arrived back at the Hilton. After dropping off the keys at the Hertz counter, he walked to the main desk and approached one of the clerks.

"I'd like to check out of room forty-two eighteen, please."

"Name, please."

"Belousov." Bonham-Carter ran the syllables together. As he spoke them, they could have fit any of a dozen spellings.

The clerk turned his back and flicked through the room files.

"Any charges since breakfast?"

"No."

"Okay, then you can just take this over to the cashier," the clerk said, handing Bonham-Carter an itemization of charges and pointing to another counter farther down the same wall.

Bonham-Carter thanked the man and walked slowly in the direction he had pointed. But he did not stop at the cashier's window. Instead, a minute later he was in the elevator and on his way to his room.

As he had suspected, the bill which the clerk had handed him indicated that the room was occupied by two men. The names in the upper left-hand corner of the bill identified them as Sakun, Paul; and Belousov, Nicolai. Beneath the two names, in the space where normally the name of a firm or corporate affiliation would appear, there was the word Exportkhleb. It meant nothing to Bonham-Carter.

Back in his room, he took the last of the beers from the refrigerator and sat down at the desk. It was Wednesday. He would have to cable Sallas.

On a piece of hotel stationery, he began to compose his message. He had bought a total of six hundred contracts of wheat at $1.51 per bushel and two hundred contracts of soybeans at $3.58 per bushel. Eliminating dollar signs and decimal points, he condensed these facts into two six-digit numbers; 600151 and 200358.

Then, opening the previous day's *New York Times* to the New York Stock Exchange listings, he began to run his finger down the column of numbers indicating how many hundreds of shares of each stock had been traded. He looked only at the second digits. Sallas had pointed out that if he used first digits, he would never find a zero. Twenty lines down, he found what he wanted. Alberto Culver had traded sixteen hundred shares. That took care of the six. He wrote down the name of the stock. Then, picking another part of the listings at random he repeated the process, stopping at Garfinckel's which had traded two thousand shares. So much for the first zero.

Inside of two minutes, he had a stock for each of the digits of the first number. He then went through the procedure again until he had six more stocks for the soybean transaction.

After dating the cable draft July 3, the date of the market day described in the paper, he wrote as follows:

AGAINST SHORT TERM MOVEMENT ADVISE
PURCHASE FOLLOWING:
              ALBERTO CULVER
                GARFINCKELS
                  DAN RIVER
                 COLLINS FD
                    PEPSICO
                  PUBLICKER
UNTIL FURTHER NOTICE ADVISE REDUCE
POSITION:
                   TRANE CO
                BLACK DECKER
                   LEVITZ FURN
               MOHAWK DATA
                    US SHOE
                HOWARD JOHN

By the time the cable reached Sallas' house, the New York Stock listings for July 3 would be readily available in Lima.

Bonham-Carter finished his beer and turned on the television set. He was pleased with the day's events. Things were going according to plan and, with the other major buyers in the market, Sallas' price projection stood a good chance of being realized. He had not mentioned the baggy suits in his cable. In rehearsing the cryptogram format, they had not envisioned the need to communicate other information. Besides, he did not yet know the identity of the other buyers.

Considering New York was the center of the television universe, the afternoon programming was a disappointment. Bonham-Carter finally settled for a closed-circuit channel on which a wire service news story was moving silently up the screen, white letters against a blue background.

According to the item, two FBI agents, one disguised as a pilot and carrying $800,000 in ransom money, had shot and killed two armed hijackers who had been holding eighty-six persons aboard a jet airliner in San Francisco International Airport. The dead men were identified as Dimitr Alexiev and Michael Dimitrov.

The two men's names had not disappeared from the screen before Bonham-Carter was putting on his jacket. Minutes later he was in a pay phone in the lobby putting through a call to the U.S. Department of State. He had decided that, if asked, he would identify himself as a reporter from the *Toronto Star.*

He was not asked. The man answering at the Soviet desk evinced no interest in having more than his name. Yes, of course he had heard of Exportkhleb. It was the Russian agency responsible for foreign sales and purchases of grain. Khleb, the man explained, was a transliteration of the Russian word for bread. Bonham-Carter had one more question. Had the man ever heard of

Paul Sakun or Nikolai Belousov? The desk officer had never heard of Sakun. But Belousov he knew. Belousov was the head of Exportkhleb.

Chapter

V

WHILE Bonham-Carter still stood in the telephone booth pondering his discovery, Nicolai Belousov was leaving the office building on Lower Broadway. Though satisfied, the Russian was weary. At fifty-two years old, his system was beginning to protest the demands made on it by his schedule.

It was not that the rigors of high-level grain negotiations were new to him, rather that they were old. Ten years earlier, in 1963, he had seen the same men from the same companies he would be seeing now. Then the meetings had been in Ottawa at the Chateau Laurier, a massive turn-of-the-century railroad hotel across Confederation Square from the Canadian Parliament buildings. They had been difficult talks—complicated by the fact that they occurred against the backdrop of a highly partisan political debate in the United States. Republican party leaders had charged a Democratic Administration with courting Communism for its willingness to extend export credits to the Russians so that the Russians could buy grain from American companies. These echos of 1950s rhetoric had stirred just enough life in dying Cold War embers to hold sales to a minimum. Belousov had been just a deputy in those days. Ultimate responsibility for the negotiations had rested on other shoulders. This time he was in charge and it was his future that would be affected by what happened in the weeks that followed.

Accompanied by Paul Sakun, a member of the Ministry of Foreign Trade, Belousov had arrived at the Madison on the twenty-ninth of June, two days before Bonham-Carter. Since then he had been in almost constant motion. In a series of discreet telephone calls, he had let out the word that the Russians were buying. Then, like a Hong Kong tailor on his annual tour of the United States, he had set up in his hotel room and prepared to receive.

And receive he had, for in midsummer of 1972 the American grain market belonged to the buyers. Indians and Africans may have died that year for lack of bread grains, but alongside the railroad rights-of-way that crisscrossed the Great Plains of the American Middle West, the storage elevators stood rafter full. And in Washington, at the Department of Agriculture—all-subsidizing inseminator of surplus—friendly men stood ready to pay for foreign disposal of the bounty without quibble as to cost. As long as these men at the department stuck to their policy of export subsidy, a foreign sale was a risk free proposition. The companies could buy dear and sell cheap, and Uncle Sam would make them whole.

Freeport was only one of a number of grain operators, who, seeing the profit in this arrangement, made the pilgrimage to the Madison. The meetings were occasions of strange contrast: on one side of the table, Belousov, agent of the world's greatest state-planned economy; on the other, Freeport and his competitors, the last of the great freewheeling capitalists, throwbacks to a more private era of private enterprise in which there were no stockholders, an era when authority and ownership resided in the same hands, and men felt responsible only to themselves.

In all half a dozen different companies had come to the hotel. And most had come several times, for there were complex terms to be worked out. Meetings had run late into the evening. The first agreement had not been completed until that morning in New York, and that purchase represented only a fraction of what Belousov had come to buy. It might take weeks before he had bought all he had to buy. He would have to endure the fatigue. If he surrendered to it, he would become careless, and he could not become careless. A slip, even the slightest hint of overeagerness, could betray him. It would not escape the grain men. They would listen to his words, but their gray eyes would be on his face, searching for the blink, the twitch, the swallow that would tell them what they wanted to know. They were not farmers looking to cover their costs; their government guaranteed them their costs; they were traders, dealers, opportunists looking for that extra cent or two cents which multiplied by millions and millions of bushels would mean the difference between big profits and small.

Belousov knew he could rely on each of the grain men to keep the size of his sales from the others; he depended on their secretive ways to prevent any one of them from sensing the overall scale on which he intended to buy. If anyone did, his game was lost. The prices would run away from him. Russia could not afford that. More importantly, he could not afford it. His government did not take kindly to failure. As the limousine whisked him back uptown toward the Hilton, Belousov rested his head on the back of the seat, closed his eyes

71]

and tried to put these thoughts out of his mind. Instead, he reflected upon the circumstances that had brought Russia once again to the West to buy grain.

Over a quarter of a century had elapsed since the end of the Second World War. For Russia, the years had been a time of rebuilding, and the advances had been enormous as the Russian worker, under the lash of external menace both real and imagined, had given his sweat without stint to the championship of his ideology.

But the bulk of Russian progress had occurred in the heavy industrial sector, in power generation, in production of steel and cement, and in the extractive industries, notably manganese, nickel, iron, chrome and the platinum group metals. Belousov had watched these gains with satisfaction, knowing that they were the foundation on which economic strength rested. Moreover, such basic production gains would be duly recorded by economists in other countries and printed up in abstracts of growth rates, capital formation and all the other indices of who is doing well and who isn't. The world would be impressed.

But if Belousov was pleased to regard the world as Russia's ideological constituency, he was also aware that his government was being forced to address a more immediate audience. Soviet housewives hungered for the rudest home appliances. For them, the Soviet economic miracle had been little more than a concrete cell in an apartment block and a bunch of numbers printed in Pravda.

The only mechanical home appliance readily available in the Soviet Union in 1970 was the sewing machine. Automatic washers, dryers and freezers were neither produced nor sold. And if one was lucky enough to get on the list for one of the Russian-built Fiats rolling off the assembly line at the new Togliatti plant, one could count on a four- to six-year wait. Belousov knew because he had seen the numbers that the Russian in 1970 was getting one-third the goods and services consumed by the average American and that he was eating only one-third as much meat. And Belousov knew, too, that the Russian was getting impatient.

For these reasons, Belousov had marked with satisfaction the new Five-Year Plan which Soviet Premier Aleksei Kosygin unveiled in the summer of 1971 in a speech to the 24th Communist Party Congress. The plan's promises had been characteristically bold. By 1975, seventy-two percent of Russian families would have television sets, seventy-two percent would have washing machines and sixty-four percent would have refrigerators. Production of automobiles would increase four times and consumption of meat would increase by one-third. It had not occurred to him at the time that the last pledge—almost a throwaway—would turn out to have a significant impact on his life.

It is part of the Western caricature that the Russian is a potato eater. In fact, the single most important ingredient of the Russian's diet is not the potato. It is bread. The average Russian consumes more than a pound of bread a day, and he eats it in a mind-boggling variety of forms. He can have *polianitsa, Ukrainka, kasha, bliny, pannkogid, palmeni, vareniki, pirozhki, kelebiaka, bulochky, palochky, pampushky, balabushky, kruchenyk, bublyky, zdoba, rohalyky, rizhok, deda's puri, khala, khorz, solomka* and *koulitch.* If he tires of these, he can have others. The Moscow central bakery alone turns out some 130 varieties.

On occasion, the Russian taste for bread has made it necessary to import grain. But such occasions have been rare. Generally, Mother Russia provides. In fact, the Russian grain harvest is traditionally the largest in the world, and accounts for the fact that the agency which Belousov headed bore the name Exportkhleb rather than Importkhleb. The Five-Year Plan announced in 1971 promised that grain production would get even greater, that annual grain yields would rise to 195 million tons from the 162 million tons averaged in the previous five years.

But there was a mouse in the Russian bread box in 1972. The mouse was the promise that meat consumption would increase from 11.4 million tons to 15.6 million per year.

It takes eight pounds of animal feed to produce a single pound of meat, and Russia's extreme climate limits severely its ability to grow corn and other soft animal feeds. To achieve its meat-consumption goals, Russia would have to use bread grains for animal feed. It did not take a sharp-eyed analyst to see that the increase in demand for animal feed was going to be as great as the projected increase in grain production. In short, if grain production fell even a little bit short of projections, the Russian pigs and the Russian people were going to be lining up at the same trough.

Under ordinary circumstances, this problem might not have been acute. Russia historically was an exporter of grains. Increases in domestic requirements theoretically could have been met by reducing exports. Reducing exports would mean loss of foreign exchange. Given the prevailing political priorities, it would have been expedient to accept that cost.

But circumstances were not ordinary in 1972. Russia's Golden Triangle—the grain-growing region cornered by Leningrad in the north, Novosibirsk in the east and Odessa in the south—had seen nothing but bad weather all year. That winter an unusually light snow cover had provided the infant wheat planted the previous September and October with little insulation against the bitter Russian cold. Winter wheat is not a frail crop. It can withstand temperatures down to five below zero Farenheit. But it got colder than that in Russia in the winter of 1972, and without the snow to protect it, almost thirty-five million hectares of winter wheat, wheat that would have yielded thirty million tons at harvest, succumbed to winter kill before the year was two months old.

That was not all. In June of 1972 a high pressure system stagnated over the Urals, its circular winds drawing air out of the Arctic, driving it like a wedge under the warmer air over the new territories in western Siberia and northern Kazakhstan, then superheating it over the desert of the Kazakh Plateau. By the time this air crossed the Caspian Sea and headed north up the Volga valley in the second and third weeks of June, it was ninety-five to a hundred degrees Farenheit and dry as dust. In the valley, seven million hectares of spring wheat planted in May collapsed in trauma, and Russia had lost another twelve to fifteen million tons from its harvest.

The economic loss was severe. But the political losses promised to be even more serious. To the Russian, the quality of his bread is one yardstick by which he measures his standard of living. Nikita Khrushchev, who should have known better, had failed to take that into account ten years earlier and had tried to cover up a bad crop by raising the extraction rate—the rate at which wheat is converted into flour. The drop in bread quality that resulted had been a factor in his downfall in 1964.

None of this had to be explained to Belousov on the Friday morning in late June when he was handed his instructions. At its regular Thursday meeting the day before, the Politburo had reached the decision to import. No one had suggested that the crop failure and the commitments made in the Five-Year Plan were his responsibility. The Planning Agency and the Politburo bore responsibility for them. But Belousov knew the system well enough to understand that blame had mercurial qualities and did not always alight where it ought. In being handed his orders, he was being told to cure an economic malady, and told by a government that had been known to hang its doctors. It might do no good to explain later that the malady had been incurable. The Soviet Union had made huge investments to develop its agriculture in the previous decade. As the prototype for collective economies the world over, it could not afford to concede failure.

Which explained Belousov's obsession with secrecy. The world commodities market was as sensitive as a smoke ring. A heavy rainfall, the discovery of a crop parasite, anything that altered the delicate balance between supply and demand would be reflected instantly in a price change. If the magnitude of the crop failure were known, the price would take an enormous leap.

That would be disaster. Russia could not afford to spend freely for grain in the West. She did most of her trade with the Communist bloc, and, as a result, held little in the way of Western currencies. To buy in volume at high prices in the United States, she would have to sell gold. That would have undesirable effects. It would depress the price of gold, which Russia as the world's largest producer of gold did not want to do, and it would deplete Russia's gold reserves, the one resource for which the West was willing to exchange precious technology. A similar dilemma had arisen before under Khrushchev, and Russia had run her gold stocks down to $1 billion. It could not happen again.

Preventing a price rise would be especially difficult because of two peculiarities of the Russian grain requirements. The Russian eats almost no noodles, no macaroni, no spaghetti nor any of the other forms of pasta common throughout the rest of the world. Russia therefore has little use for durum, the gluten-rich grain from which pasta is made. Belousov's instructions were to purchase durum only in small amounts that could be mixed with other grains and made into bread. Belousov also was instructed not to buy spring wheat because of its susceptibility to a fungus parasite known as *Claviceps purpurea*.

Under the circumstances, this latter restriction may have seemed excessively squeamish, but there was a reason. The *Claviceps purpurea* fungus contains several alkaloid drugs, among them one called ergotamine. If ergotamine is present in dough when baked, it undergoes chemical changes which convert it into lysergic acid diethylamide, better known as LSD. The Russians had happened on this discovery by accident in 1722 when an entire Russian army commanded by Peter the Great and bent on the capture of Constantinople had gone berserk on the eve of battle after eating an off batch of rye.

Because of these two restrictions, Belousov's buying would be focused on just part of the grain market, namely soybeans and hard winter wheat. The possibility of a price rise was increased proportionately. But there would be several factors working in his favor. He would be dealing with a number of companies in rapid succession. It was possible that he could complete his buying in bits and pieces before the sum of it could be learned. The companies would assist him. They would be selling him grain that they did not yet own. They would know better than to announce what they had sold. Individually the companies would keep it secret from each other in order to prevent panic buying. Collectively, they would keep it secret from the farmers until they had bought all they had promised to deliver. That was the way business was done in the United States.

Belousov had one more crucial factor in his favor. The linchpin in the Russian buying plan was the U.S. government's agricultural export subsidy. Under it, a U.S. exporter could sell wheat abroad for $1.62 a bushel and be assured of breaking even regardless of the price he had to pay to buy it, because the government would pay him the difference. This safety net was essential to the Russian strategy because the U.S. companies, knowing it was there, would be far less cautious and circumspect in making their commitments. It had been to inform Belousov that the U.S. government intended to stick by this policy that Freeport had called the New York Hilton the evening of July 4.

Belousov knew he would need continued good luck, but as he and Sakun once again entered the lobby of the hotel and headed for the elevator, he could take comfort from the fact that he had made a good start. Though they were crossing paths with him for the third time in as many days, neither man took note of the tall figure in the white linen suit and dark glasses apparently making an inquiry at the tour bus counter.

Chapter

VI

BONHAM-CARTER bought heavily on each of the next two days. By the time the market closed on the seventh, he held contracts which gave him a claim on eighteen million bushels of wheat and three million bushels of soybeans. Still, he was only some $2.2 million into his stake.

Though neither commodity's price had shown any sign of rising since his initial purchase in Washington on July 3, Sakun's telephone conversation with Freeport and subsequent conversations overheard between the Russians and other grain companies had convinced him that the price rise, when it came, would be biggest in wheat.

Before retiring for the night, Bonham-Carter composed his second weekly cable to Sallas. As agreed, it described only the transactions, making no mention of the Russian buying.

At 7:30 the next morning, the Saturday streets were almost empty. During the night, the breezes moving down the East and Hudson rivers had swept the exhausts of the previous day out to sea, and the sky above Manhattan was clear and blue. By ten o'clock, the air would again be hot and foul again. He would not care. By then, he would be somewhere over Ohio on American Airlines Flight 59 headed for San Francisco.

His decision to move on had not been made whimsically. At two o'clock the previous night, his intercom had gone dead in the middle of a conversation between Belousov and another Russian. Bonham-Carter had considered that reason enough to disengage. Anyone who could have found the wire tap could have found the room to which it was connected. He had been at the airport since four o'clock.

In more than a decade of freebooting for various employers, Bonham-Carter had seen too many hellholes to have any appetite left for danger or hardship. After the Lumumba job, having made his way north through

Kivu Province, he had been forced to hide for nearly three weeks in a tiny bamboo hostel in the otherwise deserted village of Kisoro on the border between the Congo and Uganda. The only passable road had been blocked to the west by the Belgian police in Rutshuru and to the east by the Ugandan authorities in Kabale. There had been nothing to do but wait. So he had waited. He had learned a lot in those weeks. From the Dutchman who ran the hostel he learned that there were subtle pleasures in loneliness. From walking the road east of the village he had learned that there was nothing hyperbolic about the term "impenetrable forest"—not, at least, when it referred to a wall of bamboo trunks three inches thick and two inches apart with shiny nickel-hard surfaces that made a machete rattle and turn in the grip. He had learned something about stoicism, too. Learned it from the Watusi whom he had watched arrive each night outside the hostel. Tall, silent men driven from their lands in Ruanda-Urundi by the smaller but more numerous Bahutu. Though many had been wounded, they had stood patiently in the darkened yard in front of the hostel. They had asked for nothing except water. And always, in the morning, they were gone, having taken their silence and their hardship elsewhere. He was comfortable with the memory of those three weeks, but like a dozen other experiences cherished in retrospect, he did not want to repeat them.

Difficult working conditions no longer interested him. He had long ago lost his comparative advantage in that sort of business and was content now to rely on his wits. One of the things that had attracted him to Sallas' proposition more than four months earlier had been the promise of no danger and a chance to live first class.

In Washington and New York, he had allowed his curiosity to get the better of his judgment. He was a wage earner now, and wage earners didn't need to take chances. He would be careful from now on. To one who had grown up poor in sunless London, California had seemed an uncomplicated paradise. He would see for himself. Besides, he had a compelling personal reason for going to San Francisco.

It was noon West Coast time by the time Bonham-Carter picked up his bags and made his way out to the taxi stand in the parking garage below the San Francisco International Airport terminal. There was no wait. A few minutes later, he was settled next to his suitcase in the back seat of a taxi and heading for the city.

"Where you goin'?" the driver asked.

"Huntington Hotel."

As the cab sped along the shore road toward the city, Bonham-Carter drank in the air off the Bay. It was fully twenty degrees cooler than New York and a welcome change.

The lobby was small and quietly furnished—more London than California. At the desk straight ahead, a man in a green sport jacket, his back to the door, was chatting with the clerk. He turned as Bonham-Carter approached, and for a moment before they passed, Bonham-Carter caught a glimpse of his face. The face's lumpy features hit him with the force of instant familiarity. Who was he? While the face belonged to none of the men he had seen in Washington or New York, in that brief glimpse it had seemed more Russian than Russian. Was he becoming paranoid? He was in the elevator before he finally connected an identity with the face. When he did, the face was not wearing a green jacket but a clerical collar; and he felt suddenly very foolish. He was in California now. Perhaps it happened all the time here that people bumped into Karl Malden.

"Paper, sir?" The question was evidently a formality, for the elevator operator was already handing him the early-afternoon edition.

As Bonham-Carter idly scanned the front page, a headline caught his eye: "Russians to Buy U.S. Grain." The headline spanned two wire service stories, one datelined San Clemente, the other Washington. He read quickly. The first story was sketchy, saying only that the President, while speaking that morning from the Western White House, had announced a three-year agreement under which Russia would buy some $750 billion worth of wheat, corn and other grains from the United States. The second story reported the terms of the agreement in more detail and was based on the press conference held simultaneously in Washington and conducted jointly by the Secretaries of Agriculture and Commerce.

Bonham-Carter spread the newspaper on his bed and studied the stories closely. There was something about their wording that puzzled him. Both the President and his two Cabinet members apparently had referred to the Russian buying in the future tense exclusively. There was nothing in either story to suggest that Russians had already begun to buy. The story from Washington also contained a curious quote attributed to the Agriculture Secretary. He was reported to have called it possible that, over the three-year life of the agreement, the Russian purchases might actually exceed $750 million. Why would the secretary make a statement like that? The Russians had already bought a third of that amount from a single company before the three-year period had even begun. Either the secretary was given to understatement, or he did not know what was going on. If the latter explanation were the right one, it would partly answer another question that had begun to puzzle him; it would explain why, despite all the buying that had been going on over the previous week, the price of wheat had not moved. That was not yet a serious problem for Peru, but unless some movement occurred soon, it would become one.

"Operator, could I have the listing for Ernest Winckler, please."

Bonham-Carter had showered and changed and now lay on his back on the bed. He had not seen Ernest Winckler since he and Martha left England in 1953. Probably; he would never see him again. That was the promise he had made to Martha when the baby was born. At the time she had been fearful of what the baby would look like, terrified that her punishment would be to have it look like him. When it had been a boy, she had been certain, and, on the theory that Ernest might not recognize what he could not see before him, she had made Bonham-Carter swear that he would never visit.

It had been an easy promise to keep. As far as he knew, they hadn't been within five thousand miles of each other for almost twenty years. Resisting temptation was not among his long suits, but at that distance he could manage. He had honored the promise. Now the boy would be grown and he wanted to see him. He didn't care about seeing Ernest, or even Martha; just the boy. Ernest would not be home in the afternoon. If he called now, Martha could tell him where the boy was and that would be the end of it.

The operator was back on the line. She gave him a Sausalito number. He took it down and thanked her. He dialed slowly. It was one of those phones that purred rather than rang. On the third purr, there was a pickup.

"Hello." It was Martha. Her accent was almost unchanged. "Hello, hello." He could hear her growing impatient. "Look, if this is your idea of a joke, it isn't amusing."

He listened to the click at the other end, half wondering why he had found himself unable to speak. He wasn't sure what he had expected. Certainly he had expected some change in the voice. But the voice had not changed. It was too easy to imagine the voice he had just heard saying exactly the same thing it had said to him twenty years earlier. In any event, the risk was too great. He folded the paper on which he had scribbled the number, slipped it into his wallet and shut his eyes.

When he woke it was seven o'clock. Although it was ten o'clock stomach time, the sleep had taken his appetite away. For almost two hours he walked. He walked down the hill, through the city's old tenderloin district, then around the base of the hill and back up California Street past the Fairmont and the Mark Hopkins.

The walk restored his appetite, and several doors before he reached the Huntington again he turned into a restaurant called Alexis'.

Whoever ran the restaurant obviously had made an effort to give the place the flavor of Russia, not the Russia of the men in New York and Washington, but the Russia of the czars. For the second time in a week, he found himself wondering why it was that Americans seemed never to eat in American restaurants. Maybe there weren't any American restaurants. Alexis' was elegant, expensive and slow. It was late when he got out.

Instead of heading toward the hotel, Bonham-Carter set off back down the hill. This time he was not strolling but walking with a purpose. If there were no interesting conversations on which to eavesdrop, eating alone was at least a profitable time to think. And waiters could be helpful in strange towns.

He passed the Bank of America building and continued down the hill. Several blocks farther on, he left the sidewalk and turned into the open first level of Embarcadero Center. To the right a circular stairway led to the first floor. He could already hear music coming from above.

At the top of stairs, the throbbing noise was overwhelming. Its source, a huge glass-encased sound system, was immediately inside the door. Beyond it, dancing in the semidarkness, there were maybe a hundred people, and beyond them a bar and more people. Feeling conspicuously old, he pushed through the crowd.

For half an hour he drank at the bar and watched the swirling mob of singles for a promising candidate. Next to him, two men in their mid-twenties were carrying on an argument about the San Francisco 49ers.

"Hey, buddy." What seemed to be the drunker of the two was speaking to him. "You a football fan?"

Bonham-Carter shrugged his shoulders. He'd become more interested in the television set behind the bar that was showing a color film loop of rolling surf.

"Whatsa matter, pal, you don't like football?"

"Actually, I don't know much about it."

"Where the hell are you from anyway?"

"England."

"Jesus!"

The sign on the men's room door read "No women allowed unless accompanied by their dates." He stepped up to one of the two urinals, a television screen at head level on the wall in front of him lit up with squirming images of couples having intercourse. He waited for his bladder to release its contents, wondering if one day the London pubs would install erotic movies in their rest rooms.

"Hi." He had not seen anyone else when he entered so the voice startled him. A glance in its direction told him that getting the cooperation of his bladder was going to be out of the question for the moment. He zipped up his fly and turned to the owner of the voice, a red-haired girl who apparently had just stepped from the toilet stall.

"Don't stop on my account," she said.

"I'm not, I'm stopping on my account. You want a drink? From the bar?" The girl was a stroke of luck. Though he had come to the bar with another matter on his mind, any girl who hung out in the men's room—in flagrant violation of the sign on the door—might be good for all kinds of services. Except for the little, dark-haired Peruvian confection which Sallas had provided him as a sort of contract bonus several weeks earlier, he had not been with a woman for a long time.

The girl's name was Clarissa Cox, but, as she explained on the way to the bar, she liked to be called Classie. The light was better at the bar than in the men's room and he could see that her face was heavily freckled. He put her age at somewhere close to, but under, thirty. She wore a brown pants suit and a seemingly permanent euphoric smile. Though he wanted badly to believe in his own magnetism, he had to admit that she looked mildly drugged.

"What's your name?" She spoke each word slowly as though it were a separate thought.

"Felix."

"You don't sound like you're from around here, Felix."

"No, that's right. I'm from Washington."

"Oh, really, I used to live in Washington. Or rather, I worked in Washington. I lived in Arlington."

Bonham-Carter wondered whether this girl with the dazed look was what he had come looking for—wondered whether her vacant voice would be too offputting.

"What sort of work did you do in Washington?" he asked.

"Secretary, at first. Then I got into tricks."

"Beg your pardon?

"Hmm?"

"What is tricks?"

"Oh, tricks is hooking. I was a hooker for the last two years I was there."

"I see. How was that?"

"Oh, that was great. Washington is a good hooking town. We used to work out of the Carroll Arms across the street from the new Senate Office Building. We had some very big deal customers, some very powerful guys. Course powerful don't necessarily mean you're much of a screw. Lot of them have hair triggers there, and there's plenty who can't get off at all. The girls used to like to get the big names, but the trouble was the powerfuls tend to be the older ones. Hey, we used to have a saying: you want to know what it was?"

"Please."

"We used to say that there is nothing so ideal as a powerful whose come is timed."

"That's very good. Are you in the same sort of work out here?"

"You mean am I hookin'? In San Francisco? Are you kidding? There's no business here. There's too much free competition. Besides, this is the fag capital of the world. You'd have to be an Arab boy to make a living hookin' in this town."

Classie was smiling her smile again. Having finished with the subject of hooking, she appeared content to remain silent and give herself up to whatever was working on her head. In the course of talking, they had walked out onto a raised concrete patio at the rear of the room. From there they could look north over the lower buildings toward the mouth of the Bay and Marin County. Somewhere in that direction was Sausalito, and Martha, who would be asleep, and maybe the boy.

"Classie?" He had the feeling that if he did not speak she might go on smiling and staring forever.

"Hmm?" At least she turned to look at him. Maybe she was more alert than she appeared.

"Classie, I wonder if you would do something for me . . ." He was deliberating over whether to tell her why or just what when she answered.

"Sure. I want to. I was just thinking about it."

"I'm not sure we are talking about the same thing. You see . . ."

She cut him off. "Don't worry, Felix. Like I told you, I'm not in business anymore. You'll see." As they left the bar, it occurred to Bonham-Carter that so far she had told him only what she wasn't doing in San Francisco.

It was close to two o'clock by the time they got to the street and found a taxi. Classie's apartment was half a block off California Street, some dozen blocks toward the ocean. The ride, which was mostly up and down, took five minutes. After two flights of stairs, they paused to catch their breath. The light from the street filtered through the glass bricks of the stairwell wall, and he could see that she was still wearing her rapturous smile. As they started to climb again, she took his hand and held it to her left breast. He could feel her nipple hard against the back of his hand. It was the first time they had touched.

The apartment was ninety percent pink. Walls, curtains, rug, kitchen and couch—all pink. It struck Bonham-Carter as a strange color for a girl with red hair to pick out. Classie had gone into the kitchen immediately upon entering and from where he stood in the living room, Bonham-Carter could see her leaning over the counter squeezing something that looked like an atomizer into her face.

When she emerged she walked straight toward him. He could see her eyes dilated and even glassier than they had been.

"Felix, sweetie, if you'd like to take that piss now, the bathroom is over there. When you're through, I'll be in the bedroom." She turned to go, then remembered something else. "Oh, and, Felix, maybe it's an ex-professional's idiosyncrasy, but I like to have the other person do the work."

When he entered the bedroom a few minutes later, he could see what she meant. The king-size bed was set squarely in the middle of the room. There was no headboard, nor were there any covers except for a bottom sheet. With ropes around it, it would have looked more like a boxing ring than a bed. In the middle of this expanse of white was Classie. She had taken off her clothes, which were now in a heap on the floor. He reflected that she must not have been wearing underwear, for there was none that he could see.

For a moment he wondered if Classie had taken a shower; from her knees to her neck, she appeared soaking wet. Then on the floor behind the pile of clothes, he spotted the nearly empty bottle of mineral oil. His initial reaction was a shudder. He had known women who had been almost addicted to sex with mineral oil. But they had always warmed the bottle in a sink of hot water. There was no sink in the room. It could not have been much more than sixty degrees in the San Francisco night. Classie would have smoothed the oil on cold.

Classie seemed oblivious to his presence. She lay on her back, her legs pressed tightly together. Except for two teasing fingertips, her body was motionless. For thirty seconds he remained in the doorway, uncertain of how to move. Though he was conscious of a surge of interest in his groin, he hesitated, reluctant to break her mood, reluctant as a boy is reluctant to cut in on a pretty girl at a dance because he can see over her partner's shoulder that her eyes are shut and that she is somewhere far away and will have no use for whoever brings her back.

Quietly he slipped out of his clothes. As his knees depressed the bed, Classie reached toward him with her eyes still closed. Her body heat had warmed the oil and her hand slid smoothly down his stomach until she had her orientation. Lifting her hips, she turned onto her side and pulled him down behind her, fumbling between her legs for his member with her free hand. He felt her slippery buttocks squirming backward into his crotch, then the light touch of fingernails where he could not see them. He knew he would not be an intruder that night.

"You're not circumcised, Felix."

"I know."

"That's very sane."

"Not my idea, actually."

"Very sane." Classie repeated the thought as though she hadn't heard him.

"Umm." He wasn't sure what correlation there might be between sanity and circumcision. Nor did he care. For the moment all his attention was focused on the work her fingernails were doing. If this was what circumcision felt like, in another few minutes he would be ready to sign up for the whole course.

Classie knew her business. Contrary to her warning, she was providing most of the motion, opening and closing the cleft of her bottom around his now fullblown self—and still the fingernails. After three or four minutes, the fingernails stopped and were replaced by a new and strange pressure he did not recognize.

"Have you ever had a rubber band, Felix?" Classie had disengaged and was on her back now, smiling up at him. For a moment he could not imagine what she was talking about. Then, glancing down to where her hand still held him, he saw what it was that had caused the pressure. "We used to call it 'The Congressional' back at the Carroll Arms," she added pulling him toward her. "It was a very big number with some of the older fellows."

Classie was all play and totally in control. He was just beginning to feel his body tensing in anticipation when she pushed him away and flipped onto her stomach. Her hand on his hip slowed him now, dictating rhythm like a metronome. Then she was on her back again and the cycle was beginning all over. Back-front-start-stop, the game seemed to go on forever. Bonham-Carter was perspiring freely now. His spirit was still willing, but the gymnastics were taking their toll. Just as he felt he would have to protest, Classie turned for the last time and whispered, "Now, Felix." For the first time he could feel real urgency in her body beneath him. The amateur was taking over from the professional in her and she quivered with each stroke. Her hand guided his around her flank to the cleft in her buttocks. There were no directions now, just heels digging into the backs of the thighs and hard breathing in his ear. Then the pressure of the heels was gone and he could feel her legs go rigid alongside his as she pressed her heels against the sheets to give her vaginal muscles purchase. For an instant, he could feel them squeezing him like a garrote. Then that sensation was numbed out and his legs and his loins were swimming in the warm tingly morphia of orgasm. The last thought that crossed his mind was the rubber band. Classie didn't need a rubber band. A rubber sheet maybe, but not a rubber band.

Classie was still sleeping when he awoke the next morning. There was almost nothing in the kitchen—an unopened can of coffee and some lefover garlic bread wrapped in tinfoil in the refrigerator. From these he made himself breakfast and sat down in front of the living room window to eat. His eye caught a photograph on the table. It was a photograph of a couple who looked to be in their early forties. The man was suntanned and dressed casually in a sport jacket and shirt open at the neck. The woman wore a professional, unmotherly look. The picture appeared to be at least twenty years old. He wondered if the man and woman were Classie's parents, where they were and whether they knew where she was. It was strange to think that someone anywhere might think of Classie as their little girl. What would he think of her if she were his little girl?

"Morning."

"Morning."

Classie was still naked. In the daylight she looked totally innocent—why was it his generation had insisted on defining innocence in terms of sex? All freckles from head to toe, she was still smiling, though sleep had put some life behind the smile now.

"Did you get something to eat?"

"Yes, thank you, there's some more coffee in the pot, if you want some." As she turned toward the kitchen, he could see that her back, her buttocks and the tops of her thighs were still shiny from the mineral oil. He watched them move with her steps and felt the familiar feeling in his trousers.

In a moment she was back, cup in hand. Without the

slightest hint of self-consciousness, she settled herself in one corner of the couch opposite him, tucked one ankle under her other leg and cradled the coffee in her lap. "I enjoyed that, Felix." It was said in a way that almost implied he had done her a favor. She did not ask him for an assessment and apparently did not expect one.

He watched her silently as she sipped her coffee. She seemed to feel no need to talk. He felt none of his usual morning after haste to depart.

"You never told me what you are doing in San Francisco. Have you gone back to being a secretary?"

"No, Felix, I'm not really doing much of anything. Just drifting along, waiting."

"Waiting for what?"

"I'm not sure. I suppose I'm just waiting to want to do something else. I've got some money now. Not much, but enough so that I don't have to work all the time. So I just wander around and think a lot. This is a good place for doing that. Why did you come to San Francisco? You just wandering, too?"

"Sort of."

"Maybe we should just wander around together then."

"Well, I do have business, too." Almost immediately, he regretted having spiked her suggestion. He did not see how she could get in the way of his work which it was now apparent would take only a few minutes to transact each day. It was going to take a lot of TV movies to add up to one "Congressional."

Too late, Classie had changed the subject. She seemed unaware that she had been rejected and uninterested in reopening the subject. Perhaps it was just as well. In his business, lonely was safe.

"Classie, I wonder if you would make a telephone call for me?"

"Sure. Want a cab?"

"No, I want you to call a friend of mine and find out something for me." He reached in his wallet and removed the slip of paper on which he had written Martha's number the previous afternoon. "I want you to call this number and ask for Anthony. Just say you are a girlfriend. I don't expect he will be there, so I want you to find out from whoever answers where he is. Make sure you find out where he is this afternoon. I don't want his home address if he is not going to be at home."

"Okay," she said, taking the paper from him and picking up the phone. If the request struck her as odd, she gave no indication.

The call took only a few minutes. Ernest answered. Classie jotted down the information and thanked him. Ernest had given her an El Cerrito address. She explained that it might take an hour to get there because it was two-thirds of the way around the Bay. He would have to rent a car. And he would have to hurry. It was already close to eleven o'clock.

"Who is Anthony, Felix?" She had followed him toward the door.

"He's a friend."

"Do you always have other people call your friends?"

"Nope, sometimes I meet them in the men's rooms of bars."

"You a switcher, Felix?"

"Yeah, something like that."

"If you're trying to make me jealous, it's working."

"Good-bye, Classie."

Classie had known what she was talking about when she had said the drive would take an hour. Even with the light weekend traffic, it was close to one o'clock by the time he had got through Oakland and Berkeley and was entering El Cerrito. The change from San Francisco was dramatic. This was flat land, land that had doubt-less once been part of the Bay's floor. Here there were no old town houses, no bay windows, no elegance, no charm. Instead, there were block after block of tiny square houses distinguished one from the other only by the placement of their windows and rounded Spanish doorways. The neighborhood was reminiscent of some he had seen in Australia. Those had depressed him at the time as this depressed him now.

He reflected on the best approach. Because it was Sunday, it was going to be difficult. He should have asked Classie to find out if the boy had a job. He could have waited one more day. It would have been easier to find an excuse to see the boy at his job. He pulled the car to the curb and thought. After a few minutes he took two new one-hundred-dollar bills from his wallet, slipped them into an envelope and tucked it in his jacket pocket.

The street address Classie had given him belonged to a small stucco bungalow. It had the dried lawn and generally unkempt appearance of a rented house. He rang the doorbell. The two-tone chime told him the bell was one of those wall units with the dangling metal tubes.

A girl answered the door. She was dressed in a faded Indian smock. He put her age at between fifteen and twenty. It was impossible to tell whether underneath the dress she was heavy or thin. Beyond her the living room was dark. The floor was strewn with newspaper.

"Is Anthony here?"

The girl appeared not to hear. She stared first at his face, then at his clothes, then beyond him at the car parked along the curb.

"Which Anthony?"

"Anthony Winckler."

"Just a minute." He waited for more than a minute. While he waited he rehearsed the speech he had planned. He was an old friend of his father's. He had not seen his father for many years. The money in the envelope was money that . . .

"Hi." It was the boy.

Bonham-Carter's hand went instinctively to his own face. It was as though he was looking into the mirror of the past. There were the same wide-set eyes, the same broad nose, the small teeth. The words would not come.

"I'm Anthony Winckler." There was no hint of recognition in the voice. The boy was not yet twenty. To him older people would look like older people just as Chinese people would look like Chinese people. He could not see the future as Bonham-Carter could see the past.

Their conversation took no more than a minute. The explanation for the visit, which had seemed plausible enough five minutes earlier in the car, seemed foolish and inadequate as Bonham-Carter stood on the stoop in front of the boy. In the end, he simply said he was a friend of the family and pressed the envelope into the boy's hand.

As he walked back to the car, he could feel the boy staring after him. He felt hollow and light-headed. He had come three thousand miles for this, and now it was over. He had been too numb to feel it. The worst part of it was that the boy had seemed friendly and willing to talk—if there had been anything to talk about. For the first time since he was a child, he resented his loneliness.

San Francisco failed to lift his spirits. He had half expected that crossing the Bay Bridge would enable him to put the experience of the afternoon out of his mind, but it did not. The city, which had been so appealing that morning, looked gray and unfriendly. That was the trouble with places that played strongly on people's emotions. The leverage worked both ways. By seven o'clock in the evening of that day, July 9, he was on a Pacific Southwest Airlines flight to Los Angeles.

Chapter

VII

THE experience in El Cerrito had shaken him, and, even with the change of scene, the depression was slow to wear off.

For several days he played tourist. Los Angeles was a strange city. It had no middle. At the airport tourist information desk, he had decided to stay at the Hyatt Wilshire. On the map it had looked reasonably central. Instead it had turned out to be in a neighborhood that was only in between places. Most of that first evening he spent walking up and down Wilshire Boulevard in the expectation that he would get to something.

The next morning dawned bright and blue-skied. The smog had not yet begun to build up, and from his window at the back of the hotel, he could look inland across the last flat mile of Los Angeles to the hills behind which ringed the city, which trapped the gases from millions of automobiles and gave Los Angeles its bad air and its bad name. Perched partway up the nearest hill was the old observatory where he had seen James Dean get his tire slashed seventeen years before in *Rebel Without a Cause,* where Sal Mineo had died on the steps in the night. Off to the left he could see Hollywood where he had seen other people do other things in other movies in other hotel rooms in other places, by himself.

Though he could see these things, they were a long way off. Walking was out of the question. He would have to rent a car.

It was nearly four o'clock when he returned to the Hyatt Wilshire. In seven hours, he had put almost 150 miles on the car without leaving the city. Though it was Monday and the market was open, he had resolved to put off until the next day any further purchases. What-ever the Russians might be up to, it need not concern him. He had a timetable, and he would stick to it. To im-provise was to care. And to care was to get involved. And to get involved was dangerous, as he had already had occasion once to be reminded.

"Hi." He had just opened the door to his room and was standing on the threshold. He could see the owner of the voice, but he would have recognized it anyway. It was the same voice and the same "Hi" he had heard less than forty-eight hours earlier in the men's room of the bar in San Francisco. Classie had followed him.

"How the bloody hell did you find me here?" Bon-ham-Carter was delighted and made no effort to hide it.

"I called."

"Called?"

"I called hotels. San Francisco was easy. Los Angeles was a lot harder." Classie explained that she had decid-ed to see him again, and, not knowing where he was staying, had simply begun calling hotels in San Francis-co. She had hit the Huntington on the fifth call and had learned from the desk that Bonham-Carter had left for Los Angeles. So she had followed him and repeated the procedure. When she had then presented herself down-stairs as Mrs. Bonham-Carter, the clerk had agreed to give her the key and adjust the account. She told the story as though it were the most natural thing in the world.

That evening the two of them had dinner at Alice's, a restaurant in Malibu which Classie knew about. Then, for nearly an hour, they watched a group of boys catch-ing dogfish off the end of the pier behind the restau-rant. The fish were biting and the boys, using a device resembling broad-jawed ice tongs at the end of a rope, were pulling the useless two- and three-foot creatures from the darkness forty feet below as fast as they could get the lines back down.

As he headed back down the shore road toward the city, the depression of the previous day seemed remote. Classie had removed her shoes, and she sat now with her legs tucked under her, her head resting sleepily on his shoulder. Ahead, he could see the coastline, a string of lights veering off to the right in the distance. He wondered how long it would take them to get to the end of the string, and whether they would still be in Los Angeles, and when they did whether there would be another string of lights behind the point. And he wondered, too, about the girl sitting silently next to him who seemed so easily to have made herself at home in his life, the girl who never seemed to need to be anywhere and who had followed him all the way from San Francisco and didn't even know who he was.

"How long are you going to be in L.A., Felix?" They had almost reached the hotel before she spoke.

"I don't know. Maybe a week, maybe a fortnight. I haven't any plans."

"Didn't you have business in San Francisco?"

"I had business, but I didn't have to be in San Francisco."

"Why?"

"I'm a speculator. I buy things because I think they are going to get more expensive. I can do that wherever I want to. The only thing it requires is a brokerage house, and there are brokerage houses everywhere." He wondered as he spoke if he was speaking too freely. It seemed a harmless confession. Besides, Classie seemed hardly to be listening. Shortly before they left the restaurant, she had excused herself to go to the rest room. He had thought nothing of it at the time, but he could recognize now that she was drifting off into the same state of stupefaction she had been in when he first met her. He hoped that her thoughts would not turn inward to the extent that they interfered with her performance. They hadn't in San Francisco.

Classie proved to be intimately familiar with the city. The next day, which did not begin for them until nearly eleven, was given over entirely to a sight-seeing excursion which ended at midafternoon with a swim at Venice. Whatever it was that Classie needed to bring on her glassy-eyed smile, she apparently did not need it until evening, for she was a bundle of energy and information. With surprising sophistication she explained the unique sociology of Venice's bohemian population, the curious game played in wire cages on the beach with paddles and punctured tennis balls, the bottom formations which made Venice a bad surfing beach and other beaches good surfing beaches. She took him around the point to the nude beach and lectured him on the relationship—or lack of it—between sex and clothing—or lack of it. And she told him the name of the strange brown seaweed with the round bulbs on it and explained why he would not find it were he to go to a beach on the East Coast. That night, Sallas and the Russians in New York seemed very far away.

The next morning he awoke at eight. Classie was gone. He could see the indentation still in the mattress next to him where she had been the previous night. But she was gone. No clothes, no suitcase, no note, no help from the desk downstairs when he called. He waited in the room until nearly ten, but there was no call. There was nothing to do but to go back to work.

Buying had been simple in Washington and New York, so simple that Bonham-Carter had begun to forget that caution Sallas had told him would be essential. He had had some of this complacency shaken in the San

Francisco airport the previous Sunday when uniformed agents had demanded to see his identification and had searched his bags. Though he had learned from the newspaper the next day that the checks had been ordered by the White House as a response to a rash of hijackings, the experience served to remind him that he had not left all danger behind with the Russians in New York. It had pleased him to read three days later that two more airliners had been hijacked despite the precautions. In both cases the hijackers had demanded parachutes and in both cases the planes had been Boeing 727s whose rear-facing doors and stairways made them ideal for a parachute escape.

The hijackings that occurred that July 12 were only the latest in a series that had begun the previous April, when a balding twenty-nine-year-old named Richard Floyd McCoy had demanded and got $500,000 from United Airlines before he bailed out over Provo, Utah. Two and one-half years later, McCoy, by then one of the FBI's ten most wanted fugitives, would die on a quiet street in Virginia Beach in a shootout with Federal agents. But for the time being, he was the father of a movement, and Bonham-Carter drew comfort from the government's apparent inability to stop it.

That day, a Wednesday, while Belousov and Sakun, having concluded deals with three more grain companies, were leaving New York for Canada, Bonham-Carter walked into the Merrill Lynch office in Beverly Hills and invested half of the remaining Peruvian funds.

In the previous trading session, the price of September wheat had shot up more than four cents after having moved hardly at all since his first purchase. He had taken the four-cent increase to be the beginning of the surge, and was therefore a little surprised now to find that the price since had dropped a cent. Still, there was every reason to be confident. For one thing, the wheat contracts were doing better than the soybean contracts. This fact tended to support his theory that the Russian wheat buying would outweigh in consequence any information that might have leaked out of Peru concerning the anchovy crop. It indicated, too, that prices were beginning to respond to the Russian purchases. Surely four cents was only the beginning, only a small fraction of what was to come.

Bonham-Carter thanked the broker and was about to leave when he was checked by an impulse. Sitting back down, he took out his pad of traveler's checks. By the time he got up to leave again, the venture had taken on an entirely new perspective. In a matter of minutes, he had expended $35,000 of his $50,000 advance. In its place he now held ninety contracts of September wheat in his own name and for his own account.

If Sallas was right about where the price of wheat was going, those contracts would be worth $700,000 to him. He had never before faced the prospect of that kind of money. Every time the price rose a penny, he stood to make $4500.

His step was light when he reached the sidewalk. He congratulated himself for ignoring Sallas' instruction not to carry more money than he would need for personal use. On reflection, the instruction, which had seemed unnecessary at the time, made sense from Sallas' point of view. It was a long way from Lima to the United States. Though Bonham-Carter would have $50,000 waiting for him when he finished the job, $50,000 was not much of a lever with which to control a man, who, with luck, might walk off the job with better than half a million made in the market. Of course, it was not Sallas' only lever. Bonham-Carter was all too aware of his thugs and their demonstrated ability to track people down in obscure places.

There was no reason for Sallas to know. The Swiss Credit Bank would record withdrawals made against the Bethlehem Corporation account. These records would routinely be sent to the apartment on Sonnenbergstrasse. From there, they would doubtless be forwarded to Sallas who would check the amounts against the purchases recorded in Bonham-Carter's cables. There was little opportunity for graft, but there was no way Sallas could ascertain what Bonham-Carter did with his own funds.

After he left the Merrill Lynch office, he placed a call to the Hyatt Wilshire. Classie had not returned. He was back where he had been two days earlier. Five-minute workdays in strange cities raised a problem of how to pass the time. He toyed with spending another afternoon on the beach, changed his mind and opted instead for a look at one of the old movie lots.

It was shortly after one o'clock when he parked the car outside the gate of Universal Studios. After paying the three-dollar tour charge, he joined the group of tourists milling about waiting for a guide to appear.

"My word, they certainly have a lot of policemen." An elderly blue-haired woman to his left was addressing her husband. The man, camera-bedecked and sporting a gold polo shirt, plaid Bermuda shorts and orthopedic shoes over short dark socks, nodded knowingly.

"Yes, dear, I imagine they have a lot of people who come here and try to swipe things. Remember, there is a lot of priceless memorabilia here, a lot of history."

The guide had arrived, and the tour was under way. For an hour and a quarter they roamed from one sound stage to another. They were shown a horizontal, plaster-

103]

of-paris cliff face across which some intrepid screen bravo had once crawled and sent chills up the spines of millions of moviegoers. There were plywood deserts, six-foot ocean liners and all of the other paraphernalia of cinematic deception. It was an illusion-shattering experience, and the group loved it.

As the tour moved slowly back toward the gate, Bonham-Carter noticed that the number of policemen had increased. He detached himself from the group and moved in the direction of their greatest concentration. His instincts told him that whatever lay in that direction would be worth seeing.

The police were ranged in a loose semicircle. Skirting its periphery, he found a spot that afforded him an unobstructed view of its center. His initial reaction was disappointment. He was not sure what he had expected—perhaps Marlon Brando or Elizabeth Taylor. Instead, all he could see was two rather nondescript men standing in front of a table piled high with props and bits and pieces of costume. They were clearly enjoying themselves.

He watched as the shorter of the two men, kinky-haired and bespectacled, reached up to put a Roman helmet on the head of the other. Reaching up again, he tipped the helmet forward over the man's eyes, then flashed an impish grin at the explosion of flashbulbs. In the instant of the flash, Bonham-Carter recognized who the short man was and why the police were present.

It was the President's famous Assistant for National Security Affairs, Henry Kissinger. He would not learn until he read it in the paper the next day that the taller man had been Anatoliy Dobrynin, Soviet Ambassador to the United States.

Across the lot, a limousine was waiting against the wall, and he headed in its direction. It would be a good place to watch from. He knew from reading the news-papers that the short figure who would soon be getting into the car was reputed to be better informed and more influential in the formulation of U.S. foreign poli-cy than even the Secretary of State. He wondered if Kis-singer would know about the Russian grain buying. It was hard to believe that the National Security Council with its monitoring capability through the State Depart-ment, the National Security Agency and the CIA would not keep track of the movements of foreign officials, especially Russian officials. Surely, if he knew, he would have informed the Agriculture Department and . . .

"Stop." He felt a twinge of pain as a hand on his left elbow jerked his arm toward the middle of his back, spinning him around so he could not see his assailant. Tripping over his feet, he was half pushed, half carried in a direction away from the limousine.

"Don't move." He recognized the accent. It was the same he had heard in the Madison and again in the Hil-ton. Strong hands lifted his elbows and moved rapidly up and down his sides, then into his crotch and down the insides of his legs.

"What is it, Yuri?" The voice was American. Over it, he could hear the crowd beginning to break up and feet moving in their direction.

"He was going to the car." Yuri turned Bonham-Car-ter as he spoke. "He is not armed."

"Well, just walk him to the gate, Yuri. We don't need any trouble; this trip has been bad enough already." The speaker was a slender man, no older than thirty, with dark hair and tortoiseshell glasses. For a moment he cast a world-weary glance to Bonham-Carter, then, shaking his head with the air of a man too tired to care, turned and hurried to join Kissinger and the tall man, who by then were climbing into the limousine.

During the walk to the gate, Yuri walked behind him. Neither man spoke. Yuri's size had surprised him. From the way he had been manhandled, he had expected a bigger man. But what size Yuri had was in his arms and hands. The latter, huge and heavily veined, hung, even with arms slighly bowed, to mid-thigh. At the gate, he could hear the footsteps stop behind him. He did not look around until he had reached the car. When he did, Yuri was gone.

What to do for the rest of the day? After driving aimlessly for an hour, he decided he needed a drink. Twenty minutes later, having picked up a paper in the lobby of the Beverly Hills Hotel, he was entering the Polo Lounge. The room bent around to the right like a sock. He picked out a table in the toe and ordered a double Scotch. He hadn't eaten since breakfast and the Scotch worked quickly. The alcohol, like little massaging fingers, crawled up the back of his skull, and he relaxed.

"Humphrey, Muskie Step Aside" was the paper's leading headline. The story underneath told of decisions by Senators Hubert Humphrey and Edmund Muskie to quit their pursuit of the Democratic Presidential nomination and throw their convention support to McGovern. It went on to say that McGovern was expected to win the nomination on the first ballot the following day.

Bonham-Carter read the story, but without interest. He hoped the man whose political organization was described in such glowing terms had better taste in people and policies than he had in hotels. The lobby of the Hyatt Wilshire was still filled with photos taken a month earlier when it had been McGovern's headquarters during the California Democratic primary election.

"Another drink, sir?" The waitress was a pretty Oriental girl.

He ordered another Scotch and a sandwich to go with it. He read the paper as he ate.

"Hello, I see the events of the afternoon have brought us to the same pass."

Bonham-Carter looked up at the owner of the familiar voice. It was the young man with the tortoiseshell glasses. He was grinning. His quiet dark suit contrasted strangely with the rest of the bar. From his voice, it was obvious he had been either there or in some other bar for a while.

"I thought you went with Mr. Kissinger."

"That, coming from someone who doubtless saw me get into the car with Dr. Kissinger, is a fair assumption. Indeed, it is an assumption not without some truth in it, for it was, in fact, with Dr. Kissinger that I, as you put it, went."

The young man spoke with the elaborate circumlocution of a novice drunk, concerned that his audience recognize that he was not at his best.

"But I did not went far. I put the son of a bitch in the helicopter, and he went, and I stayed, and that's the way it is going to be for a week. One whole week, I haven't seen a week I could call my own for more than two fucking years."

Bonham-Carter looked at the young man. He bore all the earmarks of privilege. Even now, in his slightly disheveled condition, the bespoke tailoring was evident.

"Do you work for Mr. Kissinger?"

"That is correct. Hey, you're English, aren't you?"

"That's right. Is it difficult working for Mr. Kissinger?"

"Is it difficult? Is it difficult? My friend, does Dracula have overbite? Is it difficult? I want to tell you, it is an around-the-clock, twenty-four-carat, Sanforized, polyunsaturated pain in the ass. Hey." The young man gestured toward the waitress. "Hey, you, Jade Flower, yeah, you, how 'bout another little pop here?" he said, thrusting his glass toward the girl who had been waiting on Bonham-Carter.

The young man's inhibitions were obviously on vacation, and it occurred to Bonham-Carter that he might be talking to a useful source of information.

"What exactly do you do for Mr. Kissinger?"

The young man's attention had wandered to the prostitutes who peopled most of the tables nearest the door.

"Hmm, what do I do?" For a moment he seemed to think that one over. Then, shrugging, responded, "I'm his pipe and bowl man." He looked at Bonham-Carter's uncomprehending stare.

"You know, he calls for his pipe and he calls for his bowl? Well, that's me; I get 'em for him. Good job for a former Rhodes scholar, don't you think?"

Bonham-Carter ignored the question. "What do you think of the Russian grain buying?" he asked casually.

"You mean the Russian grain deal? Bully for them. Bully for us. Détente and all that. Good thing all around, I should think."

"No. I mean the actual purchases."

"What purchases? We just signed the goddamn thing a couple of days ago. Hey, that was a funny deal." He was leaning forward now and speaking in a confidential tone.

"Did old Willys get fucked or didn't he? With those assholes at Agriculture and Commerce getting all the credit. You couldn't appreciate that, but it tickled the hell out of me."

The information didn't move Bonham-Carter one way or another. He had no idea who "Willys" was and didn't care. He wanted to know something else. "If Kissinger were aware of any actual buying that the Russians might have done, do you think you would know about it?"

"Damn right I would know about it. Unless it came to him in a dream, I'd have done it up in triplicate and pushed it through to Bergsten or Hormats or who the hell ever is running that shop these days."

"They have started buying, you know."

"No, I don't know." The young man's demeanor was soberer. "Look, I don't know that they have or they haven't. But I can tell you this. It isn't going to mean a helluva lot to Henry one way or the other. He doesn't give a flying fuck about trade or economics or any of that stuff. You are talking about an eighteenth-century diplomat. This is a guy who is secretly pissed off 'cause he missed the Congress of Vienna. You mention soybeans to him and you might as well have handed him a turd. If that's what you are interested in, you should talk to somebody at the Agriculture Department."

Five minutes later, Bonham-Carter was back in his car and headed for Los Angeles International Airport. At the airport, he inquired at the counter and found he would have a wait of an hour and a half. At 10:40, he took off for Washington on American Airlines Flight 278, the "Redeye."

Chapter

VIII

THE Dulles terminal was almost empty. Three hours of low-grade sleep had left him rumpled and unrefreshed. He watched the other passengers yawning and staring blankly as they lined up at the escalator. He guessed that most of them would be going straight to their offices. It was a hell of a way to start the workday.

By 9:30, having checked back into the Madison, showered and shaved, he was in a taxi heading down Fifteenth Street. At New York Avenue, the driver zigged to the right then cut left down East Executive Avenue between the Treasury Department and the White House. Another left and a quick right and they were back on Fifteenth Street, out of the heavy traffic and heading for the Department of Agriculture.

All of Sallas' warnings that the slightest leak would cause the market to adjust for the anchovy shortage had given him exaggerated faith in the market's ability to ferret out the secrets of buyers and sellers. He had not considered the inapplicability of this textbook precept to a world in which a large number of sellers were separated from a large number of consumers by a handful of tight-lipped middlemen. The grain companies, it was becoming clear, had concealed so far the fact of their sales to the Russians. They would now be covering their positions by quietly buying what they had already sold from farmers who were ignorant of the fact that there was backlogged demand one step up the line. Sooner or later the farmers would find out. When that happened the price would rise. But sooner or later could be too late. With his own investment now hanging in the balance, the timing was something he could not leave to chance; he had resolved to help the process along.

The Agriculture Department occupied several huge government buildings on the south side of the Mall. It was nearly half an hour before he located the right building and found the corridor and room he was looking for.

Five minutes later he was back in the street. It had

been a waste of time. The receptionist in the secretary's outer office had explained that the secretary was out of town and not expected back for three days. The woman had not been encouraging about the chance of seeing the secretary even then. She had not said so directly, but her tone had made it clear that one did not walk unannounced into a Cabinet member's office and expect to be welcomed.

Bonham-Carter pondered his next move. He had spent much of the trip back from Los Angeles rehearsing what he would say to the Agriculture Secretary. Finding the secretary away left him with his wheels momentarily off the rails. As he thought, he walked back in the direction of the hotel. A crowd was queuing in the midmorning heat at the door of the Washington Monument. The flags that ringed the monument hung limp against their staffs. Having traversed the Mall, he crossed Constitution Avenue and hailed a taxi southbound on Fifteenth Street.

"Commerce Department, please." Shutting the door behind him, he noted gratefully that the air conditioner was running.

"Which entrance?"

"Any entrance."

"Is the southwest gate all right?"

"That'll be fine."

"Okay, buddy, that's it right across the street."

A uniformed guard sat at a desk in the hall just inside the door, but he took no notice as Bonham-Carter entered. The secretary's name, Forest Kopke, was listed at the top of the wall directory next to the elevators. Bonham-Carter remembered the name from the wire service stories describing the press conference in which the grain deal had been announced. According to the floor plan, Kopke's office was on the fifth floor on the west side of the building. Listed under Secretary Kopke's name was the name of his executive assistant. Bonham-Carter's experience at the Agriculture Department suggested that the indirect approach might be more effective and he filed the assistant's name away in the back of his mind.

At the fifth floor he turned left. Beyond heavy glass doors, he could see the blue-carpeted secretary's corridor; it was empty. There were doors along the walls on both sides. Plaques identified the occupants of the offices on the left. There was nothing to indicate what lay behind the doors on the right. Halfway along the corridor a sign protruded from the left wall, indicating that the door beneath it led to the secretary's office. He paused in front of it for a moment, then passed it by. The plaque by the next door bore the name of the executive assistant. He opened it and entered.

The room in which he found himself contained three desks with typing credenzas. In the far corner, a bank of file cabinets was pushed against the wall. To the left, behind the door, was a squat safe. The room, which obviously belonged to the secretarial help, was empty.

"Anybody here?" There was no answer. The door in the right wall of the room gave onto another office, and, as Bonham-Carter stepped forward, he could see the end of a couch and on it a pair of feet. He stepped back and tried again, this time a little louder, "Anybody here?" He stepped forward again. The feet had disappeared.

"Hullo." The voice belonged to a sandy-haired young man in his middle twenties. Despite an obvious effort to look alert, the young man managed only to look sheepish. As he spoke, Bonham-Carter recognized the Massachusetts accent. Ten years ago, he had become familiar with it from newsreels and Voice of America broadcasts.

"Can I help you? My name is Huggins. I guess the girls are all down having coffee," he added, looking around him.

"Are you the secretary's executive assistant?" Bonham-Carter knew from the directory on the first floor that the question was superfluous.

"No, sir, I'm the special assistant—just a heartbeat away from the executive assistancy though. You want to talk to him?"

"Well, I'd like to talk to someone about making an appointment to see the secretary."

"Yeah, well, he'd be the guy. He's over here," the sandy-haired young man said, crossing the room with the desks and opening the door on the opposite side.

"Braxton, there's a . . ." He turned to Bonham-Carter. "I'm sorry, I didn't get your name."

"Bonham-Carter."

"There is a Mr. Carter here who would like to talk to you about seeing the secretary."

Braxton turned out to be a very busy young man. Their conversation which consumed only ten minutes was spread over forty minutes on account of a half-dozen telephone calls. Without mentioning how he had come upon the information, Bonham-Carter related what he had learned. In between calls, Braxton listened attentively. At the end, he excused himself and left Bonham-Carter. In a few minutes he was back.

"The secretary is tied up right now, but would like to see you. If you could stay for lunch, you could tell him what you've just told me."

Bonham-Carter agreed.

The secretary's dining room was across the hall, behind one of the unmarked doors. When they entered, a white-jacketed Pullman waiter was already busy laying three places at one end of a long table. While they waited for the secretary to join them, Braxton made small talk. Had Bonham-Carter been to Russia? No? Well, it was a very interesting place. He and the secretary had spent two weeks there in June "putting together the deal." The Agriculture Secretary was not mentioned but there were several references to "Henry" whom Bonham-Carter took to be Kissinger. Braxton explained that Secretary Kopke had been the one to sell "Henry" on the idea that a commercial deal was important to détente. There were also references to Patolichev and Alkimov, Soviet officials of unspecified responsibility. Bonham-Carter nodded with feigned interest. The names meant nothing to him. Braxton made no mention of Belousov or Sakun. If Bonham-Carter would remind him before he left, he, Braxton, would give him a copy of the secretary's report entitled *U.S.-Soviet Relations in a New Era.* Bonham-Carter would find it interesting. It represented the best thinking of the best people.

Lunch offered a choice between steak and lobster. Braxton explained that the secretary was on a high protein diet because of a running contest with the scales and that steak and lobster were all he ever ate. They had already begun to eat when the secretary entered.

"Don't get up. Brax tells me you think the Russians may have already started buying some grain," he said.

While the secretary ate, Bonham-Carter described the facts of the sale he had heard agreed to between Michael Freeport and the Russians. He also mentioned the other calls to indicate that the Midcontinental sale was only one of possibly as many as a half-dozen similar transactions between the Russians and other companies. It was difficult to gauge the reaction. The secretary was leaning over his plate and chewing vigorously. His only replies were nods which began somewhere underneath the table and caused his entire upper body to lift and fall. Bonham-Carter felt obligated to explain himself further. "It occurred to me that at least some of this buying was being conducted in secret—that if that were the case, you would want to know about it. The press reports I have seen have all been phrased in a way that implied the Russians had been holding off until the question of credit terms could be resolved."

Kopke's plate was empty now and he was ready to speak. As to whether or not the government was aware of the sales, his tactic was neither to confirm nor to deny. But he was at pains to leave the impression that CIA surveillance made undetected movements by foreign agents highly improbable. "People like to criticize the CIA," he said, giving Bonham-Carter the confiding, steady-eyed treatment, "but I tell you one thing, those guys know what the hell is going on. We get a Russian here and he can't fart but what one of our agents gets a nose full."

Lunch lasted half an hour. Though Bonham-Carter had the feeling that his information had been news to Kopke, there was nothing he could detect in the secretary's manner that indicated alarm. The only hint that he might have created some unease came when they were getting up from the table and the secretary asked him where he could be contacted if there should be any need.

They were saying their good-byes in the corridor when Braxton interrupted them by handing Kopke a light green booklet. "Good, Brax." Then, turning back toward Bonham-Carter, the secretary added, "You might want to skim through this. I think it pretty well summarizes the economic foundations of our new relationship with the Russians. It represents the best thinking of the best people."

Braxton shooed him out via the secretary's private elevator. Behind its heavy bronze doors, the elevator was richly paneled in dark wood. A sign hanging next to the instrument panel indicated the floor at which the secretary wished the elevator left. Presumably it followed him up and down the building, sparing him precious seconds of waiting. At the first floor, he thanked Braxton, walked out through a small antechamber and stepped into the hall. The hall, which had made no impression on him as he entered, now seemed stark by contrast with the fifth-floor corridor. Tired-looking bureaucrats hurried past in short-sleeved, see-through shirts, plastic pocket liners bristling with ball-point pens. Outside the building, the heat and his stomach reminded him he had had only three hours' sleep, and he headed for the Madison.

It was late afternoon when the phone wakened him. He had been asleep for several hours. The voice on the other end had been a woman's telling him that Secretary Kopke wished to speak with him. He fought to clear his head in the ten-second interval.

"Hello." Kopke was on the line. His tone seemed surprisingly friendly. He was calling, he said, to thank Bonham-Carter for troubling to come by. He wanted Bonham-Carter to know that he appreciated his consideration. He wanted Bonham-Carter to know also that he had checked out what he referred to as "the rumor."

"I didn't say anything at lunch because I wanted to confirm my understanding," the secretary said. "But the Russians' deal with Midcontinental and the other companies was a washout."

"I see."

Bonham-Carter, in fact, did not see. He had not mentioned Midcontinental's name in talking to either Braxton or the secretary, so the fact that Kopke knew the name of the company involved lent some credibility to what he said. It was unlikely that the secretary would risk a guess. Still, it was hard to understand how the transaction, which had sounded so amicable and so firm, could have been undone in so short a time. The secretary seemed to read his thoughts.

"Yeah, it came a cropper over the shipping question. The Russians are insisting on moving the stuff in their own bottoms. That's pretty typical of them, but our unions will go homicidal if we agree to it. It could take months to clear it up—that is, if we ever do clear it up."

They wound up the conversation with awkward pleasantries. Bonham-Carter thanked the secretary for the call. It had been unnecessarily decent of him. He reflected that not many Cabinet members would take the trouble to set straight someone they had never seen or heard of before—someone who could do them no imaginable good. After the secretary rang off, Bonham-Carter thought he heard a second click. He listened a second longer, then decided it was probably the woman who had first come on the line. She would have made an transcript of the entire conversation. No doubt by day's end he would be part of a memorandum for the file.

He lay back on the bed and shut his eyes. The secretary's call had left him somewhat uneasy. Setting aside the factor of his own newly acquired financial interest, he reviewed the last week's sequence of events. He felt certain that somewhere they contained inconsistency.

The more he thought about it, the less plausible the secretary's explanation seemed. If Kopke had been lying to hide the fact of the sales, how much further might he be willing to go toward the same end? People had disappeared for less. It was a risk he didn't have to take.

Having settled his mind, he wasted little time. Arising, he took his raincoat from the suitcase and laid it open across the bed. Next, he removed two shirts, shook the fold out of them and spread them on top of the raincoat, running the sleeves down the arms of the coat. He tucked razor and toothbrush into one pocket and a change of underwear into the other, then closed the coat and buttoned one button. A few minutes later he was crossing the Madison lobby, the coat thrown casually over one arm. Outside the door, he turned left and headed for the downtown area. He walked slowly, stopping at shop windows, pausing to read restaurant menus. Fifteen minutes later he strolled up to the ticket window of the RKO Keith theater across the street from the Treasury Department and bought a ticket.

Once past the second set of doors, he quickened his pace. The change from the bright street to the darkness of the theater would be temporarily blinding. He would have thirty seconds at the outside. He walked rapidly across the back of the orchestra and then down the far aisle, heading for the red light at the bottom. Within twenty seconds of the time he entered, he was through the exit door and in a corridor that emptied onto Fourteenth Street. At the curb, he hailed a cab. It was too soon to feel safe. The theater ruse would work against a single tail. If there were professionals following him, there would be several of them and one would circle the block. All he could know for sure was that if he was still being followed now, it was by someone with a car. He directed the taxi block by block. Twice he had it stop at the curb before it turned right on the amber light. After five minutes of driving in circles, he spotted a parking garage in the seventeen hundred block of M Street. Ordering the taxi to the curb, he slipped the driver a ten-dollar bill, crossed the street and entered the gaping maw. From the Seventeenth Street sidewalk, he could see over the clogged lanes of entering and exiting cars to De Sales Street on the far side of the block. No one was going to make it through there except on foot. At the far entrance of the parking garage, he cut diagonally across De Sales Street and entered the side door of the Mayflower Hotel. Thirty feet inside the door he found the stairs and descended quickly to the basement. At the end of the hall, he found the men's room, entered a toilet stall, sat down and braced his feet against the door. Through the crack between the door and the marble stall he could see without being seen. It was almost ten o'clock when he left.

Chapter

IX

AFTER Bonham-Carter had left the Commerce Department that afternoon, Secretary Kopke had immediately put through a call to the White House. He had not listened closely enough to what Braxton had told him earlier and so had agreed to the luncheon, half expecting to spend it being congratulated for his contribution to world peace and to the American farmer. He had, therefore, been slow to see the significance of the facts as Bonham-Carter related them. Their full impact had not hit him until the meal was nearly over.

For several months, Kopke had been involved in trade negotiations with the Russians. They had been by far the most significant development of his brief Cabinet tenure. Because the negotiations had both foreign policy significance and domestic political value, they had provided him an entrée to Kissinger and the other stars in the White House power galaxy. That kind of access to the White House could not be taken for granted in this Administration: not by Cabinet members, certainly not by the Secretary of Commerce. Traditionally, the Commerce Department ranked in consequence near the bottom of the list of ten Cabinet agencies. For decades, and with good reason, it had been viewed as a bureaucratic, backward-looking business apologist, dedicated to the rote articulation of free-enterprise principles and the exclusion of foreign goods from the U.S. market. The only occasions when the department made news were when it released its monthly and quarterly economic statistics.

For these reasons, the top job at the Commerce Department had never been an effective career-launching pad. Like some of the other more honorific government appointments, the Commerce slot was a post-peak post. Most often it had been filled by men whose careers had already climaxed as the chief executive officer of something like a railroad brake shoe concern or a textile mill and who sought the job as a sort of swan song that would entitle them to a decorative prefix they could carry into their golden years.

Kopke's friends had warned him not to take the job, told him that it was a dead end, argued that, if he took it, he would spend the rest of his life giving commencement addresses, cutting ribbons and looking for work. A friend from New Jersey had summed up the arguments in a ten-word telegram: "Martin Bormann is alive and hiding as Undersecretary of Commerce." Kopke had not listened. He was only forty-three and did not fit the mold. It was just possible that the patterns of the past reflected the limitations of the occupants rather than the office. It was a chance to acquire a fancy title, he could rub some of the right shoulders, pick up a little polish; it could be just the thing for a hustling kid who'd grown up poor in Pennsylvania in a town where the only man who wore a tie was the undertaker. He had got out of that town, and he had got rich doing it. He hadn't been afraid of the Commerce Department.

And he had been right. The Russian trade negotiations, together with a heavy speaking schedule, had already made him one of the most publicized Commerce secretaries in the last twenty years.

Kopke had realized the potential of the trade negotiations almost the moment he took office. Russia and the United States had been at loggerheads for all of his adult life. By his reasoning, if the United States and Russia could be given mutual economic interests, the likelihood of a conflict that might jeopardize those interests would be diminished. It was a simple idea, but timely. The President and his foreign policy advisers were already committed to making "détente" the foundation of the Administration's bid for historical immortality. Kopke's task had been to carve out a personal role in this historic design by convincing the others that in order to endure, "detente" would require solid economic underpinnings. It was neither a glamorous nor a sexy approach. And selling it to the White House, which was already intoxicated with its own magnesium-flash diplomacy, had been a slow educative process requiring a great deal of tact and persistence. But he had done it. And he had since thrown all his energies into making the idea a reality.

The reopening of commerce between the superpowers required settlement of several long-standing issues. Ever since the end of World War Two Russia had refused to repay its Lend-Lease debt to the United States. Russia had argued that whatever liability she might have incurred had been more than settled in Russian blood which the Germans had spilled on an oriental scale. To Kopke, the argument had merit. Of all of the countries that had accepted Lend-Lease aid thirty years earlier only Finland had paid up in full. Britain and France, with losses far smaller than Russia's, had been allowed to cancel their obligations for a few cents on the dollar. But he knew that the Russian Lend-Lease debt was an emotional issue in the Congress and that the Congress would have to be placated if it was to give its approval to the other aspects of the trade agreement Kopke envisioned.

Lend-Lease was therefore the key. The other issues—extension of Export-Import Bank credit, most-favored-nation treatment for Russia's exports, commercial representation, recognition of patents and copyrights and the delisting of hundreds and hundreds of restricted trade items—might be of far greater economic significance, but their resolution was still contingent on settlement of the debt.

By mid-July, 1972, negotiations on all the issues were nearing completion. The Russians, needing foreign income and consumer goods to meet impatient domestic demands, had proved remarkably tractable. The pieces had been falling nicely into place. Now the grain deal, only a week old, was threatening everything he had worked for.

The grain deal itself was not actually a part of the trade agreements that Kopke had been working on. It was the product of a parallel set of negotiations in which he had also been involved. In them the United States had agreed to extend Russia credit with which to buy grain in the private market. But if the grain deal and the trade agreements were separate, they were also related. For the Congress would look upon the grain sales as a trial run. If the grain sales went sour, the trade agreements were in trouble.

All this was racing through Kopke's mind as he picked up the phone to call the White House—this and one other thing. If what Bonham-Carter had told him was true, then the Russians were buying far more than he had anticipated. During the negotiations, the possibility that the Russian purchases might exceed the line of credit had never occurred to him. All of the bureaucratic machinery at the Agriculture Department was set up to cope with surplus. Neither he nor the Secretary of Agriculture had considered that the problem they would face might not be surplus but shortage. Now that possibility had to be considered. And if shortage was where they were headed, there was more than the trade agreement at risk. Huge purchases could drive up prices, not just grain prices at the farm but prices at the grocery store—prices of bread, prices of meat, prices of nearly everything. In an election year, that would be bad. Bad for the Administration, bad for him. He knew that, to the President, he would be part of the problem. It was essential that he be the first to get to the White House with the information. It was the loss-cutting tactic.

"Seth, I think we may have a problem."

Seth Ferguson was the chairman of CIEP, the Council on International Economic Policy, an office which made him privy to the trade negotiations. More important, by virtue of years he had spent serving the President he had inherited a multitude of other ad hoc responsibilities. Political troubleshooting was just one of them.

Though Ferguson's rank was technically lower than Kopke's his power was considerably greater for the simple reason that he was inside the White House and therefore closer to the President's ear. Unlike Kopke,

Ferguson came from money. He had all his life enjoyed the security that went with privilege and position. In the White House, security was power, and Ferguson was not in the least afraid to use it. Nor was he afraid of the man in whose name he used it. Kopke worried constantly about the impression he was making on the President; Ferguson rarely gave it a thought. To his way of looking at it, he was slumming in this White House. The President was lucky to have him. He would do the best job he could, but if the President didn't like what he was doing, then the President could throw him out and get himself a couple more yes-sir boys with their polyester suits and Arlington addresses, and they could take his place.

For five minutes without interruption, Kopke spoke into the phone, repeating what Bonham-Carter had told him about the grain purchases and extrapolating the possible market consequences for Ferguson's benefit. "I thought you would want to know right away, Seth. I'm afraid this could hurt us in November."

The November reference was obligatory when talking to one of the White House crowd. Though the election was almost four months off and the President's renomination a foregone conclusion, the Cabinet members were on notice that their every act and utterance was to be designed to further the President's political fortunes.

For a moment there was a silence on the other end of the line.

When Ferguson spoke, it was to ask a single question. "Have you checked it out?"

"Not yet, Seth. I'm going to now, but I wanted to get to you right away."

Again there was a moment of silence.

"Don't, and don't go anywhere; I'll get back to you."

Ferguson had sounded annoyed. Overlapping jurisdictions had thrown the two men together often, but their relationship had never really blossomed into friendship. The secretary wondered now how Ferguson might use his proximity to the President to turn developments to his advantage. He was familiar with the White House atmosphere and knew its low tolerance for unfocused blame.

Forty-five minutes later, Ferguson called back to say that Bonham-Carter had been right.

"Forrest, I just talked to the CIA people over at Langley, and they say the Russians have been buying like crazy for two weeks. They know all about the Midcontinental deal, and they say the Russians have also bought a pile from Cargill and Bunge. The irritating thing about it is that they talk as though we should have known all about it."

"Well, Seth, I don't know whether they expect us to check with them every day. I can assure you that nobody ever said anything to me."

"Yeah, well I don't know what's happened to communications around this place but I talked to that guy Ruby, in their Office of Economic Research, and he claims the Soviet grain shortfall was described fully in an intelligence report three weeks ago. He got the damn thing out and started reading me some mumbo jumbo about Earth Resources Technological Satellites and ultraviolet photographs and how they can spot a failing crop from the air. Honestly, Forrie, I don't know what those guys think they are over there for. The Mexicans could send an armored division into Arizona, and those bastards would put it in an intelligence report and figure that was the end of it."

Ferguson's irritation was reassuring. For the present, at least, it sounded as though the CIA were going to have to take the heat.

"Anyway," Ferguson went on, "all that's past us. The thing to do now is to make sure your source doesn't go telling his story to anybody else. If it gets to the market, there'll be hell to pay. You can bet your life Midcontinental and the others weren't selling that kind of volume from inventory. They are out there now buying from farmers who don't know what the hell is going on, and it's too late to stop it. I wouldn't be surprised if by now they had bought up damned near all the Southern crop. You know the old man isn't used to losing farm states. He figures the gap-toothed and bandanna vote is his birthright. He expects it all this year. If the farmers get wind of what's happened, somebody is going to get fucked over but good."

Kopke knew that Ferguson was right. He glanced at the date in the little window in his watch face. Too much of the harvest would be over. Already the teams of custom harvesters would have worked their combines up from Texas across Oklahoma and most of Kansas and Nebraska. Many of the farmers in those states would have put up straw and gone to soybeans or another second crop. Of the big producing states, only North Dakota, Montana and Washington remained unharvested—sixteen electoral votes among them. Releasing the information of what the Russians had bought was no longer an option. There would be no return in it.

Kopke waited for a moment, then finished Ferguson's thought for him: "I don't guess the old man is going to be satisfied with fucking some CIA report writer, is he?"

"You said it, not me."

"What do you suggest?"

"Well, for a start, you can get back in touch with this

fellow Bonham-Carter and try to convince him he's seen an apparition. Think up something plausible, something that fits in with what he knows but makes it seem inconsequential. I'll leave the words to you."

"Okay, Seth, I'll get on it right away."

"Hang on, Forrest, I have one thing that may help you. I've talked already to the Interpol people over at Treasury and they have a file on Bonham-Carter. It's old, and they are updating it now by cable. All they were able to tell me right away is that he had to be hustled out of Peru five or six years ago for reasons which were not at the time considered important enough to look into. I expect we will have more information by the end of the day, but if I were you, I wouldn't wait for it."

"Thanks, Seth, I appreciate it."

"One more thing. I put two men in the hotel and had his line tapped right after I talked to you the first time. We can't let this situation get away from us; one way or another, we are going to keep this guy quiet, so try to be persuasive."

"Right, I got you, Seth."

"I hope so, old buddy; I wouldn't want to see you with blood on your hands."

Chapter

X

TO the immediate northwest of the Capitol lies a wedge of Washington which in the summer of 1972 was almost devoid of viable commercial life. The low flatlands, bounded by New York Avenue to the north and by the Federal Triangle and Capitol Hill to the west and east, had been scraped almost clean of the red brick buildings that were once the center of the medium-sized Southern town old Washingtonians are still fond of recalling. On the area's eastern edge, Union Station stood alone like St. Paul's, London, blitzed by railroad mismanagement and hollowed out by airline competition. Or almost alone. For despite the general destruction, the station was not the only still-standing casualty of progress. Diagonally across the circle from it, along North Capitol Street, two old railroad hotels, the Pennsylvania and the Commodore, still stood, struggling to keep up with taxes by selling lunch and drinks to Securities and Exchange Commission employees, waiting for the day when the iron ball of urban renewal would deliver them from their misery.

It was to the Commodore that Bonham-Carter went after he left the toilet stall in the Mayflower. At the desk, he completed the registration card, signing his name Jean Cable and giving a New York address. He did not know for sure that he was being pursued, but if so, he knew his pursuers would check new registrations around the city. The bisexual name would give them one more obstacle. He would move again in a day or two in any event.

While the elderly desk clerk, his back turned, studied the board on which the room keys hung, Bonham-Carter took his reading glasses from his jacket pocket and placed them conspicuously on the counter top. Then with the pen he drew a single diagonal line through the prefixes "Mr." and "Miss" on the registration card, leaving only the "Mrs." If the clerk should question him, he was prepared. He had only to pick his glasses back up and pretend to recognize the mistake. There was no need. Without looking at the card, the old man slipped it into the file and handed him the key. He would sleep without worry that night. There was little chance that anyone checking new registrants would find him under the alias of a married woman.

It was almost ten o'clock when he woke the next morning. The room was not air conditioned, and in the heat it smelled strongly of dust and urine. After dressing quickly, he phoned Royer. The broker remembered him immediately and eagerly accepted Bonham-Carter's invitation for lunch. At Royer's suggestion, they agreed to meet at Le Provençal. Royer would make the reservation.

When he arrived at the restaurant at noon, Royer was waiting.

"Hello, hello. Long time no see. How you been? Good to see you." Royer spoke with the nervous excitement of a track rat watching a jockey kick home the second half of his daily double.

For five minutes the two men discussed the price of wheat futures. According to Royer, the price for September wheat that day stood at about $1.51 a bushel, essentially unchanged from the previous day and down more than three cents from its high early in the week. August soybeans, however, were up almost four cents, from $3.46 to a little over $3.50. Though Royer did his best to make the numbers sound optimistic, it was useless. The inescapable fact was that for all of Bonham-Carter's efforts to date, Peru was showing a paper loss. Worse, he was showing a loss on his own investment.

Royer sensed his mood and tried another tack. "Look, you haven't made money yet, but you haven't lost anything either. You're lucky you didn't buy last Tuesday or you would be undermargined today. This is a risky business, but I think you're going to be okay. That run-up early in the week could be the beginning of a pattern. Personally, I look for a two-steps-forward-one-step-backward market from now until the end of the year."

"What do you mean I would be undermargined?"

"Well, we gave you a five percent margin, right?"

"Right."

"So that means that when the bushel price is a dollar fifty as it was when you bought, you put up only seven and a half cents. Are you with me?"

"Yes."

"Well, that seven and a half cents—or five percent—is our protection against a price drop. What I mean is that if the price drops more than that and we don't get any more money out of you, the rest of it comes out of our hide."

"I see."

"But we would be out of business in a hurry if we waited for the price to drop the whole seven and a half cents before asking you to put up more money. Do you see that?"

"I think so."

"Right, 'cause if we did, you could tell us to go to hell and, by the time we unloaded the contract, the price might have dropped ten or twenty cents. So, anyway, Merrill Lynch has a rule that says we ask for more money as soon as the price drops by more than twenty-five percent of whatever you have put up per bushel. I mean it's not just Merrill Lynch. Any commodities broker's gonna do the same. In your case, twenty-five percent would be a little under two cents. The price drops by more than that and you're what we call 'undermargined.' That's why I say that if you had bought on last Tuesday at a dollar fifty-four, we'd be asking you for more money now."

Bonham-Carter decided he had better fill Royer in on

his other purchases. If he was going to be moving around, he could not afford to have Merrill Lynch selling off his contracts just because they could not get in touch with him. Royer listened with interest as Bonham-Carter explained the New York and California purchases. He scribbled quickly for a moment on his napkin, then spoke.

"Well, you don't have a problem yet. But that is not to say you won't. You're damn close to the twenty-five percent line with the wheat contracts you bought July twelfth at a dollar fifty-three. That's the trouble with buying on a five percent margin; you can hit the big bingo if you guess right, but it doesn't give you much room to breathe downside. Tell you what I would do if I were you, especially if you plan to keep moving around. I'd bump all your contracts to eight or ten percent—certainly I would do it with those California contracts— otherwise you may reach in your pocket one morning and all you'll feel is your leg. Incidentally, what have you been doing about your confirmation slips?"

"They've all been sent to the New York Hilton. I suppose they are piling up there. Is that a problem?"

"No, not really," Royer said; "we have all the records. As long as you can identify yourself, you won't have any problem selling. It's just that it is faster and easier if you have the slips."

After a little more discussion, Bonham-Carter agreed to accept Royer's suggestion. He directed the broker to raise his margins to eight percent on the purchases made in Washington and New York and to ten percent on those made in Los Angeles. When the calculations were completed and a check drafted, this gesture in the direction of prudence had reduced the balance of the Swiss account of the Bethlehem Corporation to slightly more than $100,000. Bonham-Carter entrusted a second check in this amount to Royer with instructions to buy with it as many wheat contracts as it would cover.

During dessert, Bonham-Carter learned another piece of disturbing information. The monthly designation given the contracts he held was not, strictly speaking, the whole truth. Royer explained that under the rules of the Chicago Board of Trade, the holder of a contract for a given month could be asked to take delivery of the commodity anytime after the last business day of the preceding month. Unless he had sold his contract by that time, he faced being assessed charges for storage, interest and fire insurance totaling more than $8.00 per contract per day. For someone holding contracts numbering in the thousands, it could get very expensive very fast. Bonham-Carter said a silent prayer of thanks for having decided to put his personal funds into wheat. The earliest possible delivery for those contracts was still six weeks away. However, the soybeans into which, on Sallas' instructions, he had put a healthy chunk of the Peruvian money were another story. They could be delivered in two weeks. It was an alarming prospect. He already had held some of them nearly two weeks during which their price had declined. Something was going to have to happen fast if things were going to work out as planned.

Before he left Royer in front of the restaurant, Bonham-Carter asked him which of the local journalists did the best job of reporting on agricultural subjects—grain in particular. Royer gave him two names which he wrote down and stuffed in his pocket before he said good-bye.

A block north of Le Provençal, he spotted a pay phone bolted into the wall of a building across the street. A minute later, the receiver pressed to his ear, he was listening to the phone's ring.

"*New York Times.*" It was the switchboard girl.

"I'd like to speak to Bill Robbins, please."

"Just a moment." He could hear the muffled tone of the extension ringing.

" 'Lo, Robbins' desk."

"Is Mr. Robbins there?"

"Haven't seen him around, just a second." Bonham-Carter could hear the party on the other end asking if anyone knew Robbins' whereabouts. "Sorry, I don't know where he is. Want me to take a message?"

"No, thank you, but you can tell me something. Is Mr. Robbins the reporter who wrote the articles about the grain agreement with the Russians?"

"Hang on." Again the interoffice conversation. "David, who's been doing the pieces on the grain deal? Is that Robbins or Bernie? Bernie, and who? Phil? Okay." The man was talking back into the phone now. "Look, the guy you probably want to talk to, Bernie Gwirtzman, is out of town, but Phil Shabecoff does that kind of stuff sometimes and you should be able to get him at home."

Bonham-Carter thanked the man at *The Times* and took down the number. Then, as an afterthought, he got Shabecoff's address as well. It occurred to him that a paper like *The Times* would receive dozens of crank calls each day. His story would be more convincing delivered in person.

At Dupont Circle he hailed a taxi and gave the driver the Chevy Chase address. It was a long ride up Connecticut Avenue. He used the time to plan his next move. Once he had got word of the Russians' buying to the press, there would be little for him to do except wait. An article in *The Times* would trigger efforts by the other papers. Certainly *The Washington Post* and *The Wall Street Journal* would feel obligated to put investigative reporters on the story. The companies would not cooperate, but their confirmation was not essential. An "informed source's" story would be more than sufficient reason for farmers to start holding their crops off the market. They were gamblers, hunch players. Instead of racing forms they consulted weather reports and almanacs. They were conditioned to act on unsubstantiated information. If there was a problem he faced, it was not with the farmers but with what Shabecoff and *The Times* might insist on in the way of proof before they went to print. On that score, he would do his best. If it worked, he was home free. There would be nothing more for him to do but hide out until time to sell his contracts. Canada would be safe. He wondered if the sales could not be made by cable and resolved to check that point with Royer.

The taxi had reached the Chevy Chase shopping center. A few hundred yards farther on it looped three-quarters of the way around the circle and turned right down a broad, tree-lined street. The taxi moved slowly as the driver peered at the street numbers. On either side there were large houses set back from the sidewalk. It crossed Bonham-Carter's mind that *The Times* must pay decent salaries.

"Shit!" It was the first word the cabdriver had spoken since Dupont Circle.

"Beg your pardon?"

"We got a cop behind us." As the driver pulled the cab toward the curb, Bonham-Carter turned to see the whirling red light and the blue and white police car stopping behind them.

"Move over." A policeman had come up on the driver's side of the cab and was motioning to him to relinquish the wheel.

"Why? What the hell is this? This is Maryland. You guys can't work here. . . ." The driver's protest was cut short by the sight of a snub-nosed revolver pointed at his groin.

A second policeman opened the rear door on the curb side and pushed in beside Bonham-Carter. "All right, let's move," he said.

As the car pulled away from the curb, Bonham-Carter noticed a small boy, perhaps four years old, sitting motionless on his tricycle. He had watched the whole episode from the sidewalk, and, as the cars passed him, he turned and followed them with his eyes until they disappeared around the corner.

On Western Avenue, the cab turned left, passed the circle again and headed down one of the numerous feeder roads which led to the main traffic artery through Rock Creek Park. Half a mile into the park, the cab slowed, then pulled to a stop at a point where the narrow, heavily wooded road widened into an observation point overlooking the creek. The police car had apparently been following them, for it now pulled alongside and Bonham-Carter was rudely transferred to its back seat. The transfer took less than twenty seconds. It was observed by no one other than the taxi driver who now stood alone by his vehicle, staring after them in mute fury.

None of the three policemen had spoken so much as a word to Bonham-Carter. Now he groped for words of his own, words that would express credible indignation. None seemed quite to fit. He had waited too long. Having been in the car already for five minutes, he could hardly come out with, "Say, what's this all about?" Though he felt absurdly passive, he resolved to remain silent for a while.

"You better call in."

The driver was speaking to the other policeman in the front seat. Bonham-Carter could hear the static as the car radio was switched on.

"Earl." The man in the front seat spoke into the hand microphone. "We got him. Picked him up on Grafton Street in Chevy Chase. He looked like he was about to stop in front of number thirty, but you better check out the whole block." The man paused for a moment, listening and nodding. "Right. Right. Okay, Earl, you get in touch with Mr. Ferguson and bring him up to date. We should be in Mount Weather by four o'clock. You can tell the guy down at DCPD we'll have the car and the uniforms back to him before he goes off duty. And thank the poor bastard, will you, Earl; he stuck his neck out quite a ways for us."

After it left the park, the police car headed north on Connecticut Avenue.

Bonham-Carter watched the houses flit by and wondered what sort of a place Mount Weather was and what they would do with him when they got there. He kicked himself for the decision in Los Angeles to invest his own money. He had violated his own first rule. He had got involved. The prospect of $700,000 had made him incautious, made him care about what he would not otherwise have cared about. Made him try to contact Shabecoff. His assignment had been to buy. What happened after he bought should not have been his problem but Sallas'.

A thought struck him. It was Friday, July 14. Sallas would be expecting his weekly cable. He wondered how the Finance Minister would react when none arrived. How long would Sallas wait before he decided that Bonham-Carter was in trouble or, worse, that he had absconded with the balance of the funds?

Chapter

XI

KOPKE did not sleep well the night of July 13. He woke at one o'clock and again at three o'clock. Finally, shortly after five o'clock, he gave up trying to sleep and crept downstairs to make a pot of coffee and wait for seven o'clock when his driver would arrive. In the hall at the bottom of the stairs, he paused and studied the shadowy circle of chairs through the door of the darkened dining room. Only a few weeks earlier he had hosted a Soviet Trade delegation and those chairs had held laughing, drinking men. During that evening, he had believed in the comradeship and cooperation to which they had drunk. He wondered now if some of those men had known of their government's buying plans at the time, if they had been laughing at him and at his innocence. He wondered, too, about White House retribution. He knew that his rickety footbridge of access—so painstakingly strung up over the past months—could be cut loose at the White House end by a single slash from any of a number of Presidential aides. Ferguson's tone the previous afternoon had made that clear. It was appalling the way the Administration had managed in just three years to emasculate the executive departments. The White House handed out Cabinet positions like costumes from a costume trunk. The authority which the costumes were supposed to confer the White House kept for itself. For those who took the Cabinet jobs, it was a no-win situation. If the Administration was guilty of a fumble or a wild pitch or of some administrative misdemeanor, somebody in the Cabinet got the blame. But when things went well, there was no credit. Credit, under the deistic formulation of the Presidency enforced by the White House gauleiters, went, ex officio, to the man in the Oval Office. Cabinet members, to the extent they were permitted onstage at all during the congratulatory ceremony, were instructed to keep their backs to the audience and to take their glory by reflection.

The inequity of the situation gnawed at him for most of the morning. It was still on his mind after lunch when the door to his office opened and Braxton walked in carrying a sheet of paper.

"Have you seen this, sir? It just showed up in my in box," the executive assistant said, sliding the paper across the desk top. "I don't know where it came from, but I suspect it's Huggins' idea of a joke."

Kopke glanced at the paper before him. It was stamped confidential top and bottom and addressed to the secretary in his capacity as surrogate campaigner for the President. It was drafted in memo format. There was no indication of its source. It read in full:

MEMORANDUM TO THE SECRETARY

Hereafter follows a foolproof plan for guaranteeing the President a landslide victory in 1972 by ensuring him dramatic increases in the proportion of the urban black and ghetto vote. These, as you know, are the people who traditionally either vote Democratic or do not vote at all. The plan would require the efforts of only one man and would cost next to nothing.

STEP 1: Someone contacts Jimmy the Greek and plants the suggestion that over the next several months he devote several of his columns to the odds on the upcoming election. Jimmy, I believe, is already on record as saying that the opposition is a 100 to 1 shot. But a few articles to that effect would fix those odds in the public mind and generate interest in the betting action.

STEP 2: Some reliable lowlife (Carlson at the White House might have some suggestions) is commissioned to go around the country seeking out the leading bookies in the major urban ghettos and suggesting that they make book on the election and promote it along with the weekly football games, boxing matches, etc. Market forces will follow their natural course and the other bookies will follow suit to meet the competition.

STEP 3: Suppose the odds open at 100 to 1 in our favor. Consider what this will mean. There will be a hundred people willing to bet on the President for every one person willing to bet on the opposition. These odds will of course tumble quickly, since, as Jimmy the Greek says, nothing but the sunrise is 100 to 1, and because not many people are going to be interested in putting up a dollar to make a penny, but the odds are still almost certain to remain better than 10 to 1. Even if the odds drop that low, you will have created a situation in which for every bet outstanding on the opposition, there will be at least 10 bets on the President. If the bettors vote their bets, and they would almost certainly do so, you will have handed the President a 10 to 1 edge among the very segment of the population whose votes he is now least likely to get.

Properly put forward, this plan should be worth points at the White House. At the very least it will give you a chance to show you're on the team.

"You've read this thing, Brax?"

"Yes, sir."

"What do you think? You think it's Huggins, do you?"

"Probably. It sounds like his sense of humor."

"Ummm, well, destroy it, Brax. I don't want it around

here. Somebody will pick it up and not know what it is. It could be hard to explain." For a moment the secretary cast his eyes over the memo again. "You know, Brax, the funny thing is that, if I sent this thing over to the White House, they wouldn't think it was humorous. They'd probably think it was a helluva good idea."

It was close to six o'clock in the evening when Ferguson's call came. The secretary had repaired to the sauna room fifteen minutes earlier and was summoned to the phone by Braxton's knock at the small glass window. He took the call on the wall phone in the tile antechamber. Despite the two large towels which Braxton handed him, the jump from 150 degrees to 70 degrees left him shivering.

"Hello."

"Hiya, having a good sweat?" Ferguson's voice was at once jaunty and smug.

"Yeah, yeah, what's happened?" The secretary wondered how much beating around the bush he was going to have to listen to.

"Well, quite a bit. For starters, your friend Bonham-Carter apparently didn't think highly of your little story about the shipping business." It was obvious that Ferguson was enjoying the conversation, for he continued in the same chatty vein. "Personally, I liked it. I listened to it on tape this morning, and I don't know that I wouldn't have bought it if it had been me in his position."

"Okay, Seth, get to the point."

"Well, the point, old buddy, is that Bonham-Carter was out of the hotel within five minutes after you put down the phone. Out of the hotel, and that was damn near the last we saw of him."

"I see. Would you mind giving me a translation of

'damn near'?" Why did he have to put up with this narrative striptease?

"Sure, Forrie. 'Damn near' means that we got him back." Ferguson, who sounded mildly irritated at having had the conclusion of his story squeezed out of him so soon, filled the secretary in on the events of the previous twenty-four hours.

The two agents stationed at the Madison had followed Bonham-Carter as far as the theater. Foreseeing the possibility that he would leave by the rear exit, one of the agents had gone to cover the rear but had been unable to circle the block quickly enough to spot Bonham-Carter before he got into the taxi. A check of the room at the Madison revealed the absent toilet articles and confirmed Bonham-Carter's flight. By morning a check of hotel registers focusing on single men without suitcases had turned up nothing but a half-dozen extremely embarrassed locals caught at their extracurricular sex.

"By nine o'clock this morning," Ferguson said, "things were looking very grim."

"So?"

"So, I asked myself what I would do if I knew what your friend knew. And I told myself, why, I'd be buying grain like a sonavabitch. The rest was pretty simple. I put five men on it and told them to check every customers' list in every brokerage house in the District, Maryland and Virginia. By noon, we'd found the brokerage house, but the guy's broker was out to lunch so we got the name of the restaurant from somebody else in the office and got a car over there right away."

"So you had him picked up?"

"Yeah, but not there. We had our men in District police uniforms, but it's still a ticklish business this snatching people off the downtown streets." Ferguson described how his men had followed the taxi to Chevy Chase and how they had made the snatch on Grafton Street.

The secretary noticed that his feet were cold from standing on the tiles. He took another towel from the stack next to the sauna room door, dropped it on the floor and stood on it. He glanced at Braxton, who was still standing in the anteroom doorway, and wondered how much he had been able to absorb from one end of the conversation. He disliked talking to the White House in front of assistants. It was better to keep his obsequious side to himself. He offered his thanks, but Ferguson was not through.

"I think we're out of the woods on this, but it was too fucking close. If that guy had gone to some schlock broker with crummy records, we might still be looking."

"Right."

"'Nother thing. We checked out the street number where we picked him up and it turns out the house belongs to a reporter from *The New York Times.* If we hadn't followed him out there, it could have been all over. You can get away with kicking the shit out of all kinds of aliens, but, buddy, you lay a glove on one of those china ass reporters and you got big trouble."

At the "shit-kicking" reference, Kopke winced. After more than a year and a half in the government, his understanding of the ways and practices of the security types to whom Ferguson referred only as his men was still based more on movies than on experience.

"Don't worry, he's going to be all right. He should be in Mount Weather by now. We'll have to hold him there for a couple of months. If you've got another minute, there are some other things you might be interested in hearing."

The secretary said he did.

"I got the Interpol report this morning, and it's got some pretty interesting stuff in it. Seems this fellow Bonham-Carter is a sort of jack-of-all-trouble type. His record goes back over ten years and he's been everything from a hit man to a smuggler. They turned up his entry papers at the Customs Bureau and they show him entering the country at Miami two weeks ago on a flight from Lima and showing a British passport. Incidentally, we checked out the London address he gave at the hotel and found nothing. Nice neighborhood, right off Berkeley Square, but the number he gave is a garage not a house."

"I see."

"Hang on, that's just the beginning. After the Interpol people found out he had come from Lima, I did a little checking with the CIA. That was very, very profitable. Turns out they've got a sizable Latino payroll which for about six years has included a Peruvian military bigwig named Ferricio. Once you get these guys on the hook, they don't have much room for maneuver, and it was no problem for the CIA's men in the embassy down there to get Ferricio to talk." Briefly, Ferguson summarized Ferricio's story for Kopke, describing the anchovy failure, the Cabinet meeting of the previous January and the hiring of Bonham-Carter.

"It's a helluva note, when you think about it," Ferguson said. "Here the Russians are buying jillions of dollars worth of wheat, and we get ourselves in a jam because a few Peruvians are running out of fish and may have to drop out of the Squanto business for a little while." Despite his chill, the secretary had to smile at Ferguson's connecting fish fertilizer with the savior of the Plymouth colony. "Anyway, there it is," Ferguson added. "From what the Interpol people say, we probably could have given him a little scare, put him on a plane and forgotten about him. According to them, his nerves are shot. They can't find any record of his having worked in the last two years. I imagine right now he is pissing in his pants out there in those spooky woods."

"Maybe so, Seth, but in my position I'll feel a lot safer knowing he is out of circulation."

"Yep, I agree. Remind me after November to take up the Peruvian aid matter. I looked it up, and those ungrateful bastards are getting more than forty million dollars this year. If I have anything to say about it, this time next year they'll be eating those little fish instead of making them into fertilizer."

The secretary could hear Ferguson still chuckling to himself as he hung up.

Back in the sauna room, he wondered whether he should have suggested to Ferguson that the government intervene to prevent further grain sales to the Russians. There would be problems, chief among them the possibility that it would necessitate public disclosure of sales already made. The risk would be great, the benefits marginal. Besides the OECD, the Organization for Economic Cooperation and Development which laid down the trading rules for the Western world, would be certain to interpret the act as a harbinger of export embargoes yet to come and protest vociferously. It would be better to do nothing and try to keep the lid on the kettle as long as possible.

The needle on the sauna room thermometer was pointing at 155, Kopke had had enough. He picked up the pitcher next to him on the wooden bench and, reaching toward the heating unit in the corner, poured several cups of water over the hot stones. As the steam sizzled off the stones, the temperature seemed to jump fifty degrees in an instant. His face and ears were burning, and he ducked his head to escape the extreme heat at the top of the room. "One, two, three, four . . ." he counted quickly to himself. At "fifteen," he kicked the door open and stepped outside.

After calling Braxton and asking him to get the car ready, he showered and dressed slowly. Despite the annoying verbal footsie he had had to play, the conversation with Ferguson had done a great deal to put his mind at rest. He was scheduled to speak the next morning in San Francisco, and the sponsors of the meeting had asked him to discuss the Soviet trade negotiations. Anticipating that the topic was one he could live off for several months, he had worked up an elaborate presentation loaded with political science/foreign policy jargon describing the negotiations in their détente context and the interdependent nexus of economic and political interests that continued efforts would fuse into a new, prosperous and stable world order. It was purest bullshit but the sort of thing that would be widely quoted and that would go down well with chamber of commerce audiences. He had worked hard on the speech and had looked forward to giving it until the Bonham-Carter episode had temporarily diminished his taste for the subject. Now, as he tightened his tie and stepped into the hall heading for his office where he would pick up Braxton and his briefcase, he could feel his enthusiasm returning.

Rush hour was over, and the green limousine made good time through the southern part of the city and out along the road to Andrews Air Force Base. Kopke was aware that some Cabinet members made it a practice to use commercial flights where possible. He admired their self-restraint, but viewed it as foolish. One of his earliest Washington lessons had been in the use of perquisites of office. They were like muscles. Either you used them or they atrophied.

Just inside the air base, the limousine turned right, following the road which ran along the backs of the hangars. From his seat in the rear, he could see planes silhouetted in the dying light on the hangar aprons, everything the Air Force flew, everything from fighter planes up to the "tubes," the modified, windowless Boeing 707s.

Half a mile down the road the limousine turned left and pulled up in front of a low sprawling building. Inside, the stark and grimy furnishings spoke volumes about the boring sameness of military life. The canteen to the right of the door might have been in Lübeck or Okinawa; it would look no different, it would serve the same food, the same burned coffee tasting of chickory.

While Braxton paused at the desk to announce the secretary's arrival, Kopke walked quickly through the crowd of thirty or forty soldiers waiting for flights which would take them back to their bases. It was one of the pleasures of Cabinet rank that he no longer waited for planes, that planes waited for him.

Outside he could see the small Jetstar pulled up a hundred yards away, its forward stairs dropped into boarding position. As he approached he could see brisk movement at the base of the stairs. Though it was almost dark, he knew that would be his departure escort snapping to attention.

"Good evening, Mr. Secretary." The chief steward was smiling down from the doorway as he mounted the stairs.

"Evening, evening, you boys all ready?"

"Yes, sir. Just waiting on you."

"I appreciate that, I do. I expect the day my number

comes up they'll let me know by having you fellas take off before I get here." He liked the military stewards. They gave good service, they didn't talk about who drank what, they didn't issue report cards. It was a refreshing change from his dealings with other parts of the government.

The plane, which in a pinch could hold about fourteen people, had been configured for only eight. On each side of the center aisle were sets of two large opposing seats. These could be converted into four serviceable beds by sliding the opposing seats toward each other until they touched and lowering the back of one of them. While they waited for Braxton to join them, the steward made up two beds in this fashion.

Once in the air, the secretary passed up the offer of a snack and wasted no time in undressing and going to bed. He was tired from the previous night. Moreover, the experience had taught him that he needed at least an hour and a half of air sleep for every hour he normally would get in bed at home.

It was pitch-dark when he awakened. The steward was gently shaking his shoulder.

"Sir, there is a radio call for you in the cockpit. I'm sorry to have to wake you up, but they said it was very important."

"Who said it was important? What time is it anyway?"

"It's two-thirty Washington time, sir, and it's Mr. Ferguson at the White House, who says it's important."

The steward turned on a low light as the secretary, clad only in his underwear, felt his way gingerly forward.

"Seth?"

"Just a minute, Mr. Secretary." The connection sounded hollow through the earphones.

There was a ten-second delay during which he felt a

mixture of apprehension and annoyance. He had to say one thing for Ferguson: the man was consensus all-American when it came to bureaucratic gamesmanship. He must have routed his secretary out of bed and made her drive fifteen miles in from Virginia to place this call so he could be the last one on the line.

"Hello." It was Ferguson's voice.

"Seth, what the hell is it?"

"Well, I got some bad news for you."

"Okay, shoot."

"I'll make it real short. Bonham-Carter has escaped."

The call was over in two minutes. Ferguson had no details to offer, and the men agreed that they would talk again in the morning.

Back in bed, the sleep would not come back to him. He asked the steward for a strong bourbon, then for more than an hour lay staring out the window at the stars.

In the wee hours of that night of July 14, more than a thousand miles from where he then lay, the Democratic Party meeting in Miami Beach would ratify its candidate's choice of a running mate.

Chapter
XII

FOUR miles north of Chevy Chase Circle, the police car, carrying Bonham-Carter in the back seat, left Connecticut Avenue, swung up onto the Washington beltway and headed west toward northern Virginia. As they crossed the Potomac, he could see the leavings of Hurricane Agnes below. The river's banks were lined with debris. Huge trees, uprooted by the force of the flood a month earlier, had been wedged between the rocks of the riverbed by the receding waters, and behind them the surface of the river was solid with flotsam and jetsam from the ravaged upper valley.

Past the bridge, they exited onto Route 193, descending quickly into a heavily wooded ravine. At the bottom of the ravine, they crossed one of the Potomac's small tributaries and accelerated up the other side. They were in horse country now. On either side of the narrow road, he could see large estates, white fences and timber jumps. Then they were back in the woods and out again and passing ordinary farms.

On the other side of Dranesville, they left Route 193 and turned onto Route 7. Taking advantage of the divided four-lane highway, the driver increased his speed. The little towns flashed by: Leesburg, Hamilton, Purcellville, Round Hill and then the mountains and they were climbing.

Five minutes past Round Hill, they left the highway and turned left on Route 601, a narrow road that led straight up the mountain. Bonham-Carter watched the odometer on the dashboard turn seventeen thousand miles and calculated that they had been thirty miles since leaving the beltway. Wherever they were taking him, it was remote. They passed a driveway on the right and next to it, a mailbox inscribed "Greyrock's Ingenuity." He noted the low stone wall that marked the edge of the property—from the look of it a sizable estate. If he got a chance, he might be coming back down the road. It would be helpful to know in advance where there was potential refuge.

Two miles farther on, he noticed a high wire-mesh fence on the left. At the same time blinking amber lights appeared ahead. The lights seemed to be in the middle of the road, but as the car drew closer, the road swerved to the right, and he could see that they were fixed to one of the roadside fence supports.

Behind the fence, he also could see now a half-dozen low green buildings and two taller tan brick buildings with red tile roofs, and then a tower, and then a gate.

The car was stopping. Uniformed security guards were coming to meet them from the glass-enclosed guardhouse that sat astride the entrance to the compound. The driver and the other man in the front seat had left the car and were talking to the guards. Several times they pointed to the car and the guards nodded. Then he was taken out. As the guards ushered him through the gate, he could hear the sound of the police car backing out of the entrance, then the squeal of tires as it accelerated back down the hill.

The guards seemed more casual than the police had been. Inside the guardhouse, he was searched. They left him his billfold, but his passport and everything that might have been used as a tool or weapon was taken from him. There were papers to fill out. Through the glass, he could see an occasional civilian walking between the buildings behind.

Though the purpose of the Mount Weather installation may have been suspected by some of the motorists who passed there and heard the strange bleeps in the low-frequency range of their car radios, it was still, in the summer of 1972, classified "top secret" by the U.S. government.

There was nothing in its early history and little in the current appearance of the eighty-five-acre property to suggest a need for that classification. Acquired in 1903 by the Department of Agriculture, Mount Weather had seen a variety of uses in the years since. The Agriculture Department had used it as a weather station until the

First World War when the Army had taken it over to conduct artillery range-finding experiments. Then, in the 1920s, it had had a brush with notoriety when President Calvin Coolidge considered making it a summer White House to which he might repair with his New Englander's constitution from the sweat bath of the capital. That never came to pass, however, and during the 1930s, Mount Weather was used as a retreat for New Deal planners and later a rehabilitation center operated by the District of Columbia Transient Relief Agency for hoboes and other unfortunates becalmed on the breezeless sea of the Depression economy.

It was not until the Cold War Years of the early 1950s that Mount Weather went underground. Acquired at that time by the Office of Emergency Preparedness, it was converted into a command post for use in the event of nuclear attack. Few physical changes were made. A helicopter pad and air traffic control tower were installed. The wire fence with its barbed-wire top was erected. And the CIA moved in to set up a communications center. But compared to the tunneled and fortified alternative emergency command post at Mount Ritchie, Maryland, Mount Weather remained a simple and somewhat shabby facility.

"Mr. Bonham-Carter, if you'll just come with me, I'll show you to where you'll be staying." It was one of the guards speaking. "I can't say you'll find it the most comfortable place you've ever been, but it's not too bad. Actually, we ain't set up here to look after people like yourself. We ain't had a prisoner here in my recollection, and I been here close to twenty years."

Bonham-Carter looked at the short smiling man, and put his age at about sixty. Despite his revolver, he had the harmless, ineffectual look that central casting generally gave to night watchmen.

Though it was nearly six o'clock, the asphalt of the driveway was still soft from the midday heat and their shoes moved soundlessly. The compound was almost deserted. As they passed the helicopter pad, he could see that an approach had been cleared for several hundred yards down the slope of the mountain. Beyond the wall of trees at the bottom of the clearing was the floor of the valley and a road. He wondered if it was the road over which they had just driven.

"I spek I should warn you 'bout Jason," the guard said. "He's one mean cuss, Jason is. I've knowed him 'bout as long as anybody has, and, I declare, I cain't find nothing to recommend about Jason. He got hisself all crippled up in the war, and I reckon he just figured he never asked for all that misery, and there wasn't no reason he shouldn't share what of it he could with other folks. Anyway, seems like that's what he's done ever since I knowed him."

"Who is Jason?"

"Jason's gonna be your guard."

The man explained that, because it was unusual for them to be asked to detain anyone on the property, there were no regular detention guards. Volunteers had been asked for from the normal security staff, and Jason had been the first taker. He would be on duty from five in the afternoon until 2:00 A.M. each day.

"This here's it."

The guard was motioning toward the door of one of the smaller green buildings, about thirty yards from the fence. They entered without knocking.

The room into which they stepped had a high ceiling and was nearly dark. Casement windows were set along the top of one wall, and from them, rectangular shafts of late-afternoon sunlight crossed to the opposite wall like huge air-conditioning ducts in which dust now

swirled from the draft. At the far end of the wall opposite, Bonham-Carter could see a partially opened door
framed by electric light behind it. As he watched, the
door opened and he could see the silhouette of a man.

For a moment none of them moved. The man, who
Bonham-Carter correctly surmised was Jason, came toward them. He was limping, and as his head and
shoulders passed through the sloping column of light
from the far window, Bonham-Carter noted that he was
older than he had expected.

There was little to talk about, and little was said. Jason
seemed confident of his business, and, after a few attempts at friendly remarks, which went largely ignored,
the first guard said good-bye and slipped out.

"Come over here."

Jason had turned the light on and was walking sideways toward a table in the corner which, along with its
chair, made up the only furnishings in the room. Keeping an eye on Bonham-Carter, he picked up something
from the table and moved it to the corner, then stepped
back and drew his revolver.

"Go ahead, pick it up," he said.

Bonham-Carter picked it up, noticing as he did so the
Exacto knife in the middle of the table.

"You know what it is?"

"It's a bullet."

"That ain't no regular bullet, young fella. That there
bullet will divide your insides into tres partes, if you get
my meaning." Bonham-Carter could see that the soft
lead slug had been split halfway down to the shell casing
by two crisscrossing cuts. Its four quarters had been
pried open at the tip like a cootie catcher. So that was
how it was going to be. He had seen dumdum bullets
with their flat ends, and he had seen hollow points and
Super Vels, and he had seen men who had been hit by

153]

them. He indicated to Jason with a nod that he understood. He could have told the old man that if he had to fire his gun he had better get close, because that homemade bullet was going to come out rolling and tumbling and wouldn't be accurate at more than thirty feet. He could have told him, too, that he had better make the first shell count, because there was a better-than-even chance the second was going to jam in the chamber. He started to return the bullet to the table.

"You hang on to that, young fella; it'll give you something to think on."

Jason was apparently satisfied that he had made his point. With his gun, he motioned Bonham-Carter toward the other room.

The second room was smaller and, like the first, almost bare. An old metal cot stood in the very center of the room. Above it, a light bulb hung from an aged fabric cord. Bonham-Carter's eyes flicked around the room, measuring its possibilities. It would be difficult for one man to move the heavy old cot across the concrete floor without making a great deal of noise. But, without something to stand on, it would be impossible to reach the room's single window high on the far wall. Someone, probably Jason, had taken an added precaution. Several dozen assorted bottles had been lined up two deep along the windowsill. The window had been designed to open inward and upward at the pull of a chain that ran over a pulley anchored in the ceiling. But any pull on the chain now would sweep the bottles off the sill and onto the floor. So long as the bottles could not be reached, they would serve as an effective alarm.

"You might as well hop on that bed and get comfortable," Jason said. "I'm gonna be right out here in the next room and I don't wanna hear no extra movin' around."

"How long am I expected to stay here?" Bonham-Carter asked.

"That ain't none of my business, and it ain't none of your business neither. I tell you this, though," Jason said, patting the gun which he had returned to its holster, "you gonna stay right here jes as long as they tell me to keep you here." With that, he backed toward the door, opened it and disappeared.

They had taken his watch from him at the guard-house, but he guessed that it was close to two hours later when the door opened again. It was Jason with a vending machine sandwich wrapped in cellophane. Though Bonham-Carter was not hungry, he welcomed the interruption. In the solitary room, he already had begun to feel like a nonperson. The circumstances of his capture had been irregular, even within his own experience. There had been no charges, no due process, no nothing. The only official papers had been those filled out at the guardhouse and they had been little more than a warehouse receipt. The Peruvians would miss him eventually, but they could not acknowledge that he was in their hire by asking questions. As far as concerned the legal authorities of local jurisdiction, he would not have disappeared because he would never have existed. He had about as much chance of help from the outside as a stowaway who had climbed out the wrong side of his lifeboat and dropped unnoticed into the sea.

He tried to recall what it had said on the small white card the immigration authorities had stapled in his passport in Miami. The card—form I 94—would have carried a date by which, on entering, he had agreed to leave the country. What was it? Had he bothered to look at it? What would happen when he failed to leave by that date? Would that trigger a search? Whatever the date had been, he felt certain that it was months off.

155]

As he ate the sandwich, he studied the room closely. It was hardly a maximum-security cell. He had been in much worse. Still, he could see no obvious avenue of escape. Perhaps the building had other rooms.

After he got up from the bed, he walked to the door and knocked lightly.

"Yeah, what is it?" The voice, partly muffled by the door, seemed to come from the far side of the outside room.

"I wonder if I could use the water closet?" He could hear a chair scrape the concrete floor and then Jason's uneven footsteps approaching.

"The what?"

"The toilet, the lavatory."

"Oh." The footsteps were moving away from the door again. "Come on out."

Jason had his pistol drawn when he emerged. With his free hand, the guard motioned down the hall to a second door which in the darkness Bonham-Carter had not noticed earlier.

The lavatory was cramped and smelled strongly of urine. In the light provided by a single bulb suspended from the top of the room, he took in its features. The toilet, directly opposite the door, was an old gravity flush model almost unchanged from the first of its kind invented by Thomas Crapper a century earlier. Though such toilets were still common in England, it was the first he had seen in the United States.

He followed its pipe up the rear wall, then across to the side wall where he could see the bottom of its porcelain water tank and the flush chain which he knew would be attached to a lever at the top of the tank. It was a pity that low ceilings had obsoleted these old toilets; sturdily constructed, with basically three moving parts, they would last forever.

He examined the tiny sink with its dirt-encrusted bar of soap and the rusted towel rack, then turned his attention again to the toilet. Despite its familiarity, there was something curious about it. The principle of its operation argued strongly for placement of the water tank directly above the bowl. Yet this tank had been placed on the side wall. That way, some of the gravitational force on which the flush depended would be dissipated in pushing the water along a horizontal course. It seemed a silly modification unless . . . unless, it occurred to him suddenly, it had been done to avoid placing the tank in front of a window.

The upper portion of the room above the light was black. Except for the reflection off the bottom of the water tank, he could see nothing. He pulled the flush chain, and, as the room filled with the sound of rushing water, stepped up onto the rim of the toilet bowl and ran his hands up the back wall.

A foot above his head, his fingers jammed something hard and solid. If there was a window there, it was sealed off. He was working blind now, running his hands over the object that had stopped his fingers. He could feel sheet metal, louvered in places. He could feel wooden supports. A mental image was forming. His hands moved quickly, taking dimensions, feeling for screws, bolts, straps, whatever the fastenings might be, then he was down and out and thanking Jason and back in his room.

Once back on his bed, Bonham-Carter began an inventory of his available tools. Most of what might have been useful—his belt, his penknife—had been taken from him at the gate. There was nothing in the room except the cot on which he lay, the bottles on the windowsill and the window chain. Without a ladder, the chain would be impossible to detach. He patted his pockets and turned up the bullet Jason had given him plus sixteen cents.

As he contemplated the possible commutations of these scant resources, he studied the bottles on the windowsill. There were old bottles and new bottles, Coke bottles, wine bottles, even a couple of old Ball jars. Jason must have turned the place inside out collecting them.

One of the bottles at the end of the front row caught his attention. In the shadows at the top of the room, it was difficult to be certain what he saw. He rose and tip-toed to the wall beneath the window for a closer look. It had not been his imagination. The bottle at the far end of the first row still had its cork.

He measured the distance. Reaching as high as he could, his fingertips reached only an inch above the sill. He could touch the bottle and he could push it back slightly, but he could not pull it forward. Nor could he risk the noise of a jump.

Returning to the cot, he removed his shoes and thrust one, toe first, into the other. Back at the wall, he found that by holding the combined shoes by the exposed toe, he could hook the back of the uppermost shoe over the top of the bottle. He switched the shoes to his left hand, freeing his right to catch the bottle when it toppled forward. Then, as an afterthought, he got the pillow from the cot and placed it on the floor beneath the window. The last precaution proved unnecessary. He caught the bottle on its first revolution, bobbled it for a moment then, sinking to his knees as he did so, smothered it with both arms to his chest.

Luck was with him. The bottle could not have been more than six months old. The cork which he removed from its neck was still fresh and resilient. Next, he took his coins from his pocket and laid them out on the bed, a penny, a dime and a nickel. He picked up the penny and pressed its rim to the mouth of the bottle. Too big. Metal and glass met with about two-thirds of the coin still exposed. Discarding the penny, he picked up the dime and repeated the process. This time the bottle accepted almost half the coin.

He put the bottle aside. Then he took the cork and, with the serrated edge of the dime, began meticulously sawing a channel along the diameter of one end.

Twice in the course of his work, when he thought he heard the chair scrape in the outer room, he quickly stuffed bottle, cork and coins under the pillow on the cot. In each instance, he waited fully five minutes before resuming work.

Within half an hour, the cut in the cork was deep enough so that the dime when inserted was obscured on its head side up to Franklin Roosevelt's ear. With the dime thus lodged, he returned the cork to the bottle, pushing until the top of the cork was flush with the glass lip. Reluctantly, the bottle swallowed the last quarter inch of cork widened by the addition of the dime. Though his thumbs ached from the effort, he viewed his product with satisfaction. If the cork held, the 180 degrees of exposed dime that protruded from the neck would make a serviceable screwdriver. He estimated the time at around ten o'clock. Four more hours until the guards were scheduled to change. He would have to let a substantial portion of that time pass in order not to raise Jason's suspicions.

It was roughly an hour later when he knocked on the door again. This time Jason did not leave his table in the far corner of the outer room. From his station beneath the light, he did not notice the bulge in the front of Bonham-Carter's trousers, nor could he see that his shoes were now secured by only two short laces at the top eyelets.

159]

Once inside the lavatory, Bonham-Carter moved quickly. Climbing back onto the toilet bowl, he located the four screws he had felt earlier. Removing the bottle from its hiding place, he set to work. The cork proved equal to the resistance and in a few minutes the screws were in his pocket. Then, gripping the metal corners on either side of the supporting L-brackets, he pushed straight upward. He could feel the muscles in his back quiver with the tension as the huge window-unit air conditioner rose off its moorings. When he lowered it again, he had moved it away from the wall perhaps two inches. With his fingers, he measured the distance that remained between the front edge of the supporting brackets and the middle of the unit. He estimated it at five inches. Most of the unit's weight would be concentrated at its back, however. That meant he might have to move it another six, perhaps seven, inches. He was beginning to lift again when he heard the outside door open.

"Howdy, Jason." The voice from the outside room was one he had not heard before. Had the changing of the guard been rescheduled?

"Hi, what do you want?" It was Jason's voice.

"Well, I just thought I'd pop in to take a leak."

"The prisoner's in the bathroom now."

"That's all right, I'll just wait if you don't mind."

"No, but I don't see why you don't just piss in the woods; the place isn't exactly crowded at this time of night."

"Okay, Jason, okay, just trying to be friendly." Bonham-Carter could hear the screen door slam as the man left.

The heat in the upper portion of the toilet was oppressive, and Bonham-Carter perspired freely with his efforts. Twice more he lifted the air conditioner and slid it farther out on its supports. After the second time, he pushed up gently on the rear of the unit. With about ten pounds of pressure it began to tip. Setting it back down, he inched it slowly forward again until it teetered precariously on the tips of the supports. Then he slid it back no more than a sixteenth of an inch.

"Hey, you hurry up in there. There's other people have to use that place, too." Jason's voice was edged with irritation.

"Yes, I'm sorry; I'll be out in a moment."

From his pocket, Bonham-Carter produced the balance of his shoelaces which he had knotted to make a single strand. He threaded one end through the metal grill in front of the air conditioner and secured it with a knot. Then, after flushing the toilet, he stretched the shoelace down and across to the chain that dangled from the toilet's water tank, threaded the other end through one of the chain links just about the level of the light and made it fast with two half hitches. At that level the shoelace would be all but invisible. After going through the motions of washing his hands for Jason's benefit, he opened the door. There was nothing left to do but to fight off the sleep and wait.

He must have dozed off anyway, for he was wakened somewhat later by a loud knocking at his door.

As he shook the cobwebs out of his head, he realized that Jason had been shouting at him for some time and that he had been incorporating the voice into his dream.

"You sonavabitch. When I call, you goddamn well better get to that door." He had opened the door and Jason, who had backed off into the middle of the outer room, was beside himself with anger. "I don't aim to get up and walk around this place every time I want to talk to you. Now, get over there," he said, pointing to the table chair which had been moved to the center of the room. "I'm gonna take a crap, and I want you where I can see you."

What followed was, in Bonham-Carter's estimation, an unpleasant and unnecessary intimacy. What worried him more, however, was the possibility, not at all remote, that the old man who sat pistol in hand hunkered on the toilet might, as his last act, get off an involuntary shot which, if it did not hit him, would nevertheless alert the other guards that something was amiss.

Bonham-Carter had killed men before, but never incidentally. Others had picked the victims. It had not been for him to decide whether they would die, only how. It had been an intellectual exercise, a question of how best to do what it was preordained would be done. His had been the morally neutral role of the professional soldier.

A noise drew his attention back to the bathroom. It was the rattle of the toilet paper roll. Jason had put down his gun on the edge of the sink and was folding a neat little square from the paper he had torn off the roll. Bonham-Carter let his eyes fall to the floor between his feet. His ears would be sufficient to keep up with events.

There was a second rattle of the toilet paper roll, and a third, and then the noise he had been waiting for—the squeak of the metal water tank lever indicating that Jason had just pulled the flush chain. Bonham-Carter looked up just in time to see 250 pounds of rusty 1950-vintage General Electric air-conditioning unit plunge out of the shadows at the top of the room. Jason had apparently been puzzled by the chain's extra resistance, for he managed to turn his head a quarter revolution. It was his last voluntary move. The air conditioner caught him on the right side of his neck just above the shoulder, its weight doubling him over and driving his head almost to the floor between his bent legs. Late the next day, the coroner in his report would describe the cause of death as an acute transection of the cervical spinal cord. The impact with his knee appeared also to have dislocated his right shoulder, for his right arm, on which he wore an old Army watch, protruded upward at an unnatural angle. Bonham-Carter slipped the watch from Jason's arm. It was 11:15. Unless the visitor of an hour earlier returned, he had almost three hours before his escape would be discovered.

Chapter
XIII

BY two o'clock the morning of the fifteenth, Bonham-Carter was outside Greencastle, Pennsylvania, heading north on Interstate 81.

The fence around Mount Weather had been high but simple enough to climb. And with the blanket from the cot thrown over it, the barbed wire had not given him difficulty. He had decided against exploring the possibilities of "Greyrock's Ingenuity," electing instead to gamble on finding a car in Round Hill. Alternately walking and jogging, he had covered the eight miles in under an hour and a half.

The town had been closed up when he arrived shortly before one o'clock, but he had located a small tow truck in a Phillips 76 station, and working by the light of the Garber's Ice Cream sign across the street, had "hot wired" its engine to life. Starting engines was a skill he had acquired by the time he was fifteen, and it had served him well. In 1942, after a six-month hitch in the merchant navy, he had found himself in North Africa with no work and a war raging around him. For lack of a better idea, he had enlisted, along with an assortment of other international misfits, in the Corps Franc d'Afrique. In due time, military service had become a series of monotonous back-and-forth treks over La Piste Forestière, a dirt road connecting Cap Serrat, on the northern coast of western Tunisia, with Sedjenane, a town twenty miles inland.

It had been a dreary experience, made tolerable only because, after the first week, he had managed to avoid making the trek on foot. Jeeps, half-tracks, scout cars; at one time or another he had driven them all. It had not mattered to him which of the three disorganized and ill-equipped armies then bleeding to death on that narrow ribbon of mud held nominal title to the vehicle. If it had an internal-combustion engine, and its hood was not bolted down, it was as good as his.

Just past Carlisle, he picked up the Pennsylvania Turnpike and headed east, crossing the Susquehanna River at Harrisburg, pushing the truck hard across the darkened countryside, ignoring the screams of the engine that was struggling against a gearbox whose ratios the manufacturer had set with a top speed of sixty miles per hour in mind.

It was 4:30 when he stopped outside Norristown for gas and to study the road map. The guards would have discovered his escape hours ago, but it would be morning before the truck was missed, and perhaps noon by the time the connection was made and an all-points bulletin sent out. By then he would have gotten rid of the truck.

An hour later he had passed Philadelphia and Levittown, and he was on the New Jersey Turnpike, and it was getting light.

The rest of the drive was a straight shot up the Jersey Turnpike to the Garden State Parkway and from there to the New York State Thruway. He cleared the New York City/Newark area a full hour before the morning rush. It was ten o'clock in the morning when he pulled into a gas station on the outskirts of Albany.

While the attendant was filling his tank, Bonham-Carter consulted the Yellow Pages in the phone booth. Then briefly he inquired about directions, nodding as the attendant counted off stoplights on his fingers. Five minutes after pulling into the station, he was out again.

The attendant's directions proved accurate. Ten minutes later, Bonham-Carter was driving through an ugly area south of the city alongside a high, dilapidated board fence. In the middle of the block, he slowed and turned through a gap in the fence, pulling to a stop in front of a small, corrugated-steel building. A freshly painted sign fixed to the roof bore the proprietors' names: Esposito & Esposito.

Inside the building, he was greeted by a man in his mid-forties, who wore a loud sport jacket with red piping around the lapels and pockets and listened silently as Bonham-Carter explained what he wanted. Then the man peered through the window at the nearly new tow truck, smiled knowingly and replied.

He could give Bonham-Carter $50 for the truck, but the machine would not be working until the afternoon. If Bonham-Carter wanted assurance that the truck would not be resold, he would have the crane throw it onto the ready stack while Bonham-Carter watched. The damage would be irreparable. Bonham-Carter agreed, and the two men stepped outside.

The whole operation took less than ten minutes. The truck was driven to the center of the yard. Its seats were removed, and it was drained of gas and oil. Then the crane's pincers bit through the windows of the cab, lifted the truck as an eagle lifts a rabbit—twenty, thirty, forty feet in the air—pivoted toward a five-deep pile of automobile carcasses and released. The truck dropped rear end first, its heavy steel towing arm puncturing the cars beneath on impact like a knife dropped point first into a piece of cheese. It was still staring skyward as Bonham-Carter turned to leave. He had found the whole operation mildly exciting. A scrapyard could probably charge admission. At the gate, he shot a backward glance at the truck perched on top of the pile. By evening, it would be a three-by-four block of steel.

At the bus station in Albany, he consulted timetables, tourist literature and maps of the surrounding area. For the moment, he was interested only in finding a quiet, out-of-the-way place where he could sleep without worrying about who might wake him up. His mind was settled by a brochure which described the virtues of an establishment called the Green Griffin Inn. It was located in Stockbridge, Massachusetts, fifty miles away. He checked the timetable. There would be a bus leaving in half an hour.

If a line were drawn from the center of Stockbridge to New York City and from there to Boston and back, Stockbridge would be at the right angle of the isosceles triangle. Over the years, the town has been sustained by that happy geometry. Tucked away in the Berkshire Mountains, it was too distant to commute to either city but close enough to benefit from the cultural and financial affluence of both. One did not have to look hard for the benefits. There were large homes in and around the town and a prosperous main street. In the summer there was the Berkshire Playhouse at the northeast end of town and the Tanglewood Music Center nearby. Residents and visitors could dine at the huge, old, rambling, white frame Green Griffin Inn, play golf at the Stockbridge Country Club or walk one of the many well-kept hiking trails through the surrounding mountains. During the winter, there was nearby skiing and, for those not athletically inclined, there was titillating street gossip about the latest famous personalities being treated at Riggs Sanitorium, across the main street, catercornered from the inn.

Several years earlier, the peaceful, well-to-do ways of the town had been threatened briefly by an infusion of hippies attracted by a young singer named Arlo Guthrie who, after living there for a short time, had made the uncivic gesture of describing the experience in a song called "Alice's Restaurant." But the town fathers and the local one-man constabulary had turned back the challenge, and, by the summer of 1972, things were back to normal in Stockbridge.

Bonham-Carter went to bed shortly after arriving at the inn. He did not awaken until nine o'clock the next morning, July 16, a Sunday. The two items of business he had to attend to would have to wait until the next day.

He passed the morning in leisurely fashion, looking in shops and strolling around the town. He walked down the main street, past an old bell tower and through the golf course to the point where a narrow bridge crossed the Housatonic River, then reversed his direction and walked to the playhouse at the other end of town. It was noon by the time he returned to the inn.

At the suggestion of the desk clerk, he took a box lunch and set out to climb the small mountain directly opposite his window at the back of the inn. The slope was gentle and the trail led straight up for half a mile then forked. He took the left branch of the fork that led to the summit and an old, abandoned fire lookout known as Laura's Tower. Twice in the course of the climb he thought he heard a stick snap somewhere behind him. Both times he stopped for a few minutes before continuing. But there was no further sound, and in the heavy foliage he could see only a short distance down the winding trail below him. Returning, he followed the other branch of the trail through a deep, boulder-strewn declivity which the trail signs identified as Ice Glen. The place was well named, for it was chilly as he picked his way through the spring-fed pools and moss-covered rocks. Even in the winter, with the leaves off the trees, there could be no more than a few hours of sunlight because of the steep and jagged cliffs which rose on either side. Now there was none.

The trail ended at a small road which he followed for several hundred yards to where it joined Route 7 leading back to town. That night he ate heartily and again went to bed early.

By ten o'clock the next morning, he had finished breakfast and was in his room at the telephone. The scrap of paper on which he had scribbled the names given him by Royer were before him on the bedside table and he was dialing.

"Information, what city?" The connection was clear.

"Kansas City, please."

"Yes?"

"Number for *The Southwestern Miller,* please; it's a magazine."

"Thank you."

While he waited for the number, Bonham-Carter composed his statement. Royer had told him that *The Southwestern Miller* was, despite its low circulation, the industry bible and the publication with by far and away the greatest influence on the grain market. The operator was back on the line now with the number. He thanked her and dialed.

"*Southwestern Miller.*" It was the switchboard girl.

"Yes, I'd like to speak to Mr. Morton Sosland, please."

"Just a moment, I'll see if he is in."

Bonham-Carter tried to imagine the layout of the office. He figured that there was a better than even chance that the girl was looking right at Mr. Sosland as she spoke.

"Hello, this is Morton Sosland."

There was something odd about the voice, a ringing, hollow quality. It was possible that Sosland was speaking through a speaker phone, that the curious noise was only the echo in the room. But he had heard similar noises before and knew that there was another, more likely explanation.

"Hello, hello."

He could hear the irritation in Sosland's voice as he replaced the receiver.

For a moment he sat still on the edge of the bed pondering his next move. Perhaps he was paranoid. The noise could well have been in the connection between the switchboard and Sosland's office. That was a risky assumption. A communications technician could have traced the call to its origin within thirty seconds. He picked up the receiver again and dialed the operator.

"Operator, I would like to place a call to Kansas City, but I would like to route the call through a London operator."

"You'll have to speak to the long-distance operator."

Moments later he repeated his request to the long-distance operator, who informed him that what he proposed would be quite impossible. Though technically feasible, it was against company policy.

He thought for a few minutes, then picked up the phone and called the long-distance operator again. This time he asked no questions but gave her a name and a London number and hung up to wait for the call-back. It came in ten minutes.

"Hello, James, it's Felix, how are you?"

There was surprise in the familiar answering voice. "Cripes, Felix, where the bloody hell are you? Still in Spain?"

"No, James, its not important to you where I am, but it may be important to other people which is why I'm calling. I need a favor."

Bonham-Carter carefully explained what he wanted. James Scrivas ran one of the most successful bookmaking operations in London. He was very prosperous and very legal, and he had one of the city's most active telephone switchboards. Moreover, he was very accommodating where friendship was involved.

Ten minutes later the phone was ringing in the offices of *The Southwestern Miller*. The girl who answered could not have known that the incoming call had been routed from Stockbridge to Scrivas' switchboard to the London overseas operator and back to Kansas City. Anyone trying to put a trace on the call would be able to tell only that it came from the offices of a London bookmaker. As an added precaution, however, Bonham-Carter announced himself to the switchboard girl as John Smith of the *London Financial Times*.

Morton Sosland, in 1972, was rounding out his fifth year as editor of *The Southwestern Miller*. An energetic Harvard graduate, he pursued the bits and scraps of information on which his subscribers' fortunes depended with a thoroughness and professionalism not often found in men who inherit their position, as he had, by dint of family control. He listened with interest as Bonham-Carter spoke.

"We are running a story," Bonham-Carter began, "about certain purchases of American wheat by the Soviet Union."

Then, under the guise of soliciting Sosland's impression of how the American public might react to the sales, he explained what he knew about the Russians' buying activity, ending with the information that the sales volume to date was at least four million tons and very likely twice that.

Sosland was stunned. Three days earlier he had quoted a speculative figure of two and three-quarter million tons in his daily news service. That, at the time, he had termed "unprecedented," as, indeed, it was. Now he was being told that his estimate covered only a third of what might actually have been sold.

"Are you certain of your figures?" he asked.

"Absolutely," came the reply.

After hanging up, Sosland regretted not having written the caller's name down. A source like that, if his information proved accurate, could be useful. The political implications of what the man said were little less than staggering. Even if the Commodity Credit Corporation dumped its available reserves into the market, it could not prevent a sharp price rise in the face of the kind of buying he just had been told the Russians were doing. It would be a serious political setback for the President if the Price Commission were forced to allow an increase in the price of bread on account of his much ballyhooed grain deal with the Russians.

Ten minutes later, Bonham-Carter was in the lobby inquiring whether there was a movie theater in the town. There was not, nor were there matinees at the playhouse on Mondays. A chat with the man behind the desk suggested nothing that without a car would help him pass the middle of the day. There was one more call he had to make, but that would have to wait until after office hours. He could use the intervening time to replace some of the clothes he had left in Washington and to pick up a new suitcase. On his way back to the inn, he stopped off at the drugstore on the main street, bought a half-dozen magazines and returned to his room.

It was seven o'clock in the evening when he placed the second call. It was to Sallas at his home. The instructions he had received had been explicit on the subject of communications with Peru. There were to be only the cables. But his current circumstances had not been foreseen at that time. Bonham-Carter was prepared to take the blame for the complications. His visit to Kopke had been ill-advised; that was clear in retrospect. Still, except for his personal problems, the plan was still intact. All the money was invested, and there was nothing to link it to Peru. He assumed that all that remained to be done was to sell the contracts at the appropriate time. That could be done through one of the brokerage firm's offshore offices. All he wanted to do now was to hear it from Sallas' mouth that he could return to Peru and collect the $50,000 he was still owed.

The phone was answered in Spanish by the maid. In a moment, Sallas was on the line. There was a hint of excitement in his heavily accented voice.

"Where are you?" were the first words he said.

Bonham-Carter spoke quickly and steadily for three minutes, eager to explain why he had not been able to send a cable three days earlier and to impress upon Sallas the perilous situation in which he currently found himself. To put the minister's mind at rest, he began by assuring him that the investing had gone without a hitch. Then, without explaining why, he described his having been seized by the policemen, the brief stay at Mount Weather and the killing of the guard. Finally, he stated his belief that the contracts could be sold abroad and that there might be no need for him to linger in the United States. He was about to suggest that he could replace his passport at the British consulate in Montreal and exit through Canada when Sallas interrupted.

"Yes, yes, I am glad that you called." The voice was surprisingly amiable. Bonham-Carter had expected irritation, but Sallas sounded almost relieved to be talking to him. "We have had a, uh, how do you say, an about-face, I think you call it, and I have new instructions for you."

Bonham-Carter listened with growing incredulity as Sallas spoke. The new instructions were for him to return to Washington immediately and, once there, to go straight to the Peruvian embassy. There would be a few papers to sign, and a Peruvian passport would be issued him. He could thereafter return to Peru at his convenience. His check for $50,000 would be waiting for him.

"Mr. Minister, I'll never get out of the airport if I do that. By now . . ." Sallas cut him off.

"It's all arranged. We have reached an accommodation with the White House. It is not as handsome as what we hoped for originally, but, in view of the fact that the prices do not appear to be rising so fast as we thought, it is quite satisfactory.

"I see," Bonham-Carter said. "If it's all the same to you, I'd feel more comfortable picking up the passport at the embassy in Ottawa."

"No, impossible. It must be Washington. The papers are in Washington already." Sallas explained that the "accommodation" called for Peru to surrender the contracts and to recall its agent in return for compensating financial considerations. But because the contracts were in Bonham-Carter's name, he would have to sign over powers of attorney in order to permit them to be liquidated. It was already arranged that the transfer would take place at the embassy in Washington.

With Sallas adamant, there was nothing to do but agree. He ended the conversation, assuring the minister that he would be at the embassy sometime the next day depending on when he could arrange transportation.

Chapter

XIV

IT was seven o'clock in the morning San Francisco time when the phone rang in Kopke's suite at the Fairmont Hotel. Outside his window, fog still shrouded the lower sections of the city. It would not burn off for several hours.

Ferguson sounded tired on the other end of the line. He must have been in his office since their conversation the previous night. If so, he would want the secretary to ask. That was the way it was in the bureaucracy. Administrators like Ferguson had little in the way of tangible product to point to. The derived their sense of self-worth from the hours put in. And they held their co-workers to the same standard. It was a vicious system, rewarding endurance over intelligence, stringing together eighteen-hour day after eighteen-hour day like beads on a thread of ambition and insecurity—a thread that could end only with failure of health or will. Kopke had seen more than one good man broken on the White House rack. Now, Ferguson, silent, was asking to be asked. He had spent the night at his desk and needed to record the fact. Without a witness, his fatigue would go for naught, an anonymous contribution, a sin against the bureaucratic advancement ethic.

"What time is it there, Seth?" Kopke was not going to play the game. Let Ferguson suffer. One man's misery was another man's merriment in the White House zero-sum game.

"It's ten o'clock; what the hell time do you think it is? Haven't you ever been to the West Coast before?"

"Thanks, Seth." They were off to a good start. Kopke listened carefully while Ferguson briefed him on what had transpired during the night.

There was not much to report. The guard had been found dead at 1:45 A.M. Saturday. The escape could have occurred anytime between then and 10:00 P.M. Friday when one of the other guards had stopped by to use the bathroom at the building where Bonham-Carter was being held. A handful of guards were combing the area but there was not much hope of their turning up anything. The likelihood was that Bonham-Carter would have hitched a ride or hijacked a car. Both possibilities were being checked out.

"Jesus, Seth, that's at least eight hours ago. He could be damn near anywhere by now."

"That's right. I guess it just depends on how resourceful your friend is. As I think I told you last night, the word we have is that he isn't very."

Kopke didn't like the reference to "his" friend. He started to object but restrained himself. Ferguson was still talking.

"One place we know he isn't going to get is out of the country. He left his passport at Mount Weather and I've had Customs lock down all the embarcation points including the Canadian crossings. He'll have to go to one of the British consular offices if he wants to leave and those are being watched."

"Oh, swell, I'm glad he's not going to be able to get out of the country. I'd hate to think of him having to pay for a transatlantic call to *The New York Times*."

"Look, Forrie, I'm trying everything I can think of to catch the son of a bitch. If you've got a better idea, let's have it. After all, he's your . . ." Ferguson stopped short of suggesting for the second time in a minute that the secretary was somehow responsible for Bonham-Carter's being on the loose.

"Anything else?"

"Let's see, did I tell you yesterday about the broker?"

"Just that he had one, and that they had lunch together."

"Yeah, well that's all there was to tell you at that point. But this morning at about five o'clock we yanked him out of bed for a few questions."

"And?"

"And, it seems it was the broker who put Bonham-Carter onto the guy at *The Times*—well, actually it was a little more complicated than that, but that was the gist of it."

"So?"

"So, I tell you this because the broker says he gave him another name at the same time."

"Who?"

"Some guy named Sosland who works for a trade rag out in Kansas City. Sosland doesn't know it, but, as of this morning, his office is wired up like a cardiac patient."

"Seth, for God's sake, it's Saturday morning. If he's trying to get Sosland, he'll call him at home. There may not be anybody in that office for two days." The conversation was not getting them anywhere. By the time Ferguson rang off, he was angry as well as tired. Kopke was right. It was a long shot that the phone tap would turn up Bonham-Carter's whereabouts anytime soon.

At 10:45, Ferguson received more bad news. The man in charge of the search at Mount Weather called to say that at 8:30 that morning a gas station owner in Round Hill, Virginia, had contacted the state police to report a stolen tow truck. Ferguson thanked the man, hung up and sat slowly shaking his head. He could have a phone tapped halfway across the country within three hours. Why the hell did it have to take more than two hours to find out that a truck had been reported stolen thirty-five miles away? He picked up the phone again and asked his secretary for more coffee and a sandwich. There was nothing to do but wait.

By midafternoon, there had been no further word. Ferguson lay on the couch in his office, his head propped against his arm. On the floor beside him, an ashtray was piled high with cigarette butts. He stubbed out yet another and glared at the television set in the corner of the room. He had just watched Lee Trevino defeat Jack Nicklaus by a single stroke and win the 1972 British Open. He knew the outcome would be popular with the press: a victory for counterstyle, one for the down and outs, the wogs of the world. Ferguson stared with patrician distaste at the little man with the black pants and the big smile, and wondered if somehow Super Mex, as he understood Trevino referred to himself, might be useful in the coming campaign. Maybe some TV spots for the Office of Minority Business Enterprises. Something like: "Eef you wand a peece of de vree anterprise seeztom, de Praysidant wanz to healp you." It might be effective in the Southwestern states; it was worth a memo at any rate. Before leaving, he called the President's appointments secretary and asked for a meeting the following morning. It was something he had hoped could be avoided. But the Bonham-Carter situation was now open-ended, and the President would have to be told about it.

At a quarter to ten the next morning, Ferguson pulled into West Executive Avenue, parked and entered through the archway of the Old Executive Office Building where on weekends the President occupied an office on the second floor. After a wait of a few minutes, he was shown in.

The President, clad in slacks and a sport jacket, at first took no notice of him. He was speaking excitedly to another aide who was seated with his back to Ferguson and who nodded repeatedly in vigorous agreement with what the President was saying.

"God damn it, Bob, this kind of stuff has got to stop." The President held the morning news summary in his lap. "It's just goddamned unfair. Am I not right?"

"Absolutely, Mr. President. After all, Mr. President, you didn't set the April seventh deadline, Congress did."

"That's right, that's right, and it's the same for everybody. We had our two-minute drill, and the Democrats had theirs. And now these candy asses are crying because we scored and they didn't. Right?"

"Right, Mr. President."

"Don't 'right me, Mr. President'; I want to know, am I right or not?"

"Yes, Mr. President, you are right."

"Well, I think so, too. I mean we may have hit a few balls close to the line, but, what the hell, that's what lines are for. All this shit about the spirit of the law gives me a pain in the ass. There is one law, and it's the same for everybody and there is nothing spiritual about it."

"That's right, it's written down in black and white."

"Look at it this way, Bob; what is the spirit of the law that says you don't go through stop signs?"

"Well, sir . . ."

"I'll tell you what it is. It is that you don't want people running into each other. Right?"

"Right."

"But these spiritualists could argue that as long as you didn't run into anybody, you would be satisfying the requirements of the law whether you stopped or not, right?"

"Right, Mr. President."

"I mean, once you start in that direction, where the hell do you stop? It's a prescription for chaos. You have to look at the words, cause there's only one set of words, and they say that you can't give anonymous contributions after April seventh."

"Right."

"Well, see if you can find somebody with some credibility to try and explain that to those bastards over there at *The Post*."

"Okay, now, what's this business about Peru?" The President had looked up and was speaking to Ferguson.

Ferguson briefly outlined the events of the previous four days, beginning with Bonham-Carter's approach to the Secretary of Commerce on the thirteenth and concluding with the escape from Mount Weather sometime during the night of the fifteenth. He explained in some detail what the CIA had learned from Ferricio about the Peruvian plan to offset their losses from the anchovy crop failure with money made in the commodities market.

"Mr. President," Ferguson concluded, "the Peruvian buying is inconsequential compared to what we now know the Russians are doing. The problem is that the Peruvian agent, Bonham-Carter, knows this, too, and already has tried to use the Russian buying to drive the price up. If he gets the word to the press, the price implications and the political repercussions could be serious."

"Good Lord!" the President exclaimed. "How the hell did we let things get this far? Isn't there anybody watching that line of credit?"

"Well, sir, they're not using the credits."

"They're not?"

"No, sir, they've been paying cash so far."

"Cash? I thought that was the whole goddamned problem—that they needed the credits. What the hell was Kopke haggling over with them for three months if they were planning to pay cash?"

"My guess is, sir, that the Russians regarded the credit issue as a question of prestige, a matter of face. They probably equate our willingness to extend them credit with first-class citizenship. They are kind of like Indians, you know, sensitive to that sort of thing."

The President had removed his glasses and, with his elbows propped on the desk, was massaging his eyes with his fingertips. Though Ferguson had seen the President in his glasses many times before, it always surprised him to see them, for they completely transformed the man's looks.

"Okay," the President continued, "let's sort out what we're talking about first off; we're talking about general price increases, right?"

"Right."

"I mean, across-the-board higher prices for food, right?"

"Right."

"But that effect is probably a ways off. I mean even if word does get out, all that stuff has to work its way up the chain of production."

"Right."

"I'm just thinking out loud now but it seems to me that it's not impossible we wouldn't get that effect—or at least all of it—until after the election."

"Quite possibly that's right."

"Okay, so, what do we have up front then? We got farmers in a couple of states who have already gotten the shaft and are going to be mad as hornets when they find out. That would be in Kansas and Nebraska and, uh . . . where else?"

"Well, Texas and Oklahoma are the other big producers where most of the crops will have already been harvested and sold."

"Shit, we've got standing Senate incumbents in three out of those four. Kansas looks safe. Nebraska's probably safe, too. Oklahoma's too close though, and Texas, shit, we lost Texas in sixty-eight by something like forty thousand votes. I'll be goddamned if we are going to let that happen again. Have you thought about that? I mean what do you suggest?"

"Well, sir, I suggest that we can't afford to wait until Bonham-Carter turns up before doing something. We are doing everything we can to locate him, but, if he is smart, it could be months. In the meantime, there is no telling what he might do to get his story broadcast. Peru has only a couple of weeks left on some of those contracts. He is not likely to stay quiet . . ."

"This doesn't sound to me like a suggestion . . ."

"No, sir, I just want to get that out as background. I think that the only thing for us to do is to go straight to the Peruvians and strike a deal."

"What do you mean?"

"I mean we get them to call their man off in return for a little consideration."

"Why the hell should we offer them anything? I mean

181]

what the hell leverage do they have? We give the bastards, I don't know what it is, but it's a fuck of a lot of money every year, millions; that isn't automatic you know. I mean, Congress would go apeshit if it knew what they were doing with it."

"Yes, sir, that's right, but I'm not sure which way that is going to cut. If we go to them and just demand that they recall Bonham-Carter, we run two risks. One is that they will figure that, because we are onto their game, their foreign aid for next year is in jeopardy whatever they do. In that case they may be even more determined to see this market play through. The other is that if they refuse to do what we ask, we are going to have to go before those committees on the Hill next year and explain why we want Peru cut off. We'll have a hell of a good case with this speculation. But we'll be hard put to explain why we tried to keep the whole business quiet in the first place if that should leak out."

"What do you think, Bob?" The President was looking at the other aide, who had not spoken since Ferguson began.

"Well, I think Seth's got a point with respect to the risk factor. I don't know what you have in mind, Seth, when you suggest that we might buy their silence for 'a little consideration,' but if there has been no significant move in the market already and they are staring down the barrel of a delivery date two weeks off, it seems to me that it might not take too much to persuade them."

Ferguson was not so confident. He pointed out that for purposes of negotiation Peru's prospective market gain was only one of the relevant considerations. "I don't think we are going to get off cheap. Once we start haggling with them, the price is not going to be set by what they stood to gain but by what we stand to lose. These guys weren't born yesterday. They know we have an election in a couple of months and they know what that means."

"Okay, look, here's the deal." From the President's tone, it was clear that his mind was made up. "We can keep our funds out of this. This is a national security issue at bottom, and the CIA has a budget for this sort of a thing. The first thing to do is to find out what kind of cash is available there. Whatever money you can free up isn't going to be anything like the losses they are talking about making up, so the cash will have to be just part one of a package. Part two is a negative incentive—or a negative, negative incentive; in other words, we promise no foreign aid retribution. That won't cost us anything either. Now, part three is not very concrete and it's going to take some smooth talking on your part, Seth. Tell this guy, what's his name?"

"Who?"

"The finance minister."

"Sallas."

"Tell Sallas that there are also a lot of little ways we can help. He's got Hickenlooper Amendment problems for starters; then there's export credits, Inter-American Development Bank funding, a whole mess of little things. Let him know that after the election we are going to put our people where it counts in all the agencies and that . . . uh, that . . . uh, you know, we'll make it worth his while."

"Yes, sir, I . . ."

"But tell him, Seth, that we want guaranteed satisfaction."

"Yes, sir."

"Now wait a second, I'm not finished yet. Guaranteed satisfaction means two things. It means we want the contracts they are holding. Tell them we will buy them at their current market value. They may not have any market value, but it's still essential that we get them because all of this goddamn hush money we're paying is going to be for nothing if we leave them still holding something that gives them an incentive to talk. Right?"

"Right."

"Okay, now, guaranteed satisfaction also means that we want this guy Bonham-Carter delivered to us. No telling what his interests are knowing what he knows. If he's got any sense, he's probably in the market on his own hook. In any event, for the next couple of months, we don't want him running around in Peru any more than we want him running around here. We want him locked up. Tell Sallas that if he doesn't like being locked up, we can think of something else. Do you understand me?"

"Yes, sir."

"Yeah, well make sure Sallas does, too. I want this thing cleared up by convention time. I don't want it hanging over my head in Miami."

"Yes, sir." Ferguson turned to leave.

"Oh, and, Seth."

"Yes."

"Call Kopke and jerk him off. I don't want him preoccupied during the campaign. He's too useful to us as a speaker. Tell him I blame this all on the CIA. We'll take care of the bungling son of a bitch after November."

As Ferguson made his way back across West Executive Avenue toward the White House, he reflected on the President's parting words. How different Kopke's position was from that of the autonomous Cabinet figures whom as a young man he had read about in the newspapers. The Achesons and Morgenthaus, the Lovetts, the Wallaces; even the Dulleses, the Gateses and Brownells. They had seemed independent men, powers in their own right. Was it only a question of perspective? Perhaps, within the court, they, too, had been pushed around, humiliated. Perhaps they, too, had served with fear and trembling. Had Harry Hopkins been a toady?

Back in his West Wing Office, Ferguson set about getting in touch with Sallas. He would have to present the offer himself. Its nature was too sensitive to entrust to a CIA intermediary. The agency had never refused to accommodate him on a request, but it would not be wise to test its pliability with a flagrantly political mission. There was no assurance that Langley and the President would see eye to eye on the definition of national security.

So, while four hundred miles to the north, Felix Bonham-Carter explored the main drag through Stockbridge, Seth Ferguson was instructing the White House switchboard—a marvel of efficiency which once, when asked to contact the Secretary of the Treasury, without ado put the call through to a commercial airliner over Kansas—to reach César Sallas for him.

Five minutes later he was listening to the rear end of a ring that was being heard four thousand miles to the south. It was a woman who answered.

"Señor Sallas, por favor." Was "por favor" Italian or Spanish? No matter, the woman would understand.

But the woman seemed not to understand. Instead of "momento" or some similar Latinate indication that Mr. Sallas would be along shortly, there was a fifteen-second stream of Aymara, an Indian dialect which to Ferguson was incomprehensible gibberish.

What to say next? He evidently had the housekeeper or the maid on the phone. There was nothing to do but keep trying.

"Señor Sallas."

Though there was no direct answer, this time he could hear the woman speaking to someone else in the room.

"Hello, may I help you?" It was a different voice, still female, but it spoke without a trace of an accent.

"Yes, I would like to speak to Mr. Sallas. I am calling long distance."

The owner of the second voice explained that Mr. Sallas was not at home and that she was Mr. Sallas' wife. If Ferguson liked, she would have Mr. Sallas return the call when he got home, which he was expected to do within the hour.

Ferguson thanked her and left a number. Since he had made a date to play tennis at twelve o'clock, he left the general switchboard number so that the call could be transferred. As he slipped into his tennis clothes and headed down the South Lawn toward the court, he wondered how Sallas would react when his return call was answered, "White House."

Of all of the perquisites which work in the White House conferred, Ferguson liked the tennis court best. Not because it was particularly a good court. It wasn't. Someone, some years earlier, had surfaced it with a rubber coating which made it far too fast for his aging reflexes. It was the court's setting he liked. Though it lay only fifty to seventy-five feet from where West Executive Avenue curved around the southwest corner of the White House lawn, it was impossible to see it from that direction because thick bushes bordered it on three sides. Glimpses of the court could be had from behind the fence on E Street, from the top floor of the Treasury Building or from the rear of the White House itself. But the only place from which it could be seen easily was from the expansive, but almost never occupied, South Lawn.

Its remoteness made the court a time island. Only there did Ferguson find it possible to separate the institution of the White House from its occupants.

The midday sun was brutal, and Ferguson, who was exhausted from a half hour of trying to keep up with a much younger and considerably more fit assistant, welcomed the ring of the phone from the box set into the fence. It was Sallas.

Chapter

XV

AS Ferguson suspected, the Peruvian Finance Minister had not recognized the name on the telephone message which his wife had handed him on his arrival home. As a result, the identifying greeting of the girl on the White House switchboard unnerved him severely.

It was not that he was totally unprepared for bad news. The fact that Bonham-Carter's weekly cable had not arrived the previous Friday had alerted him to the possibility that something might be amiss. Moreover, events already had run contrary to plans in other respects.

The attempt to falsify the anchovy data had been a disaster almost from the start. Sallas had known this since one day in early February when Alfredo Checa had appeared in his office in a state of high anxiety. The fisheries minister had had with him an envelope containing several of the information sheets on which the ministry published daily anchovy tonnage figures, broken down by processing region. The sheets which he pressed on Sallas were extensively marked up with a

187]

heavy felt-tipped pen. Someone had drawn slash marks through the entire column of figures down the right-hand margin. Alongside the obliterated column, new numbers had been scribbled in, numbers representing an almost seventy percent reduction in those crossed out. Across the top sheet, with the same pen, someone had written the words, "Fuck you, too." There was no other enclosure, but the envelope bore a Minneapolis postmark and a corporate return address. The latter indicated that it had come from Cargill, Inc. Sallas did not need to be told its significance; Cargill was the second largest grain company in the United States.

Sallas had been naïve. He had seriously underestimated the sophistication with which companies like Cargill, which dealt in substitute commodities, followed the anchovy. But the mistake did not have to be fatal. The crucial consideration, he reasoned, was not what the grain companies knew but how the price responded. Of this he easily convinced Checa, but he was by no means certain of it in his own mind.

So the ministry had quietly gone back to publishing accurate information while the two men nervously watched the daily quotes for signs that all was still well. For Sallas, it had been a nerve-racking five months. For reasons which he did not begin to understand, the prices of grain and soybeans had remained stable. The experience had raised serious questions in his mind about the impact of El Niño on the price of high protein anchovy substitutes, questions he had thus far kept to himself.

Now, however, as he waited for Ferguson to come on the line, Sallas was expecting the worst. He reflected bitterly on the irony. For almost half a year he had worried that the investment scheme might be faulty in concept. There was ample circumstantial evidence to support this concern. Now, however, disaster was bearing down on him from a totally unexpected quarter. For the call from the White House could mean only one thing: Bonham-Carter had been found out. If so, Sallas was in trouble. It was one thing to invest and fail to make a profit. As author of the investment proposal, he would have to accept a certain loss of standing. Personally, there would be some humiliation, but little else. Peru would be no worse off than if nothing had been attempted. It was not as though the other ministers had offered alternatives. Besides, with even the smallest increase in price, the contracts could be liquidated without financial loss. But it was something else altogether to engineer a confrontation with the United States government. That could be very costly indeed. Costly to Peru, because it would lose a major portion of its foreign aid; costly to Sallas personally, because there were certain to be political recriminations. He had been a spender of political capital, not a saver. Ambitious, he had operated within narrow tolerances. There was no reservoir of respect or affection against which he would be able to draw. Forgiveness was quite out of the question. He would fall in accordance with the rules by which he had risen. There was no hint of this apprehension in the voice with which he now spoke.

"Mr. Ferguson, this is César Sallas."

It was not in Sallas' nature to default, even when cornered. If there was ground to be yielded, it would have to be taken by main force. For three or four minutes, Sallas listened as Ferguson spoke. In that time his emotions ranged a spectrum from desperation to uncomprehending amazement. To begin with, the man on the other end of the line had confirmed his worst fears. The entire Peruvian plan had been uncovered, from its origin and purpose right down to its most particular details. But instead of threatening sanctions, Ferguson was offering him a deal, a deal which was insanely generous, a deal for which there seemed to be no logical foundation. Peru would have its contracts redeemed and in addition would receive a cash payment of unspecified amount; presumably the latter was to be negotiated. Instead of having foreign aid cut off, foreign aid was to be increased. And in addition to all this, Peru was to receive special trade and credit dispensations and official forgiveness for the expropriation of the International Petroleum Company. On the negative side, there was only one thing which the White House was asking. It wanted Bonham-Carter.

Sallas had not spoken since the beginning of the phone call. Now he hardly knew what to say. Ferguson's offer was a total puzzlement to him, a mystery on several levels. If the White House wanted Bonham-Carter, then it obviously did not have him. But if it did not have him already, how had it learned in such detail of the Peruvian investment scheme? Even Bonham-Carter could not have furnished it with all of the information Ferguson possessed. And why, if it knew as much as it did, was the White House making offers instead of demands? None of it fitted together. None of it made any sense at all. What did the President of the United States know that he didn't know?

"Mr. Sallas?"

Ferguson was asking for a response.

"Mr. Sallas, the President has asked me to report back to him on this conversation. The President recognizes, of course, that you cannot speak for your government without consultation, but I would like to be able to give him some idea of how Peru may respond. Is there something I can tell him?"

Sallas thought quickly. On its face, the deal was irresistible. Still, it would not do to be overeager. So far, he knew only the size of the fish he had hooked. He as yet knew nothing about the strength of his line. Ordinarily, he would not have worried. As a negotiator, he prided himself on being able to read in the tone of a man's voice how certain he was of the ground on which he stood. That was a skill, however, that was peculiarly relevant to his own culture and his own language. He had never tested its applicability across cultural and linguistic boundaries. It was too risky to rely on it now. He would have to draw Ferguson out further, test the limits of his accommodation, determine, if possible, just how badly the White House wanted Bonham-Carter.

"Mr. Ferguson." Sallas' voice was deliberate, betraying no excitement. "As you say, I cannot speak for my government. But, for myself, I have a question. It is a question I am sure our President will also want to ask."

"Yes?"

"My question concerns the foreign aid assurances."

"Yes?"

"You have suggested that Peru will be given favorable consideration in your foreign aid budget."

"That is correct."

"Yes, well, without suggesting that we discuss amounts at this moment, I must ask you what is meant by your offer. It is my understanding that the budgeting currently being done by your government is for fiscal year nineteen seventy-four, and that those budget requests will not be presented to your Congress until February of nineteen seventy-three. Moreover, I believe it is true that your Congress has not always been cooperative in meeting the Administration's requests for foreign aid funds—that, in fact, it has been the practice of the Congress in recent years to make substantial reductions. Understand that I make these observations, not

191]

because I doubt your good faith, but because these same observations will be made to me when I put this matter before the President. He and the Cabinet will ask me what assurance there is . . ."

"Whoa, Mr. Sallas, hold on, let me explain something. Your understanding of our budget process, and of the way Congress has handled foreign aid recently, is essentially correct. But you must understand the system's subtleties. When Congress considers the White House request for foreign aid appropriations, Congress is looking at programs, not at countries. We ask for a certain amount of money for this sort of aid, and a certain amount of money for that sort of aid, but there is nowhere in our budget request any country-by-country breakdown. All that Congress is able to do, therefore, is to determine the total amount of money that goes into each program. Of course, in unusual circumstances, Congress may impose certain restrictions, such as the one you are familiar with which says that we can't give money to people who expropriate U.S. property without fair compensation. But, as a rule, Congress has nothing to say about how foreign aid money is divided among recipient countries. The Administration makes those allocations at its own discretion through the agencies, and it is done after Congress is out of the picture. So I suggest to you that the problem you raise is not a real one. Not with respect to our ability to deliver, and not with respect to the timing either. Country allocations under the fiscal nineteen seventy-three appropriations are still completely flexible. You can tell your President that there is really nothing to worry about on that count."

Sallas had his answer. He had bitten the White House gold piece and Ferguson had not been offended. One thing was clear. Whatever Bonham-Carter had, it was something the White House wanted badly. He thanked Ferguson, and the two men wound up the conversation, leaving it that Sallas would call back as soon as he had had a chance to talk the matter over with the Peruvian President.

It was the morning of Monday, July 17, before Sallas could get an appointment with the President. A cold rain was falling when he arrived at the Presidential Palace at eight o'clock, and the black iron spear points which topped the palace fence glistened ominously in the morning half-light. Normally, rain was an infrequent visitor to Lima. Even in winter, when the city seemed permanently covered by clouds, there was dust in the streets, and the River Rimac ran a meandering course from bank to bank along its broad bed. El Niño had changed that. From the north, with the warm water current, had come a mantle of warm sodden air. As it slithered over the Peruvian coastal plain, the air was cooled and quickly supersaturated, dumping its excess moisture along a forty-mile-wide band of shoreline from Chiclayo in the north to Mollendo in the south. For months, the gutters of Lima had run gray with silt.

In the Cabinet room, the men were already assembled. In addition to the President, there was Ferricio, Checa and the man from SIN, the intelligence service. Except for Luis Cardona, the functionary from the Ministerio de Pesquería, whose boss would be making no presentation and whose presence was therefore not required, it was the same group that had gathered the previous January.

Without ado, the President opened the meeting with a brief explanation of its purpose, then yielded the floor to Sallas.

"Gentlemen." Eight inquiring eyes were trained on the Finance Minister. He had spent several hours the previous evening planning what he was about to say, most of it trying to devise a plausible explanation. It had come to naught. Even the most tortured logic he had been able to devise failed to explain the generosity of Ferguson's terms. In the end, he had determined that he had no choice but simply to lay the offer before the group and to seek the support from around the table which would guarantee the President's acquiescence. This he proceeded to do.

The President was the first to respond and went straight to the point.

"Mr. Minister, can you explain why the United States might make such an offer?"

"No, Mr. President, I cannot; nor can I see why Peru should refuse such an offer." Sallas hoped his answer would direct the discussion toward ground where the footing would be solid. But the President would not be directed.

"Mr. Minister, what is the current status of the investments we have made?"

"Our funds are fully invested as planned, Mr. President." It was a statement that Sallas knew he could not back up, but he could see no profit in mentioning the fact that he had received no telegram confirming what he said.

"And what has happened to the price of the commodities which we have bought?"

"Mr. President, I believe that on the last market day, which would have been last Friday—that's the fourteenth—the price of wheat was about one U.S. dollar and fifty-one cents per bushel, and the price of soybeans was about three U.S. dollars and fifty cents per bushel."

"Mr. Minister, I must say that that information makes me no wiser. What was the price at which we bought these commodities?"

"I believe our average purchase price was essentially the same."

"The same?"

"Yes, sir."

"The same as the current price?"

"Yes, sir; perhaps a few cents higher; I do not have with me the exact figures."

"Mr. Minister, if I understand what you say, we have then lost a portion of our investment."

"Yes, sir."

"We have lost money?"

"Marginally, sir."

"Marginally?"

"Yes, sir."

"Mr. Minister, how does one lose money in the commodities market if not marginally? Is not the prospect of marginal gain or loss what this speculation is all about?"

"Yes, sir."

For eight or ten chilling seconds the President did not respond. Then he spoke. "Mr. Minister, in light of what you have just told me, I am compelled to agree with you that the offer of the White House, as you describe it, is generous. Indeed, it is extraordinary."

Sallas nodded. Not since he had been in the Cabinet had he been so humiliated. Though he had feared the consequences of failure, he knew now that he had seriously underestimated the danger to which he had exposed himself by the imperious manner in which he had championed the investment proposal six months earlier. He reflected now on how much more serious his circumstances might be were there no White House offer before them to consider.

"Mr. Checa." The President was starting to go around the table. "Have you anything you would like to say?"

"No, sir, except that I do not see how we can afford to refuse what has been offered."

"Mr. Ferricio?"

Ferricio, who had been doodling distractedly on a note pad throughout the President's inquisition, indicated without looking up that he agreed with Checa.

They were down to the man from SIN, the Servicio de Inteligencia Nacional, who spoke now.

"Mr. President, I agree with everything that has been said. The proposition which has been made to us is one in which we are given a great deal, and we are asked to give up very little—one man, essentially nothing. It is, in short, too good to be true. And that is my problem with it, because, in my business, we are very cynical. Generally, propositions which are too good to be true are not true."

The man paused and shot a glance at Sallas.

"I am not suggesting, Mr. Sallas, that the terms which you have just outlined do not represent promises made to you by the White House. I suggest only that those promises may be of questionable value. I suggest further that the measure of that value will lie in the motive."

Again the man from SIN paused before going on.

"The question then becomes, 'What is the motive?' Is it economic? I do not see how it can be. As matters now stand, it appears that we may have to liquidate our investments at a loss. In any event, how and at what price we dispose of our commodity contracts would seem to be of little concern to the White House since they themselves will presumably do the same when the contracts become theirs. I challenge anyone here to provide me with a plausible economic motive for what has been offered."

There were no takers.

"Then is it diplomatic?"

Again no takers.

"No, it cannot be diplomatic. Every consideration of diplomacy militates against the White House making an offer of this nature. To begin with, the offer is covert which is contrary to the requirements of the U.S. Constitution. More important, the offer is inimical to the interests of the United States in the hemisphere. We all know that the United States is clinging by its fingernails to its commercial investments in a half-dozen countries on this continent. Nothing could be more harmful to that effort than for it to become known that the United States was discriminating in favor of Peru and against other countries in the allocation of its development aid."

"That leaves but one possibility."

"A political motive?" It was the President who asked.

"Precisely, a domestic political motive."

"But what possible connection could there be?"

"That I do not know," the man from SIN answered. "But it must be connected in some way with the upcoming Presidential election. Though it seems incredible on the face of it, the White House must regard Bonham-Carter as a threat to its election objectives. I can imagine no other issue important enough to warrant an offer such as the one the White House has made."

"This is all very well, but of what importance is it?" Sallas interjected. "I fail to see that it makes any difference why the offer was made."

"It makes the greatest possible difference, Mr. Sallas," the man from SIN replied. "If the motive is connected to the election, then the offer of the White House is in effect a campaign promise. The likelihood of the promise being honored will decline daily until November, at which time the promise will become valueless."

"Then, if we accept the offer, we must press for immediate settlement. Is that your suggestion?" It was the President asking.

"Yes and no. Clearly, it will be impossible for the White House to do anything about foreign aid or many of the other promised concessions outside the context of normal procedure. By doing so, it would risk Congressional inquiries that would undoubtedly prove embarrassing. For our purposes, it will be sufficient if we are able to secure the cash payment well in advance of the election."

From their faces, it was obvious that the other men at the table had missed this last logical turning. The man from SIN endeavored to explain.

"We are agreed that the White House motive is most probably political?"

Nodding heads.

"We are also agreed that whatever leverage we now possess in the person of Bonham-Carter, that leverage is ephemeral. That is conjecture, but it is a conjecture for which we have no rebuttal."

More nodding heads.

"Then we have but one tactic: to exchange temporary bargaining strength for permanent bargaining strength."

Dumb looks all around.

"What permanent bargaining strength?"

"Yes, I have to second Mr. Sallas' question," said the President. "What bargaining strength? It all sounds very tidy, but I haven't the slightest idea what you are talking about."

"What I am talking about is this, Mr. President," the man from SIN replied. "The United States has a very strict system of fiscal accounting. There are budgetary nooks and crannies in which expenditures may be hidden from the public. They may even serve to conceal expenditures from the Congressional committees with oversight jurisdiction. But in this latter regard, these nooks and crannies—many of which conceal funds for the Central Intelligence Agency—are by no means secure. A suspicious Congress may demand and receive a full accounting and explanation of every dollar spent by the Executive Branch. What I am suggesting is that by forcing the White House to make a substantial and politically motivated payment to Peru, we will force it to incur a permanent liability, a liability which Peru may at any time convert into a reality through the simple expedient of informing the U.S. Congress of what has transpired."

"You mean once they have paid us something, they cannot afford not to pay us everything?" asked the President.

"Precisely."

For the next half hour, the five men debated the details of the reply Sallas would make to Ferguson. The cash payment would have to be made simultaneously with the delivery of Bonham-Carter. The amount, in addition to payment for the contracts, was set at $20 million, the exact amount which had been given Bonham-Carter to invest. No specific amounts were set for the aid and other forms of compensation. Once the cash was in hand, they would be easy enough to negotiate. One additional condition was agreed to: the White House was to make the cash payment whether it received Bonham-Carter dead or alive.

It was 10:15 when the meeting broke up. Outside, the rain was still falling as Sallas ran the twenty-five feet to where his driver waited. He slumped low into the back seat and closed his eyes. The preceding hour and a half had been a personal disaster. There seemed no reason to doubt that, in time, it would have a serious impact on his career. Now he faced the prospect of calling Ferguson to relay demands that, essentially speaking, had been authorized by a subordinate. More important, he faced a problem that no one had as yet addressed. How was he going to get in touch with Bonham-Carter?

Chapter

XVI

BY the time Bonham-Carter finished talking to Sallas and rang the desk downstairs in the inn, the only evening bus for Albany had already left. The clerk, after giving him the morning schedule of buses to Albany and flights from there to Washington, mentioned that there was a closer airport in Pittsfield fourteen miles away, and offered to call. Fifteen minutes later he rang back. The arrangements had been made. Bonham-Carter had a seat on a private charter leaving at 10:00 A.M. the next day. The plane would go as far as LaGuardia, where he would be able to pick up the shuttle to Washington. He decided to repair to the bar for a drink.

It was nearly ten when he left the bar. For all of the town's charms, it was clear that night life was not a strong point. As he reached the top of the flight of stairs, he heard a door close ahead of him and looked up in time to see the figure of a woman turn and walk down the shadowy corridor in the other direction. For a moment he thought he recognized the slender silhouetted hips and legs and quickened his stride. But as the woman passed under the ceiling light midway down the hall, he could see that she had jet-black hair.

Back in his room, he undressed, considered taking a shower. Then he resolved to put it off until morning. Instead, he decided to wash out his underwear. During his shopping that afternoon, he had neglected to replace the underwear he had left in the two hotels in Washington and was down to a single pair.

Annoyingly, the light over the sink refused to respond to its pull chain. Standing naked in front of the sink, his irritation was compounded by the fact that the temperature seemed to have dropped surprisingly. In the dim glow of the overhead bulb, he huddled over his work, trying to draw as much warmth as possible from the hot water.

Hurrying, he quickly washed out his undershirt, rolled it in a towel and, after twisting the roll vigorously, shook it open and tossed the shirt over the top of the metal shower stall to dry. The effect was as though he had poured a small glass of water into a hot frying pan. With a squeaky sizzle, the shirt bounced back at him.

Kneeling cautiously on the floor of the bathroom, it took him only a few minutes to find the cause. The shower stall, obviously a recent installation, was of the preassembled variety and had been set away from the wall six inches in order to allow space for the water pipes which rose from the floor behind it. At some point after the shower had been installed, the inn must have had portions of its electric wiring replaced, for the electrician, rather than disturb the plaster, had simply used the darkened space behind the shower to route the wiring in from the corridor. Someone had worked a neat improvisation on that plan. Behind the shower stall, he could see that one of the wires emerging from the baseboard had been cut. Instead of reentering the wall a few feet further on and continuing up to the light over the sink as it doubtless had done once, the wire had been stripped and wrapped around one of the pipes. The work was crude but the intended effect had been achieved. His shower had been converted into a sort of low-voltage, stand-up electric chair. It was doubtful that the arrangement could have proved lethal. But there was no doubt in his mind that that was what someone had intended. He pulled the wire away from the pipe using the heel of his shoe and pinned it back against the wall with a rolled newspaper. As he finished up the washing, he wondered how conductive the pipes would have been and how far the current would have carried. He wondered if whoever had set the wire up had considered that he or she might be electrocuting the whole floor.

The experience left him more puzzled than frightened. Sallas had told him just that afternoon that he had made peace with the White House. Was there someone else who still wanted him out of the way? Obviously there was. Someone amateurish. The last thought was not comforting. A professional would at least be predictable.

His thoughts were interrupted by a knock at the door. It was one of the old bellhops from the lobby.

"Just want to turn on your heater." The man had crossed the room to the wall opposite the foot of the bed and was kneeling in front of an aged contraption which Bonham-Carter recognized as a gas burner. "We turn these durn things off end of May generally, but seems like we always have to turn 'em on again once or twice a summer. Sposed to go down below fifty tonight, and, tell you the truth, that'll be jes fine with me. Been too damn hot for my likin' last couple of weeks."

Bonham-Carter watched the bellhop throw the switch on top of the heater, then ignite the hissing gas at the base of the burner with a match. "Now we don't encourage folks to mess around with these things, but if it gets too hot in here, you can turn 'er off by jes hittin' this here switch. That'll turn off the pump which works off the electric. The fire'll go out by itself. If you want to cut 'er back on, jes hit the switch back the way it is now, but be sure to remember to light it. That thing is fifty years old if it's a day, but hit'll keep you warmer than wett'n your bed." The man, who seemed not to expect a tip, was still chattering as Bonham-Carter thanked him and closed the door.

He had been only half listening to the bellhop during the time he was in the room. The experience with the shower had taken some time to make sense of, but now a number of previously inexplicable events had begun to come into focus.

The bellhop was not three minutes gone before Bonham-Carter was again out in the corridor. Light shone beneath the door of the room he had seen the woman with black hair leave half an hour earlier. But he could hear no sound from where he stood. The old one-tumbler rim lock was a piece of cake, and in a few seconds he was closing the door behind him.

Inside, clothes were strewn freely about the room. Careful not to disturb anything, he cast his eyes about for something that might confirm his suspicions. None of the clothes nor other contents of the room looked familiar. On the telephone table next to the bed he found a piece of paper. Across the top of it, someone with a very deliberate hand had written a word in Russian and traced the letters over several times. In the center of the paper was a telephone number with a 212 area code. He scribbled down the word and the number. They might tell him something. Otherwise, there was nothing. He was about to leave when one further thought occurred to him. The bathroom. Ten seconds later he was back in the corridor and on his way to his room. He wondered why he had not thought of the bathroom immediately. He still could not be sure, but the evidence seemed overwhelming. He could check it by telephone.

On returning to his room he placed four calls in quick succession. The first was the number he had just scribbled down. From the directory he had already ascertained that the number was a New York City listing. He did not plan to say anything. It would be enough just to hear the answering voice. The second call was to information in San Francisco. The third to the Hyatt Wilshire in Los Angeles. The last to the same State Department number he had called two weeks earlier from the phone booth in New York. By the time he was through, there was no doubt left in his mind.

He spent the next twenty minutes packing his things. Then, having turned off the lights, he settled himself in a chair to wait. It was nearly three o'clock when he left the room. Along the length of the corridor he could see that no lights shone from under any of the doors. It took only a few minutes to locate the fuse box through which all the electric current for the floor would pass. It was old but orderly. Someone years earlier had penciled in notations indicating which of the little glass fifteen volt fuses went with which room. It was a simple matter to find the one he was looking for and to unscrew it. He figured thirty seconds to be plenty of time, but to be on the safe side he gave it a minute. Patiently, he counted off the time on the old watch he had taken from Jason. When the minute was up, he replaced the fuse, carefully wiping it free of fingerprints with his shirttail.

Bonham-Carter arrived at the airport the next morning shortly after 9:15. At the ticket counter, he learned that the owner of the plane on which he would be traveling had called in to say he would be late arriving. The flight had been pushed back to 10:30. He thanked the old man behind the counter for the information and asked about the fare.

"Dunno," the man replied. "Reckon that's between you and Mr. Mayhew. Alls I know is that Mr. Mayhew's been in and out of here three times already this summer and I ain't heard that he's charged anybody yet. He's a right generous man. I don't spec he'll be lookin' for anything but a good thank you."

Bonham-Carter watched the old man turn to help another customer. It occurred to him that in the past three days almost everyone he had spoken to had been either under twenty or over sixty—the help in the inn, the people working in the shops, everybody. What was it about towns like Stockbridge that made them hemorrhage their prime generations. He had seen the same demographic phenomenon in resort towns in Europe where the indigenous old and the indigenous young catered to the transient middle-aged. It was no wonder that such towns died in the off season; demographically they were sandwiches with nothing in them.

He bought a *New York Times* from the airport vending machine and settled down to wait. A front-page article proclaimed imminent power failure for New York City if the heat wave continued. The airport thermometer read sixty-eight degrees. Perhaps the heat wave was already ended. Perhaps it was just the morning or the mountains. He turned to the second section and looked for the commodities quotations.

On the theory that his pot would never boil if he watched it too closely, Bonham-Carter had purposely not looked in the weekend editions for Friday's closing quotes. It was Tuesday now, and he had two market days to catch up on. The news was encouraging. Soybeans were off a penny, but, much more important to him, the price of September wheat was up almost four cents. He did a quick calculation. The value of the ninety contracts he had bought for himself the previous week in Los Angeles would have increased by almost $18,000 as a result. Taking into account the two and one-half cents by which the price had dropped prior to the rise, he was ahead about $6000. Maybe it was the beginning of the run he was waiting for. He didn't bother to calculate what the four-cent rise meant to Peru. The call to Sallas had made that academic.

"Howdy, pal, you must be my hitchhiker." He looked up to see an enormous red-faced man in his middle forties, tireless in a rumpled gray and white striped cord suit. "Name's Boyden Mayhew," the man added, smiling and thrusting a huge hand in Bonham-Carter's direction.

"Felix Bonham-Carter. It's awfully kind of you . . ."

"Hell"—the way Mayhew pronounced the word it had two syllables—"don't mention it. I'll be right glad to have the company. You sound like you're from England."

"I am."

"Well, that's real good. They're nice folks up heah, but, I declare, they ain't worth a sack of cow doo doo for conversation. I been up heah a bunch of times now and seems like don't nobody want to talk about nothing but what a nice day it is and money; and if you pin 'em right down, you find out that they really don't care so much about the nice day part of it." Mayhew smiled again.

As the two men walked toward the small prop plane parked several hundred yards from the terminal, Mayhew kept up a steady stream of talk. It turned out that he was a real-estate developer from Charleston, South Carolina, who had become interested in recreational investment and was looking for land for a new ski resort.

"You ever been to Hilton Head?"

Bonham-Carter admitted that he had not.

"Well, you should, you really should. It's places like that where the money is going to be in the next ten years. You know people are real funny when they got money. You show 'em something that they need, and they're real tight about it. They'll buss theah asses to save a couple of hunnert dollars. But you show 'em something they don't need, and they spend money like they found a trunk of it in the garage."

"I see."

"That's right. People know what they need oughta cost, 'cause they been buying it all their lives. But they don't have no way of knowin' what's a good price for what they don't need. Take Hilton Head. There's people there buying houses on the beach for two hunnert and two hunnert and fifty thousand dollars, houses they maybe spend two, three months a year in."

"I see. Is that the sort of business you are in?"

"That's the sort of business I'm gettin' into. I got my sights on a little island just south of Charleston called Kiawah. Right now, it ain't nothin' but beach and swamp, and snakes and alligators and wild boars, but when it's surveyed and platted it's gonna be worth a jillion dollars."

"And you've bought it?"

"No, sir, I got me a little place on it, one of about a dozen cottages. But I'm gonna buy it; that is if the Kuwaitians don't get it first."

"The who?"

"The Kuwaitians, the A-rabs from Kuwait. They been trying to get it from this family in Raleigh who bought it for about nothing twenty years ago, but I reckon public opinion down there ain't gonna take too kindly to that. You know, we folks in Charleston are nothing if not bigoted."

"I see; and you are thinking about building a ski resort at the same time?"

"Yes, sir, gotta do it, gotta do it. With interest rates what they are today, the name of the game is cash flow."

"What exactly do you mean?"

"Hey, you ain't a businessman, I guess."

"No, actually, I'm a . . . I'm a tourist." Bonham-Carter realized that his answer was something of a non sequitur, but Mayhew seemed not to notice.

"Yeah, well, you see, the thing about a deal like Kiawah is that I am gonna have to borrow some big money to buy the place. Now, I'll get that all back and then some from selling off the lots, but a bunch of the money I figure to make from the deal is gonna come from being the rental agent for the houses that the lot owners build. That's a very profitable business, but it's seasonal. You see, Kiawah is gonna have the same problem that Hilton Head has, and Sea Island has and all of the resorts in the area have. It's nice in the fall and it's beautiful in the spring, but it ain't warm enough to swim in the winter and it's hotter than a son of a bitch in the summer."

"So there won't be any income in the winter and summer?"

"That's approximately right. And that's the beautiful thing about this New England deal. The seasonal peaks in the New England resort business are exactly the opposite from what they are in South Carolina. If I'm operating in both places, I can keep a level cash flow and stay out of the banks for my operating outlays at least. At ten percent, bank money is a hell of an expensive tit to be sucking on."

Mayhew's thirst for conversation seemed temporarily to have been slaked, and the two men rode in silence for the remainder of the short trip. From his window on the right-hand side of the plane, Bonham-Carter watched as the first traces of the city's northern suburbs appeared below, thickening slowly into subdivisions and industrial parks. Five minutes later, they were over the dense apartment blocks of northern Queens and the Manhattan skyline was clearly visible to the southwest. It was shortly after 11:30 when the plane taxied to a stop outside of Butler Aviation at the Marine Air Terminal, the general aviation facility adjacent to LaGuardia. As the two men walked from the plane, Mayhew resumed his chatter, suggesting that, as an English tourist, Bonham-Carter owed it to himself to visit historic Charleston. He would be happy to show him Kiawah anytime.

Inside the terminal, Bonham-Carter thanked Mayhew and the two men parted, Mayhew going off in search of a business associate whom he was scheduled to meet, Bonham-Carter heading for a taxi and the five-minute ride to the Eastern Airlines shuttle departure gate.

Outside there was no activity at the taxi stand, and the heat was uncomfortable. After a few minutes' wait, Bonham-Carter reentered the air-conditioned terminal and took a seat by the window where he would be able to see the arriving cars.

He had not been there two minutes when a limousine pulled up and three men got out. He watched the driver fish suitcases out of the trunk, hand them to a waiting porter, then point through the wire mesh fence toward where a half-dozen private planes of various sizes were parked on the tarmac. He watched one of the three men press something into the hand of the smiling driver. He could see their lips moving, but he could not hear. Then he watched them follow the porter through the door and walk past him into the terminal. They were halfway across the floor before the flash of recognition struck him.

It had been exactly thirteen days since he last had seen Belousov and Sakun. They had then been entering the offices of Midcontinental Grain. In that time they had changed. Both now wore light-colored summer suits as did the third man, whom he did not recognize.

He watched now as they crossed the terminal diagonally and exited by the same side door which he had entered ten minutes before. From the window, he could see them following the porter in the direction the driver had pointed to a few minutes earlier. As soon as he had a fix on their direction, he approached the desk.

"Excuse me, could you tell me who owns that aircraft?" he asked, pointing toward the white two-engined jet which the men had just reached.

"Which one is that?" The man behind the counter glanced casually over his shoulder.

"The white one."

"Fella, two-thirds of the planes that fly outta here are white."

"The one those people are getting in right now."

The man shot another glance behind him, then reached for a clipboard on the counter and began to run his finger down it.

"Let's see, according to the tail number, that there is a Jetstar and it is licensed to Cook Industries, and it is leaving here in about four minutes, so if you're supposed to be on it, you ain't got much time."

"Thank you, could you tell me what Cook Industries is?"

"Mister, I don't know who any of these people are. If I had cause to know the answer to questions like that, I'd probably have me a better job."

Bonham-Carter thanked the man and headed back to the taxi stand. This time there was no one waiting. It was 11:55 when he reached the shuttle terminal. At the information counter, he was told he could buy his ticket on the plane. Ten minutes later he was airborne.

The question of Cook Industries bothered him. The name was familiar, but he could not place it. As the plane glided over the New Jersey farmlands, over Wilmington and the top of the Chesapeake Bay, Bonham-Carter searched his memories of the past two and one half weeks for some clue to where the Russian buyers were headed. They were starting the descent to Washington when it came to him. Not Cook Industries, but Cook. One of the calls he had overheard in the New York Hilton sometime between the fifth and the seventh had been from a Mr. Cook. There had been three or four such calls from three or four different people. None had discussed terms. They had been probing in nature. But he remembered the call from Mr. Cook clearly now because he had sounded different from the others. He had spoken with a heavy Southern accent. Were the Russians now getting ready to buy grain from Mr. Cook? Kopke's story, which had never seemed plausible, must have been a deliberate lie. Would the Cook sale also be kept a secret?

The realization that the Russians were still buying left Bonham-Carter with ambivalent feelings. As a personal matter, the information was encouraging. He had already decided to hold onto his contracts, even if he had to pay several weeks' worth of warehouse and insurance charges. It seemed a worthwhile risk. Word of the Russian buying could be kept quiet only so long. With more than one grain company now seeking to cover short positions, the price would have to rise soon.

But for some reason he did not fully understand, it bothered him to see Peru foregoing its opportunity. Sallas had said that the settlement reached with the U.S. government would not provide Peru with as much as he had originally hoped for. He wondered how much less it was. He wondered if Sallas had known what he now knew, whether Peru would have agreed to the same terms. Certainly it was not solicitude for Peru's interests that troubled him. Perhaps it was no more than the knowledge that the job to which he had devoted nearly three weeks was working out less well than expected.

In the light early-afternoon traffic, the taxi was making good time. As it left the George Washington Parkway and turned right onto Memorial Bridge, he marveled at the beauty of the city approached from that angle. He also reflected on the ugly circumstances under which he had left it just five days earlier. He wondered if the U.S. government had brought up the death of the guard in talking to Sallas and whether that had been taken care of as part of the deal. He wondered whether Sallas would have felt an obligation to make it a condition of the settlement.

Suddenly, he wondered a lot of things. How had Sallas known that he needed a passport? During their telephone conversation, he had started to tell Sallas he had lost his passport, but Sallas had already known. A new passport was the pretext on which he had been told to come back to Washington—that and the need to sign the forms yielding power of attorney. But powers of attorney could be put in the mail if a signature was all that was required.

The taxi had circled the Lincoln Memorial and was heading up Twenty-third Street. Bonham-Carter wondered where the Peruvian embassy was located. If it was on Embassy Row along Massachusetts Avenue, they would be there in a matter of minutes.

He was full of uncertainty now. A half-dozen questions occurred to him at once, each suggesting answers which argued against doing what he was doing. Sallas had told him that it had been arranged for him to pick up the passport and sign the papers at the embassy. How was that possible? Sallas had not, until that moment, had the slightest idea where Bonham-Carter was and no reason to suspect that he would learn. How had he expected to get in touch with him? Either Sallas had lied to him or to the White House. Perhaps to both.

They had reached the circle at the top of Twenty-third Street. A third of the way around it the taxi turned off onto New Hampshire Avenue toward Dupont Circle. They were three blocks from Embassy Row. Frantically, Bonham-Carter struggled to give focus to the jumble of conflicting information in his head. Apart from the inconsistencies of detail in what Sallas had told him, there was something very wrong about the logic of the agreement with the White House as Sallas had described it. He felt that it would become obvious if he could calm his mind enough to think clearly.

The taxi had already rounded Dupont Circle and was headed into the 1700 block of Massachusetts Avenue, when it came to him. It had been right in front of his nose all the time. When he had talked to Sallas, he had told the Finance Minister nothing about the Russian buying. Nor had Sallas seemed aware of it. What then had Peru agreed to give up in exchange for what Sallas had termed "adequate" consideration? The contracts themselves? Perhaps. But what were they worth? Why would the White House be concerned with an investment so small compared to that of the Russians? No, the White House had been after something else. It was after the same thing that had led the policemen to grab him off the street. It was after silence on the matter of the Russian buying. Obviously, it had not said so to Sallas, or he would have known during their conversation that the Russians were buying. What then could the White House have told him it wanted? There was only one possible answer. The White House had told Sallas it wanted Bonham-Carter.

The taxi had slowed and was approaching Seventeenth Street. On the right, protruding from a balcony, he could see the familiar flag—two verticle red stripes separated by a band of white. "Driver, keep going. I won't be going to the embassy." Bonham-Carter sank low in the back seat as the car resumed speed heading for Scott Circle. He was still free, but he had been lured into dangerous territory. And he had just lost his only sanctuary. He had some quick figuring to do.

Chapter

XVII

SETH FERGUSON sat with his brown Peal loafers propped up on the windowsill. In three and a half years in the White House, he had made maybe twenty thousand telephone calls. And he had learned long ago that the three or four hours he spent on the phone each day were a lot less tiring if he spent them in the lounge chair next to the window of his office instead of at his desk. Outside the temperature was already nearing the nineties, and, for the past hour, he had watched the grounds crew dragging sprinkler hoses from one flower bed to another on the portion of the South Lawn that was visible from his second-floor office. In the winter, when the leaves were off the trees, he could see the whole lawn, and beyond it the Ellipse, and beyond that the Washington Monument. But in the winter he could see the cars on E Street, too, and the tourists. On balance, he preferred the more private summer view with its leafy protection.

It was eleven o'clock, the morning of Tuesday, July 18, and, for the first time since the previous Saturday night, matters seemed under control. He had talked to Sallas for a second time Monday afternoon, and the terms had been agreed on. In a meeting with the President later that day it had been decided that the $20 million in CIA funds would be transferred to the White House through the budget of the National Security Council to preserve the integrity of the national security cover agaist possible future challenge. All this he was now explaining to Kopke who had just arrived back from the West Coast in the small hours of the morning.

"Well, Seth, did you get the feeling that the President was satisfied with the way this thing has shaken out?"

"Yeah, I guess so; I mean they are his terms, aren't they? He made them up."

"Ummm . . . but the amount of money, Seth; that's an awful lot of money. How did he take that?"

"Listen, Forrest, you know the old man is not interested in money at this point. Besides, I don't know that twenty million isn't cheap. I forgot to tell you about the call to Sosland."

"Yes, you did."

"Yeah, well I'm sorry; but yesterday . . . I guess it was yesterday—things have been happening so damn fast around here—sometime in the morning we picked up a call to Sosland from somebody who knew the whole deal right down to the numbers."

"What do you mean from somebody?"

"I mean that the guy told Sosland his name was John Smith."

"Smith?"

"Yeah, imaginative, isn't it?"

"Did you trace it?"

"Yeah, but it didn't tell us a whole helluva lot. The call was made from a London bookie joint, but the owner of the place claims he doesn't know anything about it. I checked it out with our telephone people and they say it's possible to route calls all over the world if you can find switchboard operators who are willing to do it for you. And there isn't anything you can do about tracing them. It's not like forwarding mail where you can look at all the old postmarks. Every time a call passes through a private switchboard, all the earlier postmarks are erased."

"But you figure it was Bonham-Carter?"

"Had to be. Guy had a British accent; he said all the same things he told you. I don't see any other explanation."

"And you are expecting him to show up at the Peruvian embassy sometime today?"

"Sallas said he would."

"You figure that'll be the end of it then?"

"How do you mean?"

"Well, I mean this, Seth. It's great if we get Bonham-Carter out of circulation, but that doesn't give us any assurance that the Peruvians themselves aren't going to talk."

"Sure it does. I made it damn clear to this fella Sallas that while we were after Bonham-Carter first and foremost, we were buying everybody's silence. Besides, once they have signed the contracts over, what incentive will they have to talk?"

"None, I guess. How do we give them the money?"

"I dunno, that hasn't been worked out yet. One thing

is for sure: we're not going to brown-bag it over to the embassy."

"Jesus, I hope not. There'd be hell to pay if any of the diplomatic crowd got wind of what was going on."

"Right, and we'd probably run the same kind of risk if we send one of our people down there with it. I don't know what we'll do. Maybe we could send it down with Bonham-Carter."

"Seth, we can't hand twenty million dollars to some broken-down ne'er-do-well and put him on a bus to Dulles."

"Well, that depends on the shape he is in when we send him, doesn't it?"

"What do you mean?"

"You know what I mean, Forrie."

"Seth, I don't like that."

"Forrest, listen, be realistic for Christ sakes. We got twenty million dollars and a Presidential election in jeopardy. This is hardball. The old man isn't going to say so, but I think that is what he wants. If you want to tell him that you don't think it's worth it, go ahead. Just tell me in advance if you are going to. I think I could sell tickets to it."

"Is the old man pissed, Seth? I wanna know if he is."

"Yeah, he's pissed, sure he's pissed. But not at you. He's mad cause he figures Langley should have tipped us to what was going on weeks ago."

Having brought Kopke up to date and delivered the assurance the President had asked for, Ferguson rang off and buzzed his secretary. It was getting on toward noon. While Bonham-Carter was boarding the Washington-bound shuttle at LaGuardia, Ferguson would be taking his lunch at his desk.

At one o'clock, Ferguson called the Peruvian embassy

and asked for Enrique Solari. Sallas had given him the name as a contact. Solari was the only man at the embassy who would know who Bonham-Carter was and why he was coming. But Solari had heard nothing. He promised to call as soon as Bonham-Carter arrived.

Ten minutes later, Ferguson was climbing into one of the White House Chryslers in the West Executive Avenue parking lot. He had an appointment three blocks across town at the Office of the President's Special Trade Representative. In a moment of weakness two weeks earlier, he had agreed to attend the regular monthly session of the Interagency Trade Policy Committee's Level II group. It had promised even then to be boring. Now, when he would have much preferred to be in his office sitting by the phone, the commitment was doubly irritating.

Like most things in the government, the Trade Policy Committee was bureaucratically complex. It consisted of representatives of the Council on International Economic Policy (CIEP), the Special Trade Representative's office (STR), Treasury, Commerce, State and the Council of Economic Advisers. And it was divided into three levels: Level III, made up of low-level bureaucrats who met frequently and discussed little nitty-gritty details; and Level I which was made up of agency heads who met as seldom as possible and discussed generalities. Ferguson was a member of Level I. In fact, for the past six months, he had been the chairman of Level I. But during his term as chairman, he had made it his practice to attend occasional meetings of the other levels for the purpose of sustaining morale.

By the time the elevator delivered him to the seventh floor of the building at 1800 G Street, most of the men who would attend the meeting were already seated. He slipped in and took a place at the corner of the table, trying as he did so to be as inconspicuous as possible. He sometimes wondered if his attendance at these meetings was more inhibiting to the other men than it was morale building. If that was the case, he wished someone would say so. It was a habit that would break easily.

The main item on the day's meeting agenda was bicycle imports. The representative from Commerce had the floor. With elaborate flip charts, he described the huge increase in bicycle imports in the past several years. Since 1970, they had risen 165 percent. Graphs were produced for anyone who might be hard of hearing, and charts showing where the bicycles were coming from were distributed. Ferguson wondered as he watched the man from Commerce move his pointer down the columns of figures whether he was the department's bicycle import specialist, or whether his expertise was broader. Perhaps his professional ambit included tricycles and baby strollers. Or maybe he was truly broad gauged, an all-purpose import stopper, a man who was as at home dealing with leather-soled footwear as with textiles or sphygmomanometers. Now that last was a subject to get worked up about. Ferguson found himself wondering why the bicycle discussion had been put on the agenda. Obviously, it was all leading up to a recommendation for escape clause action and that was a matter for the Tariff Commission. Only after the Tariff Commission completed its investigation would the matter of what to do about it be submitted to the Executive Branch.

The man was really getting into his subject now. Import penetration in the bicycle market had more than doubled in the less than six years since 1966; for the first half of 1972, it was estimated at thirty-eight percent. Country by country, number by number, minute by excruciating minute, the man spun out his obvious and uninteresting story. Ferguson wrestled with mounting boredom. The room was growing increasingly close and stuffy. He doodled unconsciously on the pad in front of him, caught himself, and covered the doodle with his hand. His attention was wandering. He tried biting the inside of his cheek, but felt only pain. He groped for some aspect of the scene on which to fix his interest, anything to ward off sleep.

"Mr. Ferguson." Someone was tapping him on the shoulder.

The voice belonged to the receptionist who normally sat at the desk in the hall. She had entered behind him without his having heard. She handed him a pink telephone message slip, folded. Opening it, he glanced at the message. It was short. "Call your office."

In three minutes, he was back in the street, having declined an offer to use the receptionist's phone. He had had enough of bicycles and of the man from the Commerce Department. If the message was important enough for his secretary to have called him out of the meeting, it was important enough for him to get back to the office where he would be in a position to do something about it.

Five minutes later, Ferguson was entering the side door of the West Wing. He took the steps two at a time. By the time he reached the anteroom to his office, he was winded. It must have shown, because his secretary looked startled at his appearance.

"Okay, what is it?" He gasped out the words.

"Did you get my message?"

"Of course I got it. What do you think I'm here for?"

"I don't know who it is, Mr. Ferguson; all he would leave is a number. But he's called twice now, and he says it's very important."

"Well, get him on the line." Ferguson brushed past

her and closed the door to his office behind him. Inside, he peeled off his jacket, which was wet from the walk, and dropped heavily into the chair by the window.

The top button on the telephone console glowed yellow, indicating that his secretary was putting the call through. Ten seconds later, there was a buzz and he picked up.

"He's on the line, Mr. Ferguson."

"Right, put him on." The next voice Ferguson heard gave him a hollow, metallic feeling in his stomach. He had heard the voice just twice before, the first time in the middle of the night on Sunday when he had ordered the wire tap on the phones at *The Southwestern Miller*, the second time on Monday morning when he had learned of the conversation between Sosland and John Smith. It belonged to the man in charge of the CIA wire tap squad.

"Mr. Ferguson, I'm sorry if I got you out of a meeting"—the man spoke with an irritatingly slow drawl—"but you asked me to let you know right away if we learned anything."

"Yeah, yeah, what have you learned?"

"Well, sir, we've had another positive reading out of Kansas City."

"What the hell does that mean? You picked up another call?"

"That's right, sir; about two o'clock was when we got it. I called you right away like you said, but your secretary said you were out of the office. When she told me you wouldn't be back for . . ."

"Yeah, all right, all right, did you trace it?"

"Well, we're doing that right now, but there isn't any question but that it was the same fella as called earlier. It was the same voice and he gave the same name."

"I see."

"Would you like to know what he said?"

"Yes, of course." Ferguson's tone was sharp. How could the man run his operation so efficiently and still be so dim?

"Well, let's see, I've got it right here." There was a momentary pause and some rattling of paper. "Yeah, here it is. He said—well, a lot of this is just a repeat of what he said last time—except for this part here. He said that the Russians had bought wheat from Cook Industries." Another pause. "I guess that's about all that was new. He didn't mention any figures."

Ferguson thanked the man, and after renewing his instructions to continue monitoring the calls, he rang off.

Back to square one. For a moment he lay back in the lounge chair, and with his eyes shut measured the moves that would take him through the next several hours. Then he went to work.

The first order of business was to check with Solari at the Peruvian embassy. That took only a few minutes. Solari had neither seen nor heard from Bonham-Carter. Again he gave his assurance that he would call immediately.

The next step was to find out if Bonham-Carter had even bothered to come to Washington. That was going to be difficult. He could check the airline passenger lists and the Metroliner reservations. That was about it. If Bonham-Carter had come by car or bus or as a walk-on Amtrak passenger, there would be no record of it. He buzzed his secretary and asked for the Secret Service extension. It was worth a try.

Next he called Kopke. There would be nothing Kopke could do, but it would be a relief to distribute the anxiety a little bit.

"What is it, Seth?" Kopke's voice indicated that he suspected something was wrong.

"Forrest you don't have Bonham-Carter over there, do you?" There were muffled noises on the other end of the line indicating that a hand had been placed over the receiver. In a moment, Kopke's voice came through the line. This time his tone was hushed.

"Seth, that's not funny."

"I know. I'm sorry, but I've got something for you that's even less funny. Our boy, Bonham-Carter, is a no-show."

"What do you mean?"

"I mean he didn't take the bait. He isn't here, and it doesn't look like he intends to come. He called Sosland again at two o'clock this afternoon to tell him that the Russians are buying from Cook Industries."

"Jesus."

"Is that all you can say?"

"No, I mean he's right about Cook Industries. I just learned that a half hour ago from the CIA. Cook is flying the Russians to Memphis. I doubt if the plane has landed yet."

"Yeah, well, I'm already impressed. Maybe when this is all over we can hire him to work for us, but for the moment our problem is finding him." Ferguson briefed Kopke on his call to the Secret Service.

"What about the shuttles, Seth?"

"What about them?"

"Well, they don't have passenger lists, but we could check the boarding slips."

"Sonavabitch. Why didn't I think of that? Thanks, Forrie, I'll get back to you later on."

Checking the shuttles would require three calls, one to New York, one to Newark and one to Boston. A single call to the Secret Service took care of it. It was a good idea, but still a long shot. Boarding passengers tended to scribble their names so quickly that most were illegible. As a parting instruction to the Secret Service, Fer-

223]

guson told them to concentrate on passes with the small upright handwriting that generally indicated British schooling.

It was four o'clock when the phone rang next. Bingo. Bonham-Carter had left LaGuardia on the noon shuttle. He would have arrived in Washington shortly before one. Another call to the Secret Service, this time with two instructions: to check the car rental desks and the airport taxi logs. The first would be easy, the second would take time.

Ferguson had his answer on the first count within an hour. The rental desks of Hertz, Avis and National had each been checked. Nothing. No one named Bonham-Carter had rented a car. The man checking had looked at all the rental forms filled out between 12:30 and 2:00.

There was one more call to make, but before he made it he wanted the President's permission, and he wanted it in person. As he strode through the antechamber, he told his secretary, "Get the President's office and tell them I'm coming down. Tell them it's urgent." At the bottom of the stairs, he turned right and headed for the corridor which ran along the back of the White House, behind the reception area, past the rear door to the Roosevelt Room, directly to the Oval Office. This was one decision that he did not want responsibility for.

Ten minutes later he was back at his desk, punching at the buttons on his telephone. There were two rings, then three, then four. While he waited for the pickup on the other end, he rehearsed. He would have to be firm, definite, but he could not afford to be threatening.

"Soviet Trade Representation, good afternoon."

"Serge Neporozhny, please." Ferguson had known Serge Neporozhny since late 1969 when the Russian had first come to Washington to fill the Commercial Minister slot at the Soviet embassy three blocks north of the White House on Sixteenth Street. They had had lunch together perhaps a dozen times in the nearly three years that had intervened, and on several occasions had dined with their wives at one another's houses. Still, despite the similar functions that the two men performed for their respective governments, the relationship had been almost entirely social. Now Ferguson was going to have to make his first professional demand of his Russian friend. He hoped he could make it sound as though he were asking a favor.

"Hello." It was Neporozhny's voice.

"Serge, it's Seth Ferguson. I need your assistance." Briefly Ferguson sketched out what he knew of the Russian grain-buying activity over the previous two weeks, making it clear that the White House was aware that purchases were running far ahead of levels anticipated in the agreement that had been made public on the eighth of July. When he was through, Neporozhny spoke noncommittally.

"Seth, you must understand that such grain purchases as may have occurred are not made through my office. My office is part of the Foreign Trade Ministry under Patolichev. We are, as you know, talking with your Secretary Kopke about the problem of obtaining most-favored-nation status for our exporters and about our Lend-Lease obligations and about credits and other things, but as for the grain, that is under the authority of other departments—the Agriculture Ministry, Exportkhleb and ultimately the Politburo."

"Yes, yes, I know all that, Serge. I'm not asking you to confirm or deny anything, I'm just stating what we know to be fact, and the reason I'm doing it is that you and I and the grain companies are not the only people who know it to be fact."

"Yes." Neporozhny still seemed disinclined to volunteer anything.

"Serge, here's the point." Ferguson explained every-

thing he knew about Bonham-Carter's motives and his
movements over the previous two weeks. He saved the
essence of the message till the end. "Serge, the President's view is that sales of the magnitude I have just described, if made known, with all their ramifications, to
the public, would be inconsistent with his current political objectives."

"Yes, I think I understand."

"Good, I felt sure that you would."

"What is it that you are asking then?"

"We would like the assistance of your security people
in finding Bonham-Carter," Ferguson responded. "We
don't know how he has learned what he has learned,
but, on the surface of it, it would seem more likely that
the source of his information is Soviet rather than
American. In any event, if you will make the necessary
arrangments at your end, I will have the Secret Service
contact your people at the embassy. They will be able to
work out the coordinating details. Can you do it?"

"Yes, yes, certainly, Seth; I will get started now because the men will have to come from New York."

Serge Neporozhny had been intentionally coy with
Ferguson over the phone. The call from the White
House had come as a godsend. Though he himself had
been only peripherally involved with the events, Neporozhny knew that for eleven days the Soviet security
office in New York had had an agent following Bonham-Carter. A routine wire tap check by the security
people running cover for purchasing agents Belousov
and Sakun had turned up the bug on the New York Hilton phone during the night of July 7, and the office had
immediately followed up.

After alerting Belousov and Sakun, one of the techni-
cians had remained in the hotel to make contact and size
up the quarry. By five o'clock that morning the surveil-

lance assignment had been transferred to a more appropriate agent and the hand-off had been made at Kennedy International airport.

The agent chosen for the job had seemed ideal. Code named Postelniy, the agent, a loner, in need of money and troubled with strong and long-standing bitterness, had been recruited eight years earlier from the lists of the alienated and the disaffected nationals which the office regularly culled for prospects.

Postelniy's bitterness went back over twenty years to the summer of 1951 when as a ten-year-old, the child had spent three long weeks in the steaming hearing room of the House Un-American Activities Committee, watching in childish confusion as the people's elected representatives rewrote the First Amendment to fit the times. The constitutional subtleties had been beyond the grasp of a ten-year-old, but the child had not been too young to understand when the hearings were over that its father's successful screenwriting career had ended with them. The bitterness had come in all its fullness five years later when the call from Mommy to the fashionable and too-expensive boarding school with the news that Daddy had died that afternoon in his study in the attic. The papers the next day had been less sparing with the details.

For most of the past eleven days the monitoring of Bonham-Carter's activities had gone well. Postelniy had slipped up in Los Angeles and allowed Bonham-Carter to break contact. But that had been rectified. Bonham-Carter had been relocated the next day through the normal Washington surveillance mechanisms and the contact had been reestablished. Only the previous day, following word of the call to *The Southwestern Miller*, Postelniy had been given the order to erase.

Not an hour earlier, Neporozhny had learned from

the New York office that Postelniy was dead, gassed by a defective heating unit in a Stockbridge hotel room.

After hanging up on Neporozhny, Ferguson checked with his secretary and learned that there had been no calls from the Secret Service while he had been talking to the Russian. Checking the taxi logs would be a slow business. If the driver had gone on duty early in the morning, he would probably get off the street about four, before the rush-hour buildup. It was well past four already. That could mean the cab he was looking for was on the noon to midnight shift. Or it could mean something worse. It could mean that the driver had not recorded the fare. That had to be considered a high likelihood. Drivers forced to operate through the District's gerrymandered fare-zoning system were notorious for underreporting fares. The system wouldn't allow them to beat the customer, but it couldn't prevent them from beating the tax collector.

At six o'clock, Kopke called, and Ferguson filled him in on the afternoon's developments. Kopke seemed more anxious than he had earlier in the afternoon.

"What are you going to do now, Seth?"

"There isn't anything to do but sit here and wait."

"Okay, then, I'm coming over there," Kopke replied.

It was 6:20 when Kopke arrived in Ferguson's office. It was obvious from the rivulets of perspiration on his face that he had walked from the Commerce Department. Having wound himself up, he now seemed disinclined to stop walking and paced nervously back and forth across the office carpet.

"Have you talked to the President?" he asked.

"Yes, Forrie, I talked to him before I called Neporozhny."

"Whaddee say?"

"He said it was okay to call him."

"I mean whaddee say about Bonham-Carter not showing up?" Kopke was almost shouting. "Jesus, Seth, I don't know why you're so fuckin' cool about this whole thing. How did the President react when you told him we didn't have a clue where Bonham-Carter was?"

"He was disappointed."

"Disappointed. That's very good, Seth, disappointed—my name is Vito Corleone and I'm disappointed in you, ZAPP!" Kopke made a chopping motion with his hand as he ended the sentence. His accent was very good and Ferguson smiled.

Bored with pacing, Kopke seated himself, opened his briefcase and began riffling through a half-dozen colored folders. His mind would not focus. He looked up. Ferguson was leaning back in his high-backed desk chair, staring at the ceiling and slowly twirling a pencil between his fingertips.

"What are you thinking about?" Kopke asked.

"Bicycles."

"Bicycles?"

"Uh-huh, I listened to one of your people give a very stirring presentation on bicycles this afternoon. I had to leave before it was over, but I think he was going to suggest we raise the tariff on bicycles, maybe impose a quota."

"Yeah, well, the bicycle people are hurting."

"Lot of people are hurting, Forest."

"What do you mean by that?"

"I'm not sure. I guess it is just not clear to me how much it's fair to ask a lot of people to pay in order to spare a few people some hurt. Cause that's what you're doing with tariffs and quotas, really, isn't it? I guess what I don't understand is how you make the calculation. You can't really be objective. You can't just put the costs on one end of the scale and the hurt on the other, because how do you figure what hurt weighs? But I don't know how you approach it subjectively either. Everybody would probably agree that it was okay to raise the price of a bicycle fifty cents if it was going to save twenty thousand jobs. But how about a dollar, or five dollars or fifty dollars? Once you get into that murky subjective world, where do you draw the line, and what are your criteria? I guess that's about where we are with the textile industry right now, and I wonder if we really want to go down that road with the bicycle people, too. Where are we going to be ten years from now if we go on bailing people out like that? We're going to have half the economy riding on the back of the other half and the Japs and the Germans and everybody else who knows how to kiss a bad business good-bye are going to be eating us alive. And what is our friend the good voter going to say then: 'He ain't heavy, he's my textile manufacturer or my bicycle manufacturer'? If you think about it, that's what most of this government is about: making the winners pay for the losers. I wonder if that's what Jefferson had in mind?"

Kopke, who had stopped listening to Ferguson several minutes earlier, made no reply. For close to an hour the two men sat in silence, Kopke thumbing through his files, Ferguson twirling his pencil, occasionally sitting up to scribble a few lines on the note pad on his desk. At 8:40, they were interrupted by the phone buzzer.

"Hello, yeah, great, right, right, okay, now, I want you to cover all the airports—don't forget Friendship—cover the train stations, cover the car rentals, then I want you to start sweeping the hotels; and look, I want those taxi fleet dispatchers to keep monitoring the logs; I want all drivers listening for English accents; if he hasn't rented a car, then chances are he'll have to take another cab. Okay? Okay, you've got my home number if anything turns up. Oh, and whoa . . . the bus stations; don't forget the bus stations."

Ferguson put down the receiver and fell back into his chair. He looked at Kopke. "They found the cab, Forrest. The driver says he dropped Bonham-Carter on Ninth Street at one thirty this afternoon."

Chapter

XVIII

THERE was no sign outside the embassy that anyone was waiting for him. The building faced the street corner, and in front of the door, several cars were parked in the short driveway that angled from Seventeenth Street to Massachusetts Avenue. Next to the door, on the right, he could see a patch of light-colored stone where a plaque had recently been removed. Had he passed there six months earlier, the plaque would have been in place, identifying the building as the Australian Chancery.

The taxi passed Seventeenth Street and they were out of the embassy area. Now the avenue was lined with office buildings and apartment houses. In a few blocks, these gave way to town houses, red brick and run-down.

At Ninth Street, Bonham-Carter ordered the driver to turn right. They were entering a sleazy neighborhood of bars and pornographic magazine shops. A few minutes later, at the corner of Ninth and E streets, he paid the fare and got out. Though it was almost two o'clock, the sidewalks were still crowded with men on lunch hours from the Federal office buildings along Constitution Avenue one block south. They would remain perhaps another half hour during which time he would be inconspicuous. After that, with his suit and tie and carrying his suitcase, he would stand out among the street's off-hours complement of winos and derelicts. He needed to get to a telephone. He had been snatched off the street once already. If Sallas had made a deal with the American authorities in which he was one of the barters, there was no telling how long the embassy would wait before an effort was launched to find him. There was no certainty that someone was not already looking for him.

There were no phone booths at the intersection of Ninth and E streets. Just a parking lot, a dilapidated Army surplus store and an enormous hole in the ground which a sign nailed to the wooden fence around it announced would one day be filled with the Federal Bureau of Investigation. Two doors up from the remaining corner of the intersection was a bar with a solid wooden door reminiscent of doors on dozens of strip-tease parlors in Soho.

The bar inside was dark and throbbed with rock music provided by an overtaxed sound system. He paused in the entry and waited for his eyes to adjust. The room was long and narrow. He was standing in what probably once had been the living room of somebody's house. On the right, at about the point where the wall separating the living room from the dining room would have been, was the end of a bar which extended to the back of the building. Across from it, against the left wall, was a square platform on which a girl was dancing with obvious boredom. As the room grew lighter, he could see men seated at tables, and, along the wall on either side of the dancer, at booths. With the exception of several of the men closest to the girl who stared with shameless fixity, the clientele seemed equally bored. The girl wore only a G-string.

Bonham-Carter pushed his way to the far end of the room, shoved his suitcase under an empty table and ordered a beer. When the waitress brought it, he asked for change for a ten-dollar bill. Two minutes later he was in the telephone booth next to the men's room.

The operator's instructions were to insert two dollars at a time. It took nearly five minutes to put the call through to Scrivas. The switchback to Kansas City was much faster, and in a few more moments he had Sosland on the line. That day *The Southwestern Miller* had published its first estimate of the Russian purchases, cautiously putting the figure at somewhat over two and a half million tons, essentially the same figure that it had put out in its daily news figure four days earlier. Bonham-Carter protested that the figure was a gross understatement, that the Midcontinental sales of two weeks earlier were double that figure and that the Cook sales would push the aggregate higher still. After the conversation, Bonham-Carter remained in the telephone booth for several minutes, checking addresses in the Yellow Pages. When he returned to his table, he had two of the pages from the telephone book carefully folded in his jacket pocket.

He remained in the bar until shortly after four o'clock. Then, confident that the streets would again be crowded, he left. Outside, he walked north on Ninth Street to the intersection of F Street, checked an address on one of the yellow phone-book pages from his pocket, then headed west. Fifty yards farther on, he entered the Spranger Fashion Uniform Company. Two tiers of clothing racks lined the walls inside. He could make out scores of choir robes and vestments on the upper tier.

233]

The floor-level racks were crowded with medical whites, uniforms for waitresses, beauticians, ushers, domestics and dozens of commercial enterprises. Bonham-Carter spoke briefly with the proprietor and was shown to the rear of the store where there were shelves stacked high with folded trousers and shirts. It took only a few minutes to find what he was looking for. By 4:20 he was out of the store and heading west again on F Street.

He was relying on memory now. At the Treasury Building, he turned north on Fifteenth Street, passed the American Security and Trust Building at the corner of Fifteenth and New York Avenue and walked on toward MacPherson Square and K Street. It was familiar territory. If his memory was correct, he would be at his destination in less than ten minutes. In front of the Madison at the corner of Fifteenth and M streets, he stopped to check the address on the second yellow page from his pocket, then turned left. Two and a half blocks later he entered the same parking garage he had cut through trying to shake his imagined followers the previous Thursday. This time, however, he did not go through to De Sales Street but turned right on the narrow alley that bisected the block and entered the rear of the Madison Bank Building which faced onto M Street. When he emerged five minutes later, he wore bright red pants, a matching cap and a white short-sleeved shirt. The patch over his right shirt pocket read "Budget Rent-a-Car."

The alley was crowded with shiny new sedans. He peered in the windows of several. No keys. He tried the doors. As he had expected, they were locked. No matter. The last thing he wanted at this point was to be driving a hot car. If they were looking for him, one of the first things they would do is to get out bulletins on all cars reported stolen that day and the next.

Forty yards from the back door of the bank, the alley

made a ninety-degree turn around the corner of the building. Two hundred feet away, where the alley emptied into M Street, he could see the corner of the Budget rental office. There was no one in sight. He sat down to wait. He had been there less than half an hour when a car entered the far end of the alley from Seventeenth Street. As it approached he could see that it was an American Motors Ambassador, identical, except for its color, to those that lined the alley. He held up his hand and the driver stopped.

"Turning it in, sir?" Bonham-Carter could see the man fumbling in the glove compartment for the rental papers.

"Yup. The air conditioning don't work worth a damn." The man, rumpled, harried and in his middle fifties, was pressing the papers and the keys into Bonham-Carter's hand.

"Sorry, sir, we'll see to that. I hope it was satisfactory otherwise." The man didn't reply. He had seized a plastic suit bag from the hook above the side rear window and was hurrying off.

Bonham-Carter backed the car back down the alley, stopped to pick up his suitcase, then, at the point where the alley broadened into the parking garage, turned around and accelerated out onto Seventeenth Street. With luck, the rental company would go on charging its unwitting customer for a week before becoming concerned.

Getting out of Washington was a slow business in the heavy rush-hour traffic. He didn't mind. In his red and white uniform, he felt almost invisible. He would have had to look twice to recognize himself. As the cars on Route 95 peeled down one exit after another into the seemingly endless northern Virginia suburbs, he could feel his anxiety melting away.

It had been a memorable twenty-four hours, and he

had been lucky. He had been lucky to have left the bar in the Green Griffin Inn when he had, lucky to have seen the woman in the corridor and to have remembered her walk and the trim body he had become so familiar with. It had taken a little time to sink in, but that glimpse in the corridor and the electric shower had made a lot of things come into focus. He had already had the other pieces of the puzzle. The pink apartment. No redhead would own a pink apartment. The empty kitchen. No one could live on coffee and garlic bread. The atomizer in the bathroom at the inn. That had been enough to clinch it. Still, he had wanted to be certain. The telephone calls had done that: the heavily accented voice that had answered at the New York number, the San Francisco operator who had told him there was no listing for the name he gave her, the clerk at the Hyatt Wilshire who had checked and told him that, though the hotel was still holding an unpaid bill for Mr. Bonham-Carter, there was no record of a Mrs. Bonham-Carter having been there. Finally, there had been the call to the night duty officer at the State Department. It had taken some digging but after nearly ten minutes the man had found a dictionary which contained the word "postelniy." There had been several definitions, but the second one had been enough to settle Bonham-Carter's mind. Postelniy meant pillow talk. Classie had been sloppy, but she had almost got her job done. Sloppy people in her business were sometimes the most dangerous. He wondered what time the inn would have discovered the body. He flicked on the radio and upped his speed to over seventy. Silently, the odometer rolled on toward safety.

It was almost nine o'clock and dark when he passed Richmond. Signs ticked off the little Virginia towns: Petersburg, Stony Creek, Jarratt, Emporia, then he was in

North Carolina. It was after eleven o'clock when he pulled into a Hardee's hamburger joint on the outskirts of Rocky Mount. In four hours of hard driving he had given little thought to where he was headed. After eating and having the car filled with gas, he placed a call to Charleston information. Moments later he could hear the phone ringing at the number the operator had given him for Boyden Mayhew. After five rings without an answer he hung up. He smiled to himself, remembering that it had been only that morning that he had left Mayhew in New York. It seemed more like a week.

Outside, Bonham-Carter pulled the car to the rear of the restaurant, locked the doors and made himself as comfortable as possible in the rear seat. If he was going to Charleston, it was pointless to arrive in the middle of the night. When he awoke, it was 5:30 and already getting light. The road was empty and he made good time. He passed Fayetteville shortly before seven. A half hour later he was skimming over an awakening Lumberton on the elevated highway, then he was off of Route 95 and onto a small two-lane highway and passing a sign that told him he was entering South Carolina and the little town of Lake View. It was instant Old South—he had crossed an invisible threshold and entered the tropics. The road curved around the edge of a placid, pollen-surfaced bayou. Tall trees, festooned with Spanish moss, rose out of the middle of the water. He knew such places existed in the United States but had imagined them to exist only in Florida or Louisiana. Then Lake View was behind him and he was out of the tropics and back on the table-flat tobacco lands of shacks with rusty, corrogated metal roofs and bleak little one-story towns with Anglo-derivative names like Kingsburg and Hemingway and Andrews and Jamestown. It was eleven o'clock when he hit the steep incline of narrow and aging Grace Memorial Bridge which would take him over the Cooper River and into downtown Charleston.

After making inquiries, Bonham-Carter took a room in a small establishment called the Sword Gate Inn on Tradd Street in the old restored section of the city. At the urging of the proprietress who became giddy with civic pride at the sound of his English accent, he spent the balance of the morning and most of the afternoon walking the historic portion of the city between Broad Street and the Battery, mopping perspiration from his brow and reading the hundreds of plaques which the Colonial Dames had erected to commemorate the historic significance of everything from houses to hitching posts. At four o'clock he returned to the inn, showered, shaved and crawled into bed.

It was dark when he woke again. He tried Mayhew's number but got no answer. When he returned from dinner several hours later, he tried the number again. This time Mayhew answered. If the real-estate operator was surprised, it could not have been detected from his voice. Bonham-Carter was more than welcome to take a look around Kiawah Island. In fact, Mayhew was going out there himself the next day and would give him a ride. He could stay through the weekend if he liked. Bonham-Carter thanked him for the offer of hospitality and it was agreed that Mayhew would pick him up at the Sword Gate Inn in the morning. Before going to bed, Bonham-Carter drove the rental car down to the Battery and left it parked on the street. In the event an alert was to be put out on it in the next several days, he did not want it sitting in the inn parking lot where it could be traced to him.

Mayhew arrived the next morning driving a yellow jeep. As they crossed the Ashley River and headed south along Route 171, Mayhew explained that while there were several roads on Kiawah Island, they were little more than wagon tracks. It was possible to get onto the island in a normal car, but difficult to get around and impossible to explore the more interesting parts. A four-wheel-drive vehicle was essential.

Mayhew was in a good mood. Over the whine of the jeep's engine he filled Bonham-Carter in on the history of the Charleston area, on its famous citizens past and present, on its botanical marvels. At one point he turned off onto a dirt road and drove several hundred yards into the woods to show him what was claimed to be the largest live oak tree in the world. Bonham-Carter was content to listen and nod appreciatively. As long as they were driving away from Washington and the Peruvian embassy and the police whom he assumed would certainly be looking for him by now, he would happily look at trees, bushes or whatever else it pleased Mayhew to show him.

They were off the highway and on a smaller road now, tunneling along beneath an almost solid roof of overhanging tree limbs. Except for an occasional shack propped up on cinder blocks and the odd mule staring stupidly at them from the roadside, there was no sign of life.

"Where are we now?" Bonham-Carter asked.

"Well, this here's all Johns Island," Mayhew replied. "We been on Johns Island ever since that little bridge back there where we crossed Wappoo Creek." Bonham-Carter nodded. It was difficult speaking over the noise of the jeep. "Folks out here are right poor," Mayhew added after a moment.

"What do they do?"

"For a livin'?"

"Yes, what do they work at?"

"Don't work at nothin' much. Ain't a whole lot to

work at around here. Most of 'em got vegtubble patches and they sell some of that. The rest of it's just day work, I guess . . . when they can find it. I think the per capita income here on this island is sposed to be bout as low as it is anywhere in the country."

The road forked now, and as they bore to the left, Bonham-Carter could see in the space between the two roads the rickety hulk of what obviously had once been a combined store and gas station. An aged Dr. Pepper sign hung cockeyed from a single nail on the side wall, its enamel badly pocked in half a dozen places. Someone had shot at the sign with a low-caliber weapon. He wondered how long ago, for the building appeared to be occupied. Chickens scratched at the base of its walls, and, in front of the door, the dark earth around the emasculated gas pumps was worn smooth and free of grass and weeds.

"I imagine that the young people leave here as soon as they can?" Bonham-Carter asked.

"Some do. Some don't. Idn't that easy, cause there idn't really anywhere for them to go. Most of 'em can't talk worth a damn. They speak a dialect called Gullah, and it don't sound like nothin' you ever heard before."

Mayhew apparently preferred to discuss Charleston than talk about Johns Island, for he changed the subject. For the next ten minutes, he talked almost nonstop about the city's history, its architecture, its racial makeup and its complex social structure.

They had turned off onto a dirt road now and the trees and the shade were behind them. High brown marsh grasses lined the road on either side. Several hundred yards farther on, Mayhew stopped the jeep at a small wooden bridge and got out. For the first time that day, Bonham-Carter was aware of the heat. For a moment his sensory mechanisms seemed to go into remission as he watched Mayhew walk ahead through the bleaching sunlight toward a gate which barred the way to a narrow wooden bridge. The hum in his ears could have come from insects in the grass alongside the road. It might as easily have been the residual effect of listening to the noise of the jeep for half an hour. It was hard to tell. Then Mayhew was back, and the renewed growl of the four-cylinder engine made the question academic.

They were on Kiawah now. For a quarter of a mile past the bridge the dirt road wound through a dense thicket of live oak and palmetto laced together with all manner of vines and high-growing ground cover. Then the road broadened and became a narrow clearing several hundred yards long. On either side, houses—perhaps a dozen—were set back in the trees at roughly equal intervals. Though several of the houses had automobiles parked next to them, there were no people to be seen nor any sign of movement.

As the jeep bumped toward the far end of the clearing, Bonham-Carter studied the scene. There was little there that suggested the tropical paradise to which Mayhew had alluded on the plane ride several days earlier. Though there were several dozen palmettos in sight, the vast majority of the visible vegetation was brown and scrubby. The houses, in contrast with the wildness of the place, and the exclusivity which the locked gate suggested, were undistinguished one-story structures that managed to look cheap without looking rustic. Several, which were covered with siding in pastel, house-trailer colors, appeared to be prefabricated.

"Well, what do you think of it?" Mayhew had pulled the jeep to a stop at the far end of the clearing in front of one of the more attractive houses and was looking at Bonham-Carter with obvious proprietary pride.

"Very nice." Bonham-Carter's inventory of usable adjectives was suddenly very low. "Very private."

"Yep, but we're gonna change all that if I get my way."

Mayhew had climbed out and was wrestling with a large freezer chest which Bonham-Carter had not previously noticed behind the seat.

The path that led from the jeep to Mayhew's house was spongy underfoot. Bonham-Carter reckoned that he was walking on probably six inches of semidecomposed organic matter. He wondered if it were possible for a hot, wet climate like Kiawah's to produce new vegetation faster than the earth could digest the old, wondered if the forest would go on generating compost until it choked on its own waste. It didn't seem likely.

Inside, Mayhew busied himself putting the contents of the freezer chest into the refrigerator while Bonham-Carter studied the layout of the house. The front door had opened onto a large living room that was sparsely but expensively furnished in self-consciously masculine fashion. Directly behind the living room, separated from it only by a counter, was the kitchen and to the left of the kitchen a screened porch or breezeway which led to the bedrooms. Through the porch, Bonham-Carter could see that the rear of the house was no more than twenty feet from the forest wall.

"Is that your motorcycle?" Bonham-Carter was standing on the porch as he asked. At the foot of the stairs, resting against a tree, sat one of the most bizarre vehicles he had ever seen.

"Yup, that's some sickle, isn't it?" Mayhew called out from the kitchen. "I bought it off a fella down in Edisto Island for fifty bucks. It's some sonavabitch in the sand, I wanna tell you." Bonham-Carter believed him. The motorcycle, which must have weighed as much as a small automobile, had balloon tires approximately eight inches wide. Though its wheel radius was no greater than that of any large touring bike, the wheels themselves were solid plates of metal from rim to rim. The vehicle's most unusual feature, however, was the enormous exposed drive chain by which power was conveyed from the engine to the rear wheel. Painted all over in dull black, it reminded Bonham-Carter of motorcycles he had seen in World War One photographs.

Wandering back into the living room, he caught sight of an aerial photograph that had been fixed to the wall with architectural pins. At closer look, he could see that the photograph was of Kiawah. Even knowing what it was, it took awhile to locate the clearing and the houses. Despite the fact that the photograph was nearly four feet square, the clearing appeared no larger than his fingernail.

"Whadda ya think of that picture?" Mayhew had emerged from the kitchen and was standing behind him, drying his hands with a towel. "There's a lot of nothing in that picture; jes a lot of trees and a lot of beach and a couple of itty-bitty little houses. And you know what?"

"What?"

"I figure every square inch of that nothin' you're lookin' at's gonna be worth 'bout half a million dollars. Least half a million dollars." Bonham-Carter looked back at the photograph and tried to relate half a million dollars to the miserable steaming fingernail they had just driven through. Their current position was near the foot of the island. At about the middle of the island, at least several miles above them, a narrow ribbon of gray cut the otherwise unbroken sea of treetops from the ocean on the right to the lagoon behind the island.

"What is this? Is that a road?" Bonham-Carter traced the gray line with his fingertip.

"That's right, that's the old plantation road. Come on, grab a beer, and I'll give you the old guided tour."

The old guided tour evidently was not optional, for Mayhew did not wait for an answer. He was out the front door and climbing back into the jeep by the time Bonham-Carter could get back from the kitchen with two cans of beer.

Though the ocean had not been visible from the house, it turned out to lie only a short distance away over a low range of dunes beyond the far side of the clearing. Coming down off the soft sand of the dunes, Bonham-Carter could feel the sharp contrast as the jeep's tires hit the flat, hard-packed beach. In a few moments they were doing forty miles an hour heading north. "Best road on the island," Mayhew said, grinning.

The beach was truly spectacular. From the scale of the photograph, its size had been hard to appreciate. Bonham-Carter was struck now by its extraordinary width. From dune to waterline it measured fully 150 yards on a slope almost too gradual to be perceptible. And it stretched ahead uninterrupted as far as he could see. As the jeep roared along the virgin strand, Washington and the commodities market and Sallas and everything with which he had been preoccupied for three weeks seemed remote. He was grateful for the wind and again to be cool.

"Is there good fishing here?"

"Hmm?" Mayhew had been lost in thoughts of his own.

"Can one fish here?"

"Off the beach?"

"Yes."

"Won't catch anything this time of year. Not unless it's cooked." Mayhew caught the look of noncomprehension on Bonham-Carter's face. "Look," he said, pointing ahead of them, "you see how that beach don't slope hardly at all?" Bonham-Carter nodded. "Well, it keeps on goin' jes like that all the way out under that water. You can walk your ass off and you won't get over your waist; only I wouldn't do it this time of year or you likely to burn yourself. After the middle of July, that water's got to be way over ninety degrees. Ain't no fish who's got a choice gonna swim around in that stuff." Mayhew paused, shot a glance toward the ocean, then, after a few moments of reflection, added, "Course, I ain't a fisher, so it don't make me no difference."

"Yes, but how about the people to whom you expect to sell homes here?" Bonham-Carter asked.

Mayhew shrugged. "Well, it ain't the kind of information you want to lead off a brochure with, but it don't really matter. This around here ain't summer resort country anyway. Like I told you the other day, people'll want to come here in the spring and fall when it's nice. The hell with the summer; water's too hot, air's too hot, let 'em go somewhere else. This here's gonna be for rich people anyway."

They had been driving for over five minutes when Mayhew veered away from the waterline and pointed the jeep toward the line of trees behind the beach. As the jeep topped the dune that marked the dividing line between beach and woods, Bonham-Carter caught sight of a narrow road running directly inland. Though it looked even smaller than the gray ribbon he had seen in the photograph, Mayhew confirmed that the roads were the same. Ruts and holes and low overhanging branches held the jeep's speed to a slow crawl, and it was nearly ten minutes before they emerged in a semicircular clearing.

"Now, this here is what Kiawah used to be all about," Mayhew said, gesturing toward the back of the clearing. "That's the old plantation house."

Bonham-Carter was again at a loss for a credible expression of appreciation. The structure before him was large enough, but it hardly satisfied his cinematic definition of plantation house. To begin with, it had a red tin roof which struck him as inelegant. The porches that had once surrounded it had long ago dropped away, and their remains now lay like dirty underpants around an old lady's ankles. There was nothing glamorous about it.

"It's quite large, isn't it?"

"Yep, I reckon this here must have been quite an operation in its day," Mayhew replied. "Come on, I'll show you inside. It looks even better from the inside. Look out for snakes, though. They like to lie out here and sun themselves on these boards this time of day," he added, gesturing toward the porch rubble.

Indeed, the inside of the plantation house turned out to be considerably more impressive than its exterior. The ceilings were high and the plasterwork remarkably preserved. "If the vandals hadn't got at this place, you could move right in," Mayhew said, stepping across a large open space in the front hall floor. "It's the wood they come out here for," he added, jouncing up and down on the floor in one of the two large rooms which, with the hall, made up the first level of the house. "This here is all cypress: over a hundred and fifty years old and there ain't a crack or a squeak in it. Reckon it'll last another hundred and fifty years, too, if people'll leave it be."

From the second-floor window, they could look back

down the road they had just come up and see the ocean beyond. "All them woods you see between here and the ocean was fields once," Mayhew said, sweeping his arm across the horizon. "Probably took fifty hands to work this place when it was goin' full blast."

"What did they grow, tobacco?" Bonham-Carter asked.

"Indigo," Mayhew answered. "Indigo was the South Carolina crop, indigo and rice. Indigo was big money around here back then."

"What did they do with it?"

"Sold it."

"No, I meant what did they use it for?"

"Dye, blue dye. That's where the name of the color comes from. You oughta know that, you English folks were the first ones to use it."

"Is that right?"

"Yep, couple of thousand years ago the Celtics used to smear it all over themselves to turn blue." Mayhew obviously had studied up on the indigo business, for he proceeded to explain how several hundred years earlier a plantation such as Kiawah's would have been run. How the plants would have been fermented in huge vats of water. How the resultant yellow liquid would then have been drawn off into other vats and made to evaporate by being churned and splashed into the air with paddle wheels. And how this process of oxidation would in time have produced a fine blue sediment which would be pressed into cubes and shipped around the world.

"What put them out of business, synthetics?" Bonham-Carter asked.

"Well, synthetics didn't help, but they didn't come along till the end of the last century, and the industry was pretty much dead around here by then anyway 'cause of the war. See, the war was a lot of things to a lot of folks, but around here, it turned out to be one very expensive labor dispute. The fightin' disrupted everything to start with, then not having any more slaves made it damn hard to start up again. This house right here was actually occupied by Yankee soldiers. Come on, I'll show you." Mayhew led the way into one of the second-floor rooms off the hall and pointed to a spot on one of the walls. There, clearly written in the ornate hand of an earlier century, were the words "General Beauregard, where are you?"

"Who is General Beauregard?"

"He was one of our generals. Some Yankee must have wrote that there bout a hundred and ten years ago."

It was past noon when the two men left the old plantation house. As the jeep roared back down the beach, Bonham-Carter's thoughts turned to the days ahead. He would be safe on the island. There was nothing to worry about on that score. But he could not remain there forever. Soon, passport or no passport, he would have to make a run for it. Back at Mayhew's house they ate a light lunch of sandwiches washed down by more beer. Then Mayhew announced that he had to be getting back to town. It might be as much as a week before he would have a chance to get to the island again, but he assured Bonham-Carter that he was welcome to stay on as long as he liked. Bonham-Carter thanked him, and, after receiving instructions on where to find clean sheets and where to hide the front door key, he watched the jeep drive back down the narrow clearing and disappear into the narrow road that led back to the bridge.

Mayhew had been right about the water. It was too hot to be refreshing, a fact that rendered the beach also useless. Aside from one morning's worth of exploring, during which he encountered no fewer than seven

[248

snakes, Bonham-Carter hardly ventured out of the house during the next several days. Once, during the heat of the afternoon, he heard what sounded like the noise of a motorcycle engine coming from the direction of the beach. But no motorcycle ever appeared, nor did he ever see a trace of whoever owned the cars parked alongside the other houses in the clearing. Mostly, he passed the daylight hours in the cold shower, in the kitchen or lying on the living room couch pouring over old magazines most of whose pages had been fused together by the humidity.

It was late on the afternoon of Sunday, July 23, when Bonham-Carter next heard from Mayhew. The jingle of the telephone surprised him, for though he had been in the house for four days, he had not yet noticed the wall unit hidden behind the bedroom door. Mayhew was calling to tell him that his business would be taking him out of Charleston for several weeks. He wondered what Bonham-Carter's plans were. While he was welcome to stay on, without a car there would be no way for him to get more food, since the nearest grocery store was at least ten miles away.

Bonham-Carter raised the possibility of his using the old motorcycle he had seen behind the house.

"Yeah, it works all right," Mayhew said, "but it's a sonavabitch to start, and you might have trouble with it once you got to the road. Look, I'll tell you what. If you don't mind dropping me off at the airport tomorrow morning, you can keep the jeep. I ain't gonna be needing it in Canada."

At the mention of Canada, Bonham-Carter forgot about the jeep. Further conversation revealed that Mayhew was flying to Canada the next morning to look at alternatives to the New England deal on which negotiations were moving slowly. When asked, he readily agreed to take Bonham-Carter along, and it was arranged that he would pick him up the following morning at nine.

Charleston's general aviation facility proved to be only slightly larger than the one at Pittsfield. The small two-engine plane looked friendly sitting on the runway, and it struck Bonham-Carter as he climbed into it that, for the first time in almost a month, he was entering a familiar environment.

For a hundred miles from Charleston to Wilmington, their flight course followed the coastline. Then the plane turned inland on a line that would cut off the coastal hump of eastern North Carolina. At the airport, Bonham-Carter had bought a newspaper which he now turned to to check the market. The news was good. September wheat had risen another two cents the previous Friday. He was halfway through his mental calculation when he remembered that Royer had told him the newspaper quotes reflected an average price, that the no. 1 grade of hard winter wheat he had bought sold at a one-cent premium over the newspaper price. Making this adjustment, he went back to his calculation. The paper profit on his own investment worked out to $31,500. It was not the $50,000 which Sallas owed him and which he would now never collect, but it was a lot of money. And it was nothing compared to what the Peruvian account would yield were he to decide to liquidate that too when he got to Canada. The last thought was tempting, but it would be extraordinarily dangerous. True, Sallas had probably double-crossed him, and he owed Sallas nothing. Still, if he were to walk off with over $20 million in Peruvian funds, Sallas would hunt him down for certain. It was a decision that did not have to be made that day.

"What are all those triangles?" Bonham-Carter had to

almost shout the words. With Mayhew at the controls, conversation was more difficult than it had been coming down from Pittsfield with a hired pilot.

"What triangles?" Mayhew answered over his shoulder.

"Those orangish dirt triangles down there," Bonham-Carter said, indicating with his finger that he was speaking of the ground.

"Oh, those, they're not triangles, they're diamonds, baseball diamonds. If they made 'em right, most of that dirt would be grass, but in little towns like this they don't bother with grass."

Bonham-Carter nodded. "They must fancy baseball quite a lot to have so many of them."

"Yep, they do," Mayhew yelled back; "baseball's big in this part of the country."

Talking was too much effort. Bonham-Carter propped his feet up in front of him and leaned back to finish his newspaper. In five minutes he had dozed off. He was wakened by the sound of Mayhew's voice.

"Excuse me, I'm afraid I fell asleep," he said, sitting up.

"That's all right. I was just radioing our position to the air traffic controller. FAA regulations. They gotta know who we are and where we are." Bonham-Carter glanced out the window and was surprised to see that their altitude had shrunk less than a thousand feet.

"Are we in Canada already?"

Mayhew shot a smile over his shoulder. "Not hardly. This ain't no Gulf Stream Two you're ridin' in. That's Washington down there. We gotta gas up." Out the right-hand window, Bonham-Carter could already see the top of the Washington Monument coming into view above the wing.

Bonham-Carter could feel the tension in his throat as

he asked the next question. "What did you mean when you said you had to tell them who we were?"

"I just give 'em my tail number."

"Do you have to give them your name?"

"Naw, they have that already. You have to give the plane's registration and tail number and the passenger list at your point of departure when you file your course. Then all that stuff just gets forwarded up the line. All I did just then is tell 'em that we're here like we said we'd be. You never done any flying?"

"So, in other words, they know both our names?"

"That's right. Got to. If I was to run into that monument over there and we was both burned to roast-toasties, the government wouldn't want to have to read the back of your watch to find out who you were." Mayhew seemed pleased with his explanation, for he gave Bonham-Carter another smile.

Two minutes later the plane touched down at the south end of National Airport and began the long taxi to the Page Terminal at the far end of the runway. Bonham-Carter did not have time for further conversation. His suitcase was open on the seat opposite him and he was busy stuffing his pockets with his essential portables. If his fears were well founded, he could not afford to be encumbered.

They were still a hundred yards from the terminal when he saw the black Chevrolet sedan waiting just inside the storm fence at the runway's western edge. As Mayhew taxied the plane toward the yellow lines that marked the refueling slip, Bonham-Carter could see the sedan accelerate rapidly out onto the apron on a line paralleling their course. In a matter of seconds they would be alongside each other and separated only by a row of eight or ten parked planes. He could afford to wait no longer. Seizing the door's release lever, he gave a sharp downward thrust, hurling his body outward in the same motion. His momentum, combined with the braking action of the plane, sent the door crashing forward into the rear of the wing. Though momentarily stunned, he clung to the lever. He could feel the asphalt tearing at his shoes now. Then he was free of the plane and running. Skirting the plane's left wing tip, he made straight for the terminal. Out of the corner of his eye, he could see the sedan peeling back to try to cut him off. He had them beat. The problem was what to do when he got to the terminal.

Chapter

XIX

A PARTY of three men with briefcases issued from the terminal twenty feet ahead of him. The door had just begun to close when he reached it and he crossed the threshold without breaking stride. Ahead, he could see a second bank of glass doors and through them the parking lot beyond. Twenty heads turned and followed him across the dark linoleum tile floor. His mind was a blur. Which door to pick? Which way would it open? Where were the push-pull signs? He hit the middle door at full speed with both arms extended. It gave, and he was outside, standing at the bottom of a U-shaped driveway. To his right, twenty yards away, two long black limousines sat parked bumper to bumper against the curb on the exit arm of the driveway. Their drivers, dressed in gray livery, stood, backs to him, behind the second car, chatting with the unhurried ease of men who had just sent their masters packing. They never turned. A double forearm shivver caught them squarely in the center of their backs, lifted their feet from the pavement and pitched them forward onto the trunk of the rear limousine. Before either had sorted out what had happened to him, Bonham-Carter was in the lead car and screeching away from the curb.

At the top of the U, he swung right onto the airport access road and mashed the accelerator to the floor. He heard the automatic transmission drop to a lower gear and felt the big Cadillac lift its nose and begin to plane. He hit the George Washington Parkway doing ninety miles an hour, drifted sideways through the lane of merging traffic and settled along the median strip. He was doing slightly under a hundred miles an hour now. At that speed the limousine had no road feel at all, only a floating sensation. But speed was important. The men in the black sedan at the airport did not worry him. Their car was inside the fence. That would cost them fifteen seconds at a minimum. They could be no closer than half a mile behind him. But they would have a radio, and already they would have alerted other cars. The highway was a trap. He had to get off, and fast. It was still early afternoon. He had fortune to thank for that. Two hours later and he would have been lucky to make half the speed he was making.

At the Fourteenth Street bridge, Bonham-Carter cut back across the inside lane and headed up the ramp. He was forced to move slower now in the heavier traffic. Ahead he could see the bottom of the city looming. Once over the bridge, he would not have to worry about roadblocks. But the limousine would be conspicuous. He would have to ditch it quickly. He bit his upper lip nervously and was surprised at the metallic taste. A wipe with his finger showed blood. He must have smashed his nose on the airplane's door when it crashed into the wing. There had been no sensation.

As he cleared the bridge and swung left up Fourteenth Street, there was no sign of his pursuers in the rearview mirror. He was about to dump the limousine and hail a taxi when a movement to his right caught his eye. An automobile had bumped down off the curb directly across the street from the Bureau of the Mint and had forced its way into the lane of traffic behind him, four cars back. It was a black sedan. For an instant it appeared to be the same one he had seen at the airport. He turned left on Constitution, accelerated one block and turned right on Fifteenth Street. It was not the same car. This car had diplomatic plates. But there was no question that it was following him. And now, after the turns, it was just two cars behind.

Bonham-Carter lowered his speed. Outrunning the following car would be hopeless in the city. He pulled alongside a green and white two-tone sedan and slowed until he was running parallel to it. If he could not lose the car behind him, at least he could prevent it from passing and cutting him off. He needed time to think. The black sedan was directly behind him now and he could see two men in the front seat. He could not afford a stop for any reason. If he encountered a red light, he would have to run it and try to hit a gap in the crossing traffic.

At I Street, the green sedan slowed. It was turning left. He jammed his right leg to the floor not an instant too soon. The black sedan had swung around the turning car and was accelerating. He could see its grille not ten feet behind in his side mirror. The two cars hit the K Street intersection at sixty miles an hour, still accelerating. He could feel the whumph as the crown of the cross street jammed the big radials up into the limousine's undercarriage. Then the steering wheel went feathery in his hands and the car was momentarily weightless coming off the other side.

A block ahead a truck was entering the oncoming lane of traffic from an alley on the left-hand side of the street. Instinctively, he veered in its direction. As the left flank of the limousine passed within inches of the truck's fender, he could hear screeching brakes behind him. Then he was turning left on M Street, and, for the first time since he had left Mayhew staring after him from the plane, he knew where he was going. Deliverance had come to him in strange ways before. But never in a message written on a truck. The idea was brilliant. He was slowing to turn left again by the time the sedan reappeared in the rearview mirror. In twenty seconds he had circled the block and deposited the limousine by the curb next to the alley from which the truck had emerged. The sedan was not yet in view when he entered the modern office building one door up from the corner of Fifteenth and L streets. The elevator door was already open. As he pressed the button that would take it to the fifth floor, he felt a wave of relief sweep over him. He was in probably the safest place in Washington.

Ferguson had been eating a late lunch when he got the first call, the one that told him Bonham-Carter had eluded the Secret Service men at the airport. For the twenty minutes since, he had been on the phone almost constantly, berating the officer in charge, demanding up-to-the-minute status reports, asking about the bridges, the train station, the northern and western traffic arteries.

It was an explosion of frustration that had been building all week. Ever since the previous Tuesday afternoon when Bonham-Carter had failed to show up at the Peruvian embassy, things had been chaotic. To begin with there had been a half-dozen conversations with Sallas, reciprocal charges of bad faith followed by conciliation and pledges of mutual cooperation. Then there had been the business of constantly running the traps, checking the city's access and egress points, checking the hotels, the flophouses, the various municipal refuge centers, even the jails, checking with the taxi companies for passengers with British accents. The whole process had been the more wearing for the fact that Ferguson knew there was only a slim chance that Bonham-Carter was still in Washington.

Now the phone was ringing again.

"Hello. Right." It was the Secret Service again. "You've got him? The Russians have got him? He's where? Where? Shit!" Ferguson's hand dropped to his lap with the receiver still in it. "Fuck, shit, cunt, suck." He repeated the words again as a cathartic. He couldn't believe it. This guy Bonham-Carter was too much.

"Okay, look." Ferguson had picked up the receiver and was speaking in a composed voice now. "You say he's at *The Washington Post;* are there any of our men around there? No? Good. Good. Let's keep it that way. I don't want a Secret Service man within a block of that place. There are only two or three ways in and out of that building and we can let the Russians cover those for the time being. If that son of a bitch thinks he's found some kind of political asylum in there, he's got another think coming. I'll have him out of there on a murder warrant in an hour."

Ferguson hung up the phone and immediately asked his secretary to get Kopke on the line. In a few moments he heard the familiar voice on the other end.

"Forrest, listen carefully. I don't have time to explain

but I want you to do something. I want you to get Bart Rowen on the phone and get him over to your office right away. Tell him there's been a break in the trade negotiations, tell him anything you want, but get him out of the building. And, Forrie, have somebody else over there; call Marilyn Berger and do the same. If either of them is at their office, I want them out, pronto. I'll explain later." He slammed down the phone. That took care of the only two reporters at *The Post* who would be well enough briefed to handle competently Bonham-Carter's story about the Russian grain buying if he chose to tell it. For the moment, all he needed was a one-day delay. By morning there would be no Bonham-Carter. Someone on the national desk at *The Post* might have a pile of notes, but the notes would not check out. High Administration sources would contradict them when Rowen or Berger called the next day for confirmation. Where could *The Post* turn then? And why should it bother? A newspaper like *The Post* could heat its offices on the crackpot tips it got every day.

Ferguson need not have worried. The possibility of arrest for the murder of the old guard at Mount Weather had also occurred to Bonham-Carter shortly after he reached *The Post* newsroom, and he turned his attention directly to the matter of his next move.

Bonham-Carter estimated his sanctuary would last half an hour, maybe less.

At the end of the hall leading away from the lobby, a red light indicated the exit. He was halfway between the second and third floors when a slight tremor shook the concrete stairwell. It was followed by a sustained hum. The presses had been started. They would be running off the back sections of the paper for the next morning. At the first-floor level he turned down a corridor that skirted the hollow center of the building. A long horizontal window of the sort that is installed in factories for the benefit of industrial tourists punctured the wall on one side. Through it he could see huge rolls of newsprint spinning as they fed the multicolored monster that whirred and clicked and spun and thundered as it printed, folded and assembled the papers that he could see sliding out the far end in stacks which were carried off on a belt through a hatchway in the far wall beyond which, doubtless, there were or soon would be trucks that would carry the papers to assigned points around the city. So fascinated with the process was he that it was almost a minute before he realized the significance of what he was looking at. Forty feet farther on, the narrow corridor made a ninety-degree turn to the right and led along the back of the central press room, ending at a steel door. It was unlocked and he slipped through. He was standing now in a large square storage room piled high with cardboard boxes. Catercorner across the room, in the right-hand wall, he could see another door. He crossed to it and pushed it slightly ajar. A blast of warm air greeted him. He was looking across a concrete platform set into the building but enclosed on only three sides. On the open side of the platform he could see the alley. His guess had been right. He was looking at the loading dock. The alley would be the same alley the truck had pulled out of five minutes earlier. At the far end of the platform a similar truck sat parked, the floor of its open rear end flush with the lip of the platform. Later there would have to be more trucks. But how much later? *The Post*'s first edition would not be going out until evening. His watch told him that it was only 3:30.

He closed the door and turned his attention to the storage room. It would be a simple matter to conceal himself among the boxes. Sequestered in a corner behind six feet of cardboard and whatever the boxes contained, he could remain hidden until thirst brought him out. Remain hidden, that is, from anyone who did not strongly suspect that he was there. Unfortunately, he could not count on that. His pursuers would suspect. They would certainly move the boxes. The storeroom was an obvious hiding place.

Bonham-Carter weighed the meager store of alternatives. For the moment escape was impossible. He would have to hide. But where? Whatever he decided on would have to meet two criteria. It would have to offer a reasonable chance of success, and it would have to offer some opportunity for a second move in the event that it failed. The best hiding place would be too risky if, like the storeroom, it left him no secondary recourse.

Five minutes later, having made up his mind, he stepped out onto the platform. Behind a plate-glass window in the far wall, he could see several workmen. Their backs were to him and from their motions they appeared to be playing cards. He kept to the back wall, walking quickly. The alley alongside the loading dock was empty. There probably would be a lookout at the end of the alley where it emptied into Fifteenth Street. If so, the lookout's view of the platform would be totally obscured by the truck parked at a right angle to the wall now only twenty feet away. Bonham-Carter could hear the voices of the men behind the window as he quickened his pace.

He was directly behind the truck now. It was empty. There would be no hiding in it. The right side of the truck abutted the building wall, leaving a slit of less than half an inch through which he could see down the alley to the street. He moved closer. Forty yards away, he could see a muscular figure stationed at the corner. The man, leaning casually against the building, commanded a view of both Fifteenth Street and the alley. Bonham-Carter studied him for a moment. There was something familiar about the slope-shouldered simian outline. Then, moving quickly to the left side of the truck, he hooked his fingers over the edge of its roof three feet out from the edge of the platform and gave a light jump. As his body swung outward along the side of the truck, he lifted his feet and calves behind him, then dropped to the ground next to the truck's left rear tire. To anyone standing on the far side of the truck, the entire operation would have been invisible.

For a second he paused to collect himself. The next move would expose him to danger. It would last no more than two or three seconds, but it was the one moment in his plan when he would be vulnerable to being seen. It would have to be done as quickly as possible. Gripping the tire for added thrust, he hurled himself low along the ground, slithered between the rear of the tire and the platform's low forward wall and rolled hard to his left. The move left him breathless, less from the exertion than from the nervous tension. He lay perfectly still, looking up at the axle of the truck encased in grease and dirt six inches above his nose. There had been no shouts, no sound of footsteps from the end of the alley where he had seen the man leaning against the building. After twenty seconds, he relaxed, satisfied that he had not been seen. With the floor of the truck's baggage compartment pressed flush against the dock, he could not be seen from above. Lying below the rear axle and parallel to it, the tires would block any view of him from the ends of the alley. The only way someone might see him would be by stooping to look underneath the truck from the front or the side. There was that danger, but the only alternatives that had occurred to him had been worse. He braced his feet against the inside of the truck's left rear tire and arched his back slightly to smooth the rumples of his jacket beneath him. It was going to be a long wait. He might as well be comfortable.

After the second call from the Secret Service announcing Bonham-Carter's disappearance into *The Washington Post,* Seth Ferguson had canceled all afternoon appointments, intending to concentrate his attention solely on the matter which in eleven days had come to obsess him. It had been a mistake. Within the hour, his men, armed with a warrant, had combed *The Post* building from corner to corner and had turned up nothing. At 4:30, Ferguson had given the order to have the Secret Service men who had been called to the area returned to their original details, leaving only the Russians, who could not embarrass the Administration politically, on watch outside *The Post.* Shortly after six o'clock, with no further reports in, he put through a call to Kopke and suggested that the Commerce Secretary join him at the White House. Kopke would want to be briefed, and it would give Ferguson something to do. The silence of the telphone was becoming intolerable.

It was twilight and almost completely dark underneath the truck when Bonham-Carter heard the first noise—a heavy thump, followed a minute later by another thump and the sound of men's voices coming from above him. They had begun to load the truck. The thumps would be the newspapers being tossed onto the floor in bales. Four or five other trucks had pulled up alongside during the previous several hours, and he could hear more thumps and more voices coming from farther down the platform. Inching sideways to get clear of the round bulge of the truck's differential, he rolled onto his stomach and peered down the alley toward Fifteenth Street. It had been five hours since he had looked at the same scene through the slot between the building and the wall, but the man had not moved. Silhouetted by the lights of the building across the street, he still leaned against the corner of the building.

Five hours had given Bonham-Carter ample opportunity to study the underside of the truck and to think about what he would have to do. Technically, it was feasible. The only question was whether, at his age, he still had the necessary arm strength. Several probing attempts using the rear axle as a facsimile had convinced him that, with the surge of adrenalin that would probably come, he could manage it.

The sound of a starter motor farther down the dock told him that one of the trucks was already loaded and ready to go. He would have to move. Rolling onto his back again he slid quickly forward. In a few seconds he was lying directly beneath the drive shaft which ran down the middle of the truck from engine to rear axle. Lifting his legs, he slid his feet over the rear axle so that he was straddling the drive shaft upside down, then lowered his legs again until he felt the cold of the round steel axle casing in the curve of his Achilles' tendons. By locking his arms around the drive shaft, he would be able to lift himself clear of the ground by six inches, bearing about a third of the weight on his ankles. If he could hold on, he would ride out of the alley like Ulysses out of Polyphemus' cave.

The truck engine had been started. Above him a short grinding noise indicated that the gears had been engaged. Throwing his arms over the drive shaft, he grabbed the inside of each elbow with the opposing hand and pulled them to him. His body came free of the ground in the nick of time. For an instant the forward jerk of the truck caused his arms to slip rearward and he felt the back of his jacket brush the asphalt. The jacket! He should have thought to remove it. It would hang below him—maybe eight or ten inches—and it was too late to do anything about it.

The truck was away from the loading dock and it gathered speed as it moved down the alley. Already his forearms ached. He had not figured on the vibration. The effort was far greater than he had anticipated. His arms throbbed. He fought a temptation to spare them by gripping the drive shaft with his legs. That would be instant disaster. Though the shaft was sheathed in heavy metal casing at the point where his arms were locked around it, between his knees it was naked rotating steel, broken in the middle by the interlocking forks of a five-inch universal joint. It was that joint he had to worry about. If he allowed either leg to close on it, he could forget his other problems. It would take a chunk out of his calf the size of a tennis ball.

As the truck swung out of the alley and up onto Fifteenth Street, its heavy leaf springs flattened, dropping the payload to within six inches of the rear axle. He could feel the pressure on his toes and winced to think what would have happened to his feet had the truck been moving faster or been more heavily loaded. There was no time to worry about it. He could hear shouts now coming from the sidewalk and the sound of running feet. He had been spotted. As the truck rounded the corner and headed west on L Street, he shot a glance toward the curb. Only the tires of parked cars were visible. The pain was excruciating. Sensation was draining from his hands. In a moment he would lose control of them. They would be numb. He would hit the pavement without ever knowing he had released his grip. How long had he hung there? Fifteen seconds? Fifty seconds? Nothing was registering. An instant later the road seemed to go to corduroy under him, and his grip was gone, and he was rolling, waiting for the pain to overwhelm him.

It seemed he had been rolling for a long time before he realized that there was something peculiar about the surface beneath him. Then he struck something solid and could roll no farther. He was lying on his stomach. He opened his eyes slowly, half expecting to find that they were already open—that the darkness he had been looking at was due to nothing more complicated than being dead. The sight before him only held the issue in abeyance. He was looking straight down into a strange and dimly lit netherworld full of concrete pipes, pools of water, huge mounds of loose earth and strange-looking machinery. Was this hell? How deep was hell? This looked like seventy to eighty feet.

He lay there for perhaps ten seconds before it dawned on him where he was. He was lying in the middle of Connecticut Avenue atop the Metro construction site. What had felt like a corduroy road and had shaken him off the bottom of the truck had been just that—the timbers with which Connecticut Avenue had been surfaced because of the cut-and-cover construction going on below.

A screech of brakes cleared his head of any remaining cobwebs. The black sedan had pulled to the curb at the L Street stoplight and two men had jumped out. For an instant, Bonham-Carter considered the Metro. The gap in the timbers surrounded by the sawhorses which had interrupted his roll was large enough to slip through, but no ladder was in sight. A jump would be suicide. There was nothing to do but run for it.

Every muscle in his body objected to the directions he now gave them. Whether he had injured himself in the fall from the truck, he could not tell. There was no pain, only the feeling that he was running through water waist high which sucked at his legs with every step. Perhaps his mind was racing so fast that his legs seemed slow only by contrast. It didn't matter. He could hear the feet behind him drawing closer.

To his left, across the peninsula formed by the intersection of Connecticut Avenue and Eighteenth Street, he could see naked girders against the street-lit sky. He veered in their direction. A moment later he was behind a plywood retaining fence and picking his way through a darkened construction site.

The concrete slab underfoot was littered with rubble. He moved with care, conscious that in the darkness silence was a better ally than speed. Wires dangling from above tore at his clothing. He lifted an arm, holding it before his forehead to shield his face. Twice his forearm cracked against concrete columns. At the center of the building he could see the glow of electric light and veered away from it to avoid becoming a silhouette. Too late. His pursuers had had the same thought. Unconcerned with noise, they had moved faster and had flanked him. A guttural shout rose on his left, followed by an "oof" and the sound of a body colliding with a stationary object. Bonham-Carter was running now, running toward the light which he could see came from a stairwell in the center of the building. He took the stairs four at a time. It was an open chase now; no more chance for deception. The stairs emptied into a rectangular room, a sunken lobby. A single light bulb, encased in protective wire mesh, hung on a black rubber cord from the ceiling. Ahead, he could see its reflection in a half-dozen huge panes of glass crisscrossed with Xs of masking tape. Thirty feet away to the left, the end wall was blank. To the right in the opposing wall, three holes yawned where one day there would be elevators. The only exit was ten feet to his left, a tan metal door held ajar by a wooden wedge underneath. A swipe of his foot sent the wedge skidding into the middle of the room. In an instant, the door had slammed shut behind him and he was stumbling through the subterranean darkness.

It was shortly after nine o'clock when the Secret Service called Seth Ferguson in his office in the White House West Wing. Ferguson listened for a moment, then cupped his hand over the receiver and spoke quietly to Kopke, who had spent the previous three hours there sitting in the lounge chair by the window, staring blankly out across the darkened South Lawn.

"The Russians have got him," Ferguson said. "It's the Secret Service; they say the Russians have him in the basement of a building in the eighteen hundred block of M Street."

Ferguson listened carefully to what was being said on the other end of the line. When he spoke again, it was to give instructions. His tone was emotionless, matter-of-fact. Bonham-Carter was to be killed, not right away, but that evening. How it was done could be left to the Russians. Killing was an area in which he had every confidence in their competence. But it had to be done by midnight. The Secret Service would collect the body at around one, after the streets had cleared. By then he wanted the Russians gone. It was important that there be a safe time interval. If a District policeman should stumble on them in the process of removing the body, the Secret Service men were instructed to say they had received an anonymous tip. It would not help to have to explain the presence among them of a couple of Russian strong-arm men.

Ferguson could see Kopke squirm with discomfort as

he repeated the instructions for a second time to make certain the man on the other end had missed nothing. One o'clock. It was understood. Ferguson would be waiting in the Mayflower bar, and would expect a full report as soon as the body had been removed. He hung up the phone and shot a wink at Kopke. The gesture was lost on the Commerce Secretary, who sat now with his forehead cupped in his hands staring at the carpet. There would be time later to minister to his squeamishness. For the moment there were more pressing matters. He would have to call Sallas, bring him up to date and make arrangements for delivery of the money. The Secret Service dragnet would have to be disassembled. Finally, he would have to call Andrews Air Base and schedule a military flight for the morning. All that would take some time. He had better get started if he wanted his payload to reach the Canal Zone the next day. As he picked up the phone, he wondered how Sallas would feel about getting his money and his man in the same box.

Bonham-Carter had not got twenty feet into the basement room before the rattling of the latch bolt announced that the door had locked behind him. He could hear excited voices on the other side. The two men would be discussing what to do. He tiptoed back toward the door. The voices were lower now. Then they ceased all together and he could hear the sound of feet ascending the stairs again.

His eyes adjusted slowly to the darkness. He could make out now that he was standing in a large, low-ceilinged room. From what he could see, there were no windows. What little light there was came from a three-quarter-inch reveal at the bottom of the door he had just entered and from a dozen or so four- or five-inch holes in the concrete slab above his head. The latter, he assumed, had been left to allow passage of the electrical wiring. They were too small to be of any use to him.

Motionless, he glanced about him. Building materials lay strewn about the floor—stacks of oil-coated panels which, when locked together with steel pins, would have made the forms into which the room's concrete supports were poured; steel reinforcing rods in all sizes; perforated steel tape for binding insulating material around the pipes, piles of five-by-eight plywood sheets and the collapsible pico beams which would have supported the plywood sheets while the concrete ceiling above was poured on top of them, supported them until the concrete had cured. Rising onto his toes, he felt above him with his fingertips. The ceiling was still warm. The slab would have been poured within the last week. The plywood sheets probably had just been stripped down that day. There would not be a second floor above it yet. That would explain the light that filtered through the holes.

Another light caught his eye, this one on the floor three feet from where he stood. He reached toward it. It disappeared, only to reappear again as he withdrew his hand. He reached again, this time allowing his hand to move all the way to where he had seen it. The surface was cold and smooth under his touch. Glass. Small panes of glass, maybe twenty of them piled on top of each other. Taking a pane from the stack, he turned back toward the door. The slit of light that had been over a yard wide a minute before was now half that. It did not surprise him. He was on his belly now, head to the door, feet pointing back into the room. Carefully, quietly, he slipped the glass along the concrete floor toward the bottom of the door and the remaining light. When he was satisfied that the forward edge of the glass was halfway under the door, he cocked his head to the side and, supporting himself on his palms, lowered his right eye until he felt the slick surface on his temple. The forward two inches of the pane made a near perfect mirror. Using it, he could look under the door, directly across the lobby to the plate-glass wall on the opposite side. The second reflection, from the glass wall back to the door behind which he lay, told him what had happened to the rest of the light. Seated in front of the door, knees drawn up in front of him, head resting just below the doorknob, was the lookout from the alley behind *The Post.* Carefully, Bonham-Carter studied the face. He was sure he had seen it before, before that day. Mentally, he went back over the nearly four weeks since he had arrived at Dulles, the days at the Madison, the period he had spent in the Hilton in New York, the brief stay in San Francisco, the week in Los Angeles. That was as far as he had to go. When he stood up he was sure. The man who now sat quietly on the other side of the door was the same man who had grabbed him on the movie lot in Los Angeles. It was Yuri.

He would have to work quickly now. The second man would have gone for help. There would be very little time. The question was, what to work at? He cast about him for anything that might suggest a means of escape. A survey of the room, which had grown progressively lighter to his eye, turned up nothing that he had not noticed initially. No windows and no door save that through which he had come. Except for the horizontal water pipes along the ceiling, every standing structural element was concrete. There was nothing that he could break down, nothing except the door itself; and Yuri was behind that.

He turned his attention to the pipes. They crossed the room in two separate clusters of three each, one cluster running from side to side, the second from the rear of the room to a point directly above the door where they passed through the wall and out into the lobby. Concentrating on the latter group of pipes, he examined carefully the manner in which they were hung. Reaching up, he locked his fingers over one of them and lifted his feet. The insulating material was dusty and hard to hold, but the pipe showed no sign of movement. It would support more than his weight. Well distributed along its length, it might support a great deal more than his weight. It gave him a thought.

He estimated the distance from the level of the pipe to the middle of his thighs at six feet. Doubled, that would be twelve feet. Make it thirteen feet. Better too long than too short.

Next the metal tape. Using his body as a measure, he wound off what he estimated to be thirteen feet. The tape proved more supple than he had expected and its edges were treacherously sharp. It was nearly five minutes and more than a hundred back-and-forth folds later before the first length separated from the roll. There had to be a faster way.

There was. He would not have to break the tape. He cursed himself for the lost time. A minute later, having looped the end of the tape over the pipe and back on itself, he was standing three feet inside the door, hands above his head, completing the fourth consecutive slipknot. Then, having unwound a dozen or so more feet, he looped the spool over the pipe a few feet farther into the room and, clutching the spool tightly in his lap, sat in the resulting makeshift swing. He could feel himself drop slightly as the knot above him tightened. There would be greater slippage later when greater weight was added, but he was satisfied that it would hold.

The rest was simple. The pipe to which he had knotted the tape was hung from steel brackets set into the ceiling at four-foot intervals along its entire length. At each of these, Bonham-Carter looped the spool over the pipe again, allowing enough slack so that between each bracket the tape hung to within four feet of the floor. Each time he made a new loop, he worked the tape several times around the bracket to prevent slippage. It took him five minutes to complete the job and to knot the tape again at the end. When he was through, a total of eight loops hung from the pipe leading to the door. Though they were four feet above the floor, he was counting on them to drop at least a foot when pulled taut.

The next step would be more difficult. Along one wall of the room he located the pile of reinforcing rods he had noticed earlier, and began to feel his way through it. He would need a long one. At least thirty feet. And it would have to be heavy gauge. He quickly isolated the most promising portion of the pile and began to check for sharp ends. Though the rods themselves were uniformly cast within their respective size groupings, their ends, where they had been chopped into different lengths, varied enormously. None were pointed, but some ends had much sharper and more jagged edges than others. In a few minutes he had found one that satisfied all his criteria—slightly over thirty feet, one and a half inches in diameter and unusually pinched at its end. It was all he could do to get it onto his shoulder. Its ends did not clear the floor until he was almost standing. Its entire weight, which he could never have supported with his arms, he estimated to be close to three hundred pounds.

Staggering under the weight, he carried the rod to the far end of the room. The rest of the operation, working the rod foot by foot through the loops, took nearly ten minutes. When he was through, he was exhausted, but he had before him the rude mechanism he had envisioned when he started. The reinforcing rod, all nearly three hundred pounds of it, hung in the loops, parallel to the pipe that supported it from above. As he had anticipated, the rod was slightly less than three feet from the floor. That was perfect. It would rise several inches before it did its business.

Bonham-Carter returned to the door, dropped to the floor and again pressed his face to the pane of glass. Yuri had not moved. Rising again, he returned to his apparatus and sighted along the rod. He had purposely picked the pipe farthest away from the hinged side of the door. The bolt side of the door was more likely to give under impact. That would have been reason enough to hang the rod where he did. But it was not his only reason. He also had a score to settle with Yuri.

Bonham-Carter tried to estimate how long it had been since he had heard the second Russian climb the stairs. No more than half an hour. If he had gone only to telephone, he would be back any minute.

As he started the slow back-and-forth motion going, the makeshift battering ram swung smoothly in its slings. The first impact would have to do it. He could not let the rod touch the door by accident before he had thrown his entire weight behind it. That last swing would have to travel at least a foot or two farther than the one before it. Gradually he increased the length of the swing. The rod was only a foot from the door now. He was surprised at how little effort it took to move it. The arc of the rod was increasing four inches at a swing. At that rate, he could afford only two more swings before he would have to go for the payoff. In anticipation, his fingers tightened, feeling for the gaps between the rod's little ridges, gaps which would give the best possible grip. All his attention was focused now on the space occupied by the tip of the rod. The last swing had been just three inches from the door. That was the last dry run. The backswing was complete. The rod was starting forward. Now! This was for all of it. His eyes closed with the strain. He never saw the rod's crimped and jagged edge part the thin steel of the door's inner panel. But he heard the rip of the rod's rough ridges as they tore through the aperture, and he heard the ping as the latch bolt sprung.

As he staggered into the light, he also heard the pounding of feet on the stairs, and caught a glimpse of the second Russian reflected in the plate-glass wall opposite before the collision of their bodies stunned him and he went to the floor with the other man under him and the welling apprehension that it might all have been too late.

The Mayflower bar was nearly empty at 1:15 when the Secret Service man delivered his report to Seth Ferguson and Forrest Kopke. It was straightforward: Bonham-Carter was dead; his body, bagged in plastic, had been removed and was ready for disposal as Ferguson wished. The Secret Service man was not inclined to detail, nor were his listeners inclined to ask questions. The cause and estimated time of death had been given. It had been bloody. But that was not unexpected considering who had done the job. It was enough to know that there had been no slipups.

Connecticut Avenue was deserted as the two officials left the hotel and began the five-block walk to the White House. For two city blocks neither spoke. It was Ferguson who finally broke the silence.

"Look, Forrie, I know what you are thinking. Four years ago I'd have felt the same way myself. But you

learn, Forrie, you learn. You learn that nothing worthwhile gets done without somebody getting hurt. That's
life. It's not a simple zero-sum game, but the fact of the
matter is it works sort of that way. You can achieve
things at a certain rate without asking anybody else to
give up anything. But sometimes that rate isn't fast
enough, and then something or somebody does have to
give. Do you see what I mean?" Kopke didn't answer.
He had stopped in the middle of Farragut Square and
was standing at the base of the statue staring up at the
hero of Mobile Bay and at the stubby mortars surrounding him. "Forrie, what I mean is that if you take what
we've done and you weigh it against what we did it for,
there's no comparison. Don't you see that?"

"Yeah, I see that."

"Well, then what's your problem; why don't you say
anything?"

"I dunno, Seth, I guess I've got a different problem.
You never saw the guy. I talked to the poor bastard for
forty-five minutes. I broke bread with the son of a
bitch." For a moment Kopke paused before going on.
"You know, Seth, I can still see his face. I guess I just
don't like imagining it with a reinforcing rod sticking
out of his mouth."

"Oh, for Christ's sake, Forrest, how about that poor
old fart he squashed to death up in Mount Weather? If
you want to cry about somebody, cry about him. What
you need is a nightcap. Come on, we'll go to my place."

Epilogue

Some footnotes are in order:

Item: Shortly after eight o'clock on the morning of July 25, a member of the Laborers Union, Local #106 working in the employ of the Majendie & Cookson Construction Company on a site at the corner of Eighteenth and M streets, N.W., discovered the body of a man concealed behind a stack of sheetrock. The body bore no identification. The D.C. coroner's report issued that afternoon noted multiple injuries including scrotal ecchymosis and acute subdural hematoma. In lay language, the dead man had been kicked in the balls and hit over the head. The latter injury was listed as the cause of death, placed at some time before midnight of July 14. The matter was processed routinely by the Homicide Division. It was not until noon on Thursday the twenty-seventh that a linkup was made between fingerprints and photographs taken of the body at the morgue and those contained in a missing persons file submitted to the Police Department by the Soviet embassy on behalf of two employees assigned to the Soviet Trade Mission located on Fifth Avenue in New York City and described in the forms only as security personnel. The file, as it relates to the other of the missing Russians, one Yuri Kurashov, remains open on the records of the District of Columbia Metropolitan Police Headquarters at 300 Indiana Avenue, the department having to this day received not a single iota of further information.

Item: In the early afternoon of July 26, one day after the discovery of the body of the first missing Russian, but one day before its identification as such, an unusual event occurred. A U.S. Army Huey Cobra helicopter, flying without markings, rendezvoused with a Peruvian destroyer in the Bay of Panama to deliver an ammunition caisson containing $20 million in cash and the body of a man with long veiny arms and a gaping hole in the back of his head. This delivery, made to unwitting officers of the Peruvian navy acting on high instructions, was witnessed and later attested to at a gathering of part of the Peruvian Cabinet by one Luis Cardona, an assistant to the Minister of Fisheries.

Item: That same afternoon, in Quebec, the Montreal office of Merrill Lynch Pierce Fenner & Smith Inc. made the largest single commodities transaction in its history, selling Chicago Board of Trade contracts for soybeans and no. 1 hard winter wheat in the total amount of $22.4 million for a customer named Felix Bonham-Carter with impeccable credit credentials confirmed by computer through the Washington office. Following the transaction, completed shortly after one o'clock, the head of the commodities section closed up shop for the day and took his staff of four brokers and two secretaries for an afternoon of drinking and dinner which ran to over four hundred dollars.

Item: On the morning of July 27, a tall man in his late forties boarded an Air Canada flight for Rome at Montreal's International Airport wearing five hundred dollars' worth of new clothes which he could have been seen purchasing the previous afternoon at Brisson & Brisson on Sherbrook West, a few blocks from the old section of the city. The Rome customs official, had he been inclined to notice such things, would have been surprised at the man's fine dress, for the man's passport identified him as Yuri Kurashov, an employee without special title of the Soviet Trade Mission in New York City. Had he not been hurried, he might also have noted the fact that, while the passport picture matched the face before him and bore the impression of a seemingly official stamp, the passport's physical description data described a man fully six inches shorter than its holder. Further perusal of the Russian passport would have shown that the man presenting it had been in Canada for only twenty-four hours.

All of these facts, along with demands from Peru for compensation for the missing contracts, eventually found their way back to the office in the White House West Wing and from there were relayed to the President and to the Commerce Department. But it was the end of July before their full import was absorbed. By then, things had changed in Washington. On July 28 the heat wave had broken, and with it much of the fever that had made those twenty-four days in July what they had been. With the contracts liquidated, Peru's incentive for talking was gone. Wagging tongues could still hurt, but the election was looming and there were other problems on the horizon which, in the White House argot, were more "shootable." The matter was not dropped entirely. A search was ordered and the appropriate instructions were given the appropriate security agencies. But the pace was desultory. By the time the election rolled around, the Interpol file in the little room in the basement of the Treasury Department showed no entry past July 27, the date the man carrying Yuri Kurashov's passport had cleared customs at Leonardo da Vinci Airport in Rome. Eventually, working with information obtained from the Russians, the Secret Service would find its way to San Francisco and from there to the bungalow in El Cerrito. It was mid-December by this time, and there the trail ended. The hippie girl who answered the door remembered the boy, but he had left. Left two months earlier without saying where he was going. Left after receiving in the mail a cashier's check for $20,000 from a bank in Switzerland. No, she did not remember the name of the bank, nor had she read the letter that had arrived several days before he left. Finally, in early February, all searches were summarily called off by the White House. Congress was gearing up for an investigation of abuse of executive power. It would not be wise to have anything ongoing that could lead to trouble. With that, the bizarre case of Felix Bonham-Carter came to an abrupt halt. But the repercussions from the Russian grain buying had only begun. Eventually, César Sallas' projection would prove prophetic. In August, the Russian buyers would return to the United States for a second round of buying. By the middle of that month the price of hard winter wheat would go to well over two dollars. By the end of the month, the Agriculture Department would have abandoned its export subsidy as economically and politically insupportable. Before the price rise was finished, it would surpass Sallas' estimates and go to over three and a half dollars. Though it would not help Peru, it would prove the partial undoing of other actors in the story. Before the new year was two months old, Kopke would be out of office. In July of the new year and again in October, the Senate Permanent Subcommittee on Investigations would raise questions in hearings about the secrecy with which the buying had been conducted. Though the questions would come too late to affect the election, they would eventually undermine the standing of Seth Ferguson. Within a year of their completion, he too would have left the government.

But that would all come much later. By then, much else would have happened, and the events of July 1972 would have been eclipsed by other, more important events. There would be few people who by then would remember. Sallas—he would remember. His plan had not been executed exactly as expected, and it had caused him some humiliation for a few difficult days, but it had worked out in the end. The profits from the contracts were never realized; but in February 1973, just as the search for Bonham-Carter was being called off, Peru and the United States signed an agreement settling the old expropriation dispute and freeing the Exim-bank to lend money in Peru once again. The result: $620 million in loans for the Cuajone Copper Mine Project. The price: ironically, $22 million paid in compensation to the owners of the expropriated International Petroleum Company—almost the exact value of contracts with which Bonham-Carter had disappeared. Sallas would leave the Finance Ministry in 1973. Then, after a fourteen-month hiatus, he would, in February 1975, be named Premier, Commander in Chief of the Army and Minister of War.

An old lady in Front Royal, Virginia, would also remember. She would have a gravestone to remind her. Remind her of the day she had been called by the man at Mount Weather and told that her brother Jason, whom she had not seen for twenty-five years, would be arriving that afternoon and would require attending to.

Somewhere, someone else would remember. He alone would remember all, for he alone would have known all. He would be closing in on fifty, probably showing gray hair unless he had found some way that money could ward it off. Possibly he would have a young man with him. Probably he would have a different name, too. At the price, the hyphen would be easy to part with. He would remember. Remember and wonder how the others had fared. Wonder what Sallas was thinking, wonder if Yuri and the other Russian had also had sons, wonder if the couple in the photograph in San Francisco had cried for their daughter, wonder if the anchovy had started running again.